Dani

CHASING

CASEY

SAVE A horse,
ride A drummer :)

Jane Anthony

Cover Design by:
Marisa Shor, Cover Me Darling

Editing by:
Candice Royer

Proofreading by:
Jenny Sims, Editing4Indies

Formatting by:
Christine Borgford, Type A Formatting

For . . .

. . . everyone who has supported me on my journey so far.
. . . all those who read my first book
and loved it enough to ask for more.
. . . my brother and his constant antics and laughter.
. . . my husband for allowing me to live out my dream.
. . . anyone who has had the courage to follow their heart.

Thank you.

Prologue

"Y OUR TIE IS crooked."

My sister sets down the small bouquet of dai-sies she's holding to adjust the tie she's making me wear. I feel like a dumbass getting dressed up for an empty church, but it's important to Jillian so, by default, it's important to me, too.

"Remind me again why you and Jameson didn't just do this shit at the courthouse."

She finishes my tie and steps back, cocking her head as she inspects her handiwork.

"Because. Mom and Dad were Catholic. They'd have want-ed it this way."

Jillian has this insane notion that our parents are watching over us from somewhere better, some place beyond the clouds or whatever. It's fairy tale shit, but it makes her feel good, so I just go with it. I know the truth, though. I walked along the edge, and I can tell you firsthand; there isn't anything on the other side. Nothing good anyway.

"Yeah, I suppose so." I pick up her daisy bouquet and hand it to her. "I'm sorry you got stuck with me walking you down the aisle instead of Dad."

"I'm not," she replies, taking the flowers from my hand. "You're every bit as important to me as he was."

Today, my little sister is getting married—to my best friend.

The only two people I care about in the entire world are running off with each other, leaving me in the dust. I'm happy for them and all, but being the odd man out is lonely. For so long, it was just the two of us in that big house together. She was my partner, my friend, and someone who always had my back. Jillian understands me in a way no one else ever has.

Ever since we were kids, protecting her has been my number one priority. She relied on me. I avoided relationships because I was all she had. I swore I'd always take care of her. And I have. But in a few minutes, I'll be passing the job to Jameson.

He's a great guy, and he loves her. I should be thrilled, but instead, I feel . . . lost. We're still close, but the dynamic is different. It used to be Jillian and me against the world. She looked up to me, idolized me. Everywhere I went, there she was. It was a good feeling—I'm not going to lie. But as she grew up and moved on from needing a big brother to needing a man, I no longer fit the bill. I became obsolete.

She tugs at the bodice of her plain white gown, the very one our mom wore. Just like the old framed photos Jill keeps scattered around the house, the memories of our mother have faded over the years. Still, they look so similar. Jill's grown into a carbon copy, a mirror image of the woman taken before she got the chance to see us grow. But now, seeing her in that simple satin dress—one that, much like Jill herself, is pretty without any embellishments—I can visualize exactly how our mom looked as if she was standing in front of us.

Jesus, what the fuck is wrong with me? Thinking about this shit has me choked up . . .

"One thing I am regretting is this dress choice. I can barely breathe in this thing."

Regrets. Sometimes, I have so many I feel like I'm drowning. I'm twenty-six years old, and I've done nothing with my life. I go to work, fix cars, and go home to my empty house. The only thing I have is my music, and even that depresses me these days. What's the point in playing if no one's there to listen?

"Stop fidgeting. You look beautiful. You can go back to your ripped up metal tees in an hour."

"Why, Mr. Morello, is that a compliment?" she asks, smiling.

"It's a special occasion. Don't get used to it," I deadpan and look right past her, but the corners of my mouth turn up, giving away my stone façade.

"You're an ass!" She laughs and smacks my chest.

Jill tells me that I'm too picky, but I know what kind of woman I want. One who allows me to be myself but makes me strive to be better. A trustworthy partner who's going to stick by me at all costs, who understands me, sees beyond the lost little boy, and brings out the man I know I can be. I want what Jill has found with Jameson, what our parents had. Love. Real, true, can't-live-without-each-other love. I refuse to settle.

"It's about that time. You ready to give me away?"

I extend my elbow, and she slips her petite hand into the crook. "Nope."

Chapter 1

AJ

"COME ON, BIG boy. Come for mommy."

The woman beneath me—Alyssa, I think she said her name was—hasn't stopped with the baby talk since I stuck my dick in her twenty minutes ago. I'm cool with kinky sex, but this mother-son fetish shit is about to make me lose my hard-on. It doesn't help that she's well into her fifties and has a kid my age. As usual, tequila starts with great intentions and ends with nothing but bad ideas.

"Ut-oh. Is wittle AJ having trouble? Maybe mommy needs to take over?"

No, definitely not. Mommy needs to shut the fuck up so I can come and get her the hell out of my house. I flip her onto her stomach and hoist her ass in the air, pushing her face into the pillow just long enough to blow my load in silence.

Tired and panting, I roll to the side, praying to God that she gets up. Instead, she settles into my bed and gets comfortable. *Fuck.* Why do I keep bringing these one-night stands to my house? Now, I have to be the dick who tells her to leave, and I hate that. Especially since they can come back to The Wreck and find me.

"So, uh, you okay to drive, Alyssa?" Hopefully, she gets the hint.

The flint of my Zippo sparks in the dimly lit room as I light the tip of my cigarette. It's the only thing I have that belonged to my mother. It was a gift from my dad before they got married. The pad of my thumb grazes over the deep etching in the front: *AM & GD Forever.* Ironic. Anthony Morello and Gabriella Donofrio didn't live long enough to see forever.

"The name's Alice," she says, rolling toward me and grabbing my Marlboro Red with two spindly fingers. *Like it matters.* The cherry glows bright orange as she takes a long drag, smoke curling out of her nostrils like a dragon.

"That's what I said," I lie, taking back my smoke and switching it to the opposite hand. Sharing a cigarette in post-coital bliss is a little too intimate for me. It's the kind of shit you see in romantic comedies after the guy and girl finally get together before something tears them apart again.

Alice reaches for me, but I'm already halfway off the bed and on my way to the bathroom to dispose of the condom. "Your band was awesome tonight," she calls from the bedroom.

"I wasn't with the band. I'm the sound guy." The second it comes out of my mouth, I cringe with regret. *Me and my big fucking mouth.*

"Oh! So I know where to find you when I want to see you again!"

Dammit.

The Wreck is a local hotspot for up and coming bands to gain exposure. I've been working there Saturday nights for a few months now, in addition to my regular job at Morello and Tate Restoration. The pay is shitty, but it's a fun job and comes with the nice fringe benefit of easy sex. The girls are pretty docile by night's end. Whoever isn't paired off by the time the lights go on is generally liquored up and ready to go home with whoever is behind door number two. Yeah, I'm an asshole . . . Save the feminist spiel. I already know.

"I was hired for the night. Usual sound guy didn't show." It's easier to lie and hope Mrs. Robinson doesn't check up on me. If she does, I'll worry about it when it happens. Right now, I just need her to go.

Disappointment hits me when I walk back into the room and find her still in my bed. Jesus, you bang one old lady, and she clings like a genital wart. "So, uh, I hate to do this, but my girlfriend's going to be home soon. You should probably get going."

"Your girlfriend?" Her eyelids narrow. The haggard look on the woman's face tells me this isn't her first trip to the rodeo. She sees right through my bullshit.

"Yeah. She's kind of nuts. It's best if you're gone by the time she gets here," I reply, swirling my finger at my head for effect.

Dropping the girlfriend is something I only do when absolutely necessary. Making up fake girlfriends is the equivalent of telling your boss you have a dead relative to get out of work. You don't want that kind of karmic juju coming back to bite you in the ass.

Alice grumbles something about me being an asshole before rolling out of my bed and grabbing her shit, but I don't stick around to watch the walk of shame. Instead, I head to the kitchen and poke around for something to eat. One thing I miss about living with Jill is the food. She kept the fridge well stocked and always had bowls of leftovers individually wrapped with instructions. She idiot proofed shit for me. It was awesome. All I have in here is cold pizza, some bread, and a six-pack.

I slam the fridge door, nearly jumping out of my skin when I see what's-her-face hovering behind it in the dark. Chick snuck up on me like a ninja.

"You're just as bad as my son is. He never takes anything

seriously, either. Everything's a party to you people." She stands, arms crossed over her chest defiantly, hip jutted out. In this light, she can almost pass for a younger woman instead of the aging beauty queen with over-processed hair and too much lipstick standing before me.

Once upon a time, this lady was probably a knockout. Bet she had dudes lined up around the corner, but somewhere along the lines, she ended up like this. Lonely. Desperate. Willing to go to bed with anyone just to feel connected to another human being for a few hours. How does this happen to a person? If I don't start changing my ways, I'm going to end up like this.

Who am I kidding? I already am.

"We had fun, Alyssa. Let's not spoil it," I warble around a mouthful of cold pizza. The last thing I need right now is a lecture from Mother Time. She doesn't know shit about me, and if she did, she'd know that I take everything seriously. Too seriously, in fact. It's the reason I took the job at The Wreck to begin with. I hoped working around music would help me relax.

Music has always had a calming effect on my soul. Whenever shit in my head got too loud, banging away at my drums chased it away and put everything into perspective. Ever since the accident, my shoulder hurts too much to wail on them the way I used to. Yet another regret in a string of many.

Speaking of regrets. I casually try to shove my current one toward the door without making it too obvious that I'm literally throwing her out at this point. My buzz is gone, I have a headache, and her two-pack-a-day voice is starting to grate on my nerves. I want to go to bed and forget this ever happened.

Opening the door, I usher her through it as she snaps her name at me for the second or—who am I kidding, probably fifth—time. "Adios, Alyssa," I say to myself as soon as the door closes with her on the other side.

★ ★ ★

MUSIC WAILS FROM the backyard as I pull past the shop into my sister's driveway. The gravel crunches under my feet, while loud howling guitar riffs and growling vocals waft through the warm evening air.

"No more Twisted Sister!" I shout, straddling the picnic bench across from her.

Jillian smacks the volume on the speaker, turning it to a less ear-splitting decibel. "The prodigal son returns! And he looks like shit!"

"Rough night," I grumble, fishing for a beer in the cooler. *Hair of the dog, right?* "What are ya cookin'? Smells good. I'm starving."

Ever since I moved out, Jillian insists we get together for Sunday dinner. Yet another tradition she claims she does for our parents' benefit. It's not enough I have to see her and Jameson every day at work, but I have to spend time with them on my day off, too. Personally, I think she worries I'm not going to eat unless she feeds me. She's an old Italian grandma trapped in the body of a twenty-five-year-old.

"Good because Jameson grilled enough sausage to feed an army."

"You talkin' shit about me out here?" Jameson emerges from the house, sliding the screen door shut behind him.

"S'up, man?" I chuck my chin, imitating his greeting.

Jillian tilts her head with a wry grin. "Yeah, I was telling AJ how much I hate you."

Jameson snorts. "That's not what you were saying this morning."

"Gah . . . I'm already hungover! Don't make me puke." I shake away the disturbing imagery Jameson loves to put in my head.

The initial thought of my little sister and my wayward best friend didn't exactly thrill me. Considering the hell I put these two through, a little light-hearted ribbing is the least of my worries. Still . . . gross.

Jillian rolls her eyes and laughs. "How was the band last night? Any good?"

"Eh," I say, curling my lip. "Classic rock. The place was full of middle-agers."

"Tell me you didn't bag an old lady last night." Jameson shakes his head and uses the edge of the table to pop the cap off his beer bottle.

"She wasn't that old!"

He cringes. "You'll stick your dick in anything, won't you?"

"What can I say? I'm a giver."

"You're disgusting. You're never going to have a quality relationship if you keep eating at the taco truck," Jillian shoots.

"Whatever." I tip my beer to my lips. My delusional sister seems to think a secret pool of women is out there just waiting to be discovered. Just because she was lucky enough to meet her significant other as a kid doesn't mean the same fate is in the cards for the rest of us. It's rough out there.

A screeching cry blasts through the little speaker box on the table, taking the unwanted attention off my love life for the time being. "Zakk's up," Jillian announces with a sigh. Her exhausted eyes scream *Calgon, take me away* as they roll toward Jameson.

My nephew came barreling into this world about six months ago and hasn't stopped screaming since. Kid has a metal set of pipes, a guitar player's name, and a front man's attitude. When he hits puberty, my sister is fucked.

"I'll get him."

I step out of the spotlight and into my childhood home. Every time I come back here, I can't help but feel weird. The bones of the house are the same, but everything inside has been changed. The worn hardwood floors seem even older next to the new furniture. Mom's old lace curtains are gone, replaced with sleek modern panels in vibrant colors. New photos depicting a new life have replaced the childhood photos of Jill and me that used to grace every wall. A new life where I may as well not even exist. But I do. And if these walls could talk, they'd tell stories about the family that was here before. A family that loved each other with a fierceness so bright they literally burned themselves out.

"Hey, Lil' Shredder," I say, poking my head in the room. The very one I once called mine. The walls are the same shade of midnight blue, but all my shit is long gone. Toys, books, and baby paraphernalia of all kinds lie strewn about. Zakk stops screaming and shoots a drooling toothless grin in my direction. "You just wanna join the party, huh, kid?"

He reaches for me. As I lift him from his crib, I see the drumstick sheets I bought the day Jill told me she was pregnant. Instinctively, he clings to my side as I cradle him in the crook of my elbow. "You got me out of some this-is-your-life crap I wasn't interested in dealing with. You got my back." He responds by blowing a raspberry in my face, bubbles of saliva popping around his tiny lips. I nudge my finger into his pudgy stomach as big gales of cackling belly laughter explode from him.

I love this kid. More than I thought I was capable of loving another person. Whenever I've given up hope on having any kind of life, Zakk reminds me that some things are definitely worth fighting for.

Chapter 2

Casey

"YOU'RE NOT GOING to believe this!"

My roommate crashes into my room at lightning speed. Light from the living room filters in through the doorway. I crack open one eye and see her bouncing from foot to foot.

"Marisa, it's three in the mornin'. Can I *not* believe it at a more reasonable hour?" I roll over and pull the covers over my head.

"No! I'm way too wired to sleep. If I don't tell you now, I risk not being able to tell you tomorrow, so you have to hear it now!" Marisa is babbling a mile a minute and not coming even remotely close to using her indoor voice. She gets like this every time she comes home from The Wreck. Pumped up on loud rock 'n' roll and far too much vodka. Sometimes, it's better just to let her get out what she needs to say rather than bother to argue with her. She always ends up winning anyway, and it takes twice as long.

"Fine. Hurry up then get out," I whine.

"Lady Roger got into a huge fight with one of the customers tonight."

"You're right; I don't believe it. Good night." I yawn, adjusting my covers again.

"That's not all!" she yells, pulling my comforter back. *Mental note. Crash Missy's party at eight a.m. tomorrow.* "Frankie D. said he's tired of Lady Roger's bullshit and fired her. The Wreck needs a bartender. The job is yours if you want it!"

Now, I'm awake.

I sit up in my bed, allowing my eyes to adjust to the dark. The sliver of light from the doorway reflects off Marisa's disco ball earrings, casting millions of tiny shining fractals dappling across her face. "You got me a job at The Wreck?"

"Yes! He's desperate. Needs someone who can start tomorrow. I told him you'd fit in perfect!"

I don't know whether to kiss her or kill her. I don't fit in at The Wreck. At all. On one hand, I seriously need a job. I've been out of work for weeks now, and whatever savings I have is starting to get dangerously close to the red zone. But on the other hand, my interest in being that entrenched in the rock scene is even smaller than my bank account.

"Look, I know what you're thinking, but it's not going to be like that, okay?" Marisa says, reading my mind.

She knows exactly what I'm thinking. Musicians are dogs. Everyone in that God forsaken industry is only out for themselves. No one cares who they hurt. "It's just tending bar two nights a week. No one has to know about you and Davis. Just do your job, collect the tips, and come home."

"All right, fine," I say, defeated.

Marisa claps her hands and does a little shuffle on the spot. "Awesome! You'll love it! And now, we'll get to hang out on the weekends!"

Silver linings.

★ ★ ★

AT EXACTLY FIVE minutes to seven, I pull open the heavy wooden door of the abandoned warehouse currently known as The Wreck. It's dark and reeks of stale beer and sweat. This time of the evening, the place is a ghost town, but later, there will be so many bodies in here, they'll have to turn people away at the door. It's insane how busy this place gets. Hopefully, the patrons are good tippers.

"Hello!" My voice echoes through the wide empty space, while my Cavender boots thump on the ancient hardwood. Cowboy boots in a rock club might be a little contradictory, but they cost a small fortune, and I love them. "Anybody here?"

An enormous dark wooden bar stretches along the entire length of the wall at the back of the place. Bright lights shine below the rows of bottles behind it, making the liquor inside them glow. A door at the end bursts open and a stout man with a five o'clock shadow comes barreling through carrying a rack of clean glassware.

"Oh, I didn't hear you come in." All the glasses clink together as he sets the rack down on the bar top. "You must be Marisa's friend."

"Yeah, I'm Casey Grainger. Are you Frankie D.?"

"Yep. Frankie DiLorenzo. Thanks for coming in on such short notice," he says, extending a furry hand across the bar. His sleeves and collar reveal more hair beneath. The man is like a sweaty werewolf. "Marisa told you I need someone who can start tonight, right?"

"Yep. That's no problem."

"Excellent. Come around back. Let's see what you can do." Frankie walks to the end of the bar and opens the trapdoor to come out into the main space, while I take his spot in the back. "It's mostly a beer and shot crowd, but I need someone who can work fast. Get 'em in, get 'em out."

"Of course." I wait as Frankie sets up an iPod on the edge

of the bar and moves his thumb along the screen. The loudest, heaviest guitar riff I've ever heard blasts through the tiny speaker and emits through the cavernous space.

"Okay!" Frankie shouts over the music. "Get me two Coors Lights and two shots of Jack!"

Jumping to action, I scramble to the coolers, grabbing the beers and popping the tops off the bottles before setting them down in front of him. Then I turn toward the booze behind me and swipe the Jack Daniels off the shelf to set up the shots.

He doesn't acknowledge the drinks in front of him. The siren wail of music blasts through my brain as he fabricates another order. "Gimme a vodka cran and a rum and Coke!"

I lean across the bar, straining to hear him over the overwhelming noise and try to read his lips. I whip toward the bottles again, snatching the rum and vodka with both hands. The metal scoop chills my skin as I slam it into the well two consecutive times, filling the glasses to the brim with ice and pouring the booze with each hand simultaneously.

The sudden quiet seems deafening when Frankie cuts the music. "Nice work," he says, raising his bushy eyebrows. "I think you'll fit in here just fine."

"Thanks." I smile.

"You're cute too. A big change from Lady Roger. The guys will appreciate that."

Oh, hell no. "I don't know what Missy told you, Mr. DiLorenzo, but I'm not here to be leered at. If that's the kind of establishment you run, then you'd best find someone else." I grab my purse and start toward the end of the bar, but his hand on my forearm stops me.

"No, you misunderstand me. Look." Frankie reaches for his phone, gives the screen a few swipes, and then slides it across the bar. "That," he says, pointing at the screen, "is Lady Roger."

A smile and a flush spread across my face. "Oh."

Whenever Marisa would come home talking about Lady Roger, I imagined some busty old biker chick with frizzed out hair and a neck tattoo. I was way off. Staring up at me is the biggest, blackest transvestite I've ever seen in my life.

He laughs. *"Great bartender, terrible hothead. Just couldn't take the drama anymore."*

"I get it. I'm sorry. It's just—"

Frankie raises his hand, shaking his head as he walks behind the bar. *"Hey, no worries. We all have our crosses to bear."* He grabs a shirt from a shelf underneath and hands it to me. *"I have one shirt handy. I'll order you a couple more if you decide to stay after tonight."*

Over the course of the next two hours, I get a crash course in everything Wreck related, from drink costs to how to bounce a disorderly customer. My head is spinning by the time the other employees arrive.

"Hey, Case." Marisa strolls in, all fire and boobs. *"Nice shirt."*

Piles of flaming red hair sit atop her head in a crazy modern-day beehive with curly tendrils coming down around her face. Her leather vest does little to cover her chest and is practically see-through in the back. Anyone else would look completely trashy in this getup, but for Marisa, it works. She's glamorous. It's what attracted me to her in the first place when we met seven years ago. Not only that, but she's tough and mouthy. The perfect best friend. The peanut butter to my jelly. When shit went south in my life, Missy was the one who dusted me off and got me the hell out of Dodge.

"Hey, Miss! How come you don't have to wear one of these dumb tank tops?" I whine, toying with the ties in the front.

"I let Frankie D. look at my boobs at the holiday party last year. Not my finest ten minutes, but he's let me wear whatever I wanted ever since." She meets me behind the bar and mixes

up two Southern Comfort and lime shots. *"Here's to your first day in the salt mines, bitch,"* Marisa toasts, clinking one tiny glass into the other and then downing the shot.

The crease in my brows makes her laugh. *"You have thirty minutes until the hornets come buzzing in here demanding blood and beer. Take the shot. It will give you an edge."*

I throw it back and wash out the glass in the sink. *"Atta girl!"* she cheers, slapping me on the back.

"Missy, who's your friend?" A hulking beast of a man comes behind the bar, crowding the huge space with his girth.

"Hey, Bits, this is Casey, our new bartender. Casey, meet Bits, the bouncer-slash-I.D. checker-slash-resident fat bastard."

I look up—way, way up—into the guy's smiling face. Most of his teeth are missing, save for one rotten shard right in the front, and he has a dent in his forehead. *"Welcome to the crew."* He smiles, shaking my hand with his sweaty ham hock.

"Thanks. Nice to meet you."

"Rhonda coming in tonight?"

"Don't know. Don't care," Marisa answers, tinkering with the glasses behind the bar.

Missy blows through lovers as quickly as I change my underpants. Men or women, she doesn't discriminate. She claims having sex is like going to the gym—you should do it every day and never use the same equipment twice.

"Great! I guess this means I'm taking tickets tonight too . . ." Bits keeps talking, chastising Marisa for shitting where she eats, but the guy who just walked in the door somehow makes the enormous man disappear.

He's dark, dressed in black from his ball cap to his work boots. Even his face has a thin layer of black stubble dotting his chiseled jawline. Not enough to call a beard but enough to make him look tough and swarthy.

"Miss," I whisper, taking my friend by the arm. "Who's that?"

Bits rolls his eyes, while a smile splits Marisa's ruby lips. "That gorgeous hunk of man meat, my dear, would be AJ."

Chapter 3

AJ

"AJ!" MARISA'S VOICE bounces off all the walls in the empty warehouse. This place has excellent acoustics, which isn't always a good thing. "Get your cute little booty over here!"

I peer across the room in the direction of Marisa's raspy voice. She's tried to get an invite back to my house on more than one occasion. She has one hell of a bod and a pretty nice face too, but I know way too much about her extracurricular activities to risk dipping my toe in that water. Babe's a total man-eater.

Bits, however, is completely in love with her, in spite of her revolving door tendencies. As usual, he's next to her, leaning against the bar and trying to pretend he's not salivating at the sight of her tits in that strip of leather she calls a shirt. He slides past her to take up his post at the front door, and like the moon passing the sun in a solar eclipse, he reveals the gorgeous blonde who was completely overshadowed by his rotund ass.

Who the hell is that?

Golden hair falls long and wavy over her bare shoulders. She's wearing one of Frankie D.'s signature Wreck Me tanks.

It's too big, which explains the T-shirt under it, but I can tell from here that she's got something good hiding beneath all that black cotton. Normally, I'd just wave at Marisa and go about my business, but this is way too intriguing. I have to see the rest of her.

Blue eyes reel me in as I approach the bar. They aren't just any blue; they're the color of the sky on the sunniest summer day. Bright, beautiful, hypnotic.

"Hey, Marisa. What's up?"

"AJ, meet Casey. Casey, this is AJ, the sound tech."

Casey smiles as she says hello, but I'm too entranced by the dimples on her cheeks to return the pleasantry. Instead, I offer a tight-lipped grin and a curt nod, like a scared boy who's afraid of girls. I've never been nervous around girls. Even when I *was* a boy.

I find my voice and finally open my mouth. "So you're the one replacing Lady Roger, huh?"

"Yeah. I'll be tendin' the bar in her place." This girl has the sweetest voice, with a sexy twang that shoots from my ears to my dick in an instant. She's definitely not from around here.

"Damn. I was hoping to ask her out."

She raises her brows for a second, her clear blue eyes landing on Marisa. "Case, he's kidding."

Casey's Betty Rubble giggle hits me right in the chest. *Damn! She's gorgeous* and *cute.* She doesn't say anything else, just stands there with a little grin on her face as four dudes in leather come strolling in. "It's show time," I announce, tipping my hat for effect.

The band comes directly to the bar, as usual. All these guys are the same. The order goes booze, girls, music. No one seems to take their craft seriously anymore. It's a damn shame.

"Hey, guys! You must be Butchered at Birth." I offer my hand to leather dude number one.

"Yeah. I'm Droz," he answers, shaking my hand. "This is Joe, Marc, and Dan."

"AJ. I'm the sound engineer. You guys need help with your equipment?"

"Nah, we got it."

"All right, then. Once you're all set up, we'll roll through sound check before bodies start filling the joint."

The band starts getting all their gear set up on stage as I begin running the cables. The Wreck is a great place for a cover band because it has its own sound system. The stage comes equipped with its own speakers and lighting, so the band literally only has to bring their instruments and amps. Talent isn't even required most nights.

Fifteen minutes later, the band is set up, and I'm running around the stage miking the guys and setting up the monitors so they can hear themselves when they're playing. Good live sound engineering requires more than plugging in some amplifiers and turning a few volume knobs. It demands knowledge of acoustics and electronics, combined with the skills of the artists, to work with a band and give them the sound they want. Every venue is different, and each brings its own challenges to audio engineering, but it's my job to tame the acoustics and bring the musicians' efforts to the audience.

When there's one band playing, like tonight, this job is cake. I set the stuff up once, make sure it's mixed, and leave it alone. It's when several bands play back to back that it gets a little hectic. I have ten minutes to set up the board, and if the sound isn't stellar, the band will bitch that they can't hear themselves. Musicians are so friggin' testy.

Marc, the drummer, starts banging away at the kick drum, setting up the sound levels. Once he's happy, I move on to the guitarist, the bassist, and then the singer. If the shit ain't tight, the guys will whine, the customers will leave, and Frankie D.

loses money. My job is as important to the live performance as any guy on this stage. It has to be perfect.

"All right, guys, let's hear something."

As the band kicks off their first song, my hands move across the board, turning knobs, moving faders, and making sure the lighting effects pop at the exact moments they're supposed to. By the time I'm done, everyone's happy—just in time for Frankie D. to open the front doors.

The hoard of people waiting outside pours into the venue and instinctively congregates around the bar. I love this. The thrill of the show. The adrenaline pumps through my veins as the thundering crack of the snare cuts through the buzzing of the audience. Every thud on the bass drum is a punch to the face—and this guy's doing double time, stomping his right foot on the pedal while his left foot destroys the high hats in flawless synchronicity. He's an animal—arms flailing, they crash down on the cymbals and tom-toms with zero remorse.

The crowd flows like water, drifting toward the stage as if heading toward the rapids. They move, and bounce, and bang their heads, screaming and shouting along with the songs they know. Droz doubles over as he shrieks out the next lyric. The bass line booms with evil resonance, vibrating the floor like an earthquake rumbling under my feet, and the guitar screeches from the bleeding bite of fingers flying over the frets at lightning speed. All the while, I'm glued to the board, making sure every note they hit is on key.

This shit gets inside you. Music is a language all its own. Either you know it, or you don't. Rock 'n' roll in its pure animal form strangles the hell out of you until you can't breathe, yet you still beg for more. Years of study can teach you theory and scales, but it can't teach you this. This is hunger, need. By the time the set is over, my body is electric, and my brain feels like it's melting from the sheer volume. It was a damn good show.

The crowd disperses like roaches when the lights go on. As quickly as they came in, they filter out. A handful of stragglers loiter by the bar, and some girls wait for a few moments with the band.

Right about now, I'd be eyeballing the leftover ladies, but as I help the band break down their equipment, I can't stop glancing at the bar. The neon glow behind the bottles creates a shining halo of blue around Casey's face, making her eyes pop even from this distance. She's alone. Either Marisa's on dish detail, or she met someone. My money's on the latter.

A split second after returning to my work, a shout, a screech, and a crash bring my attention right back. Casey stands behind the bar in open mouth shock, gaping at a dude swaying on his feet on the other side. I drop the cables and run to the bar. *"What the hell?"*

"I told him he was cut off. I offered him a water, and he threw it at me!"

Her slight Southern twang turns into a full blown, Deep South drawl as her irate voice goes up an octave. She's drenched. Her hair hangs wet and lifeless, dripping onto the soaked tank top. Now is not the time to be noticing how hot her body is under said tank top, but I'm a guy, and she's hard not to notice.

"Bits!" I shout, grabbing the drunk by his shirt and locking his arms in a full nelson. *"Didn't your mother teach you manners, asshole? Apologize."*

He jerks, trying to free himself from my grasp, but he's hammered and sloppy and trips over his own feet instead. I wrench him tighter, and he cries out.

"I said apologize."

"Sorry." The smell of booze floats off him as he mumbles out his forced apology.

Bits's big ass comes waddling through the doors, filling the space as he stands there. *"S'up, Morello? Need some help?"*

"Yeah, man. Make sure this guy gets out the door. Call him a cab; don't let him drive."

Rule number one: never let the drunks drive home. I've made enough mistakes in my lifetime. I don't want that on my conscience as well.

Bits's bear paw wraps around the drunk's bicep as he drags him to the door. I turn back toward Casey, who's shivering in her wet shirt and trying hopelessly to dry off with a bar towel.

"Here." Grabbing the neck of my tee, I whip it over my head and hand it to her across the bar.

She arches her brow, her eyes dropping to my bare chest for a split second before coming back to my face again. "Nah, I can't take your shirt. I'll be fine."

"You're soaked. Take the shirt and go change," I insist.

"Did I miss something?" Marisa saunters through the back doors, followed by a tweaker wearing a Mohawk and an "Anarchy in the UK" tee.

"Yeah, you missed something! You left Casey out here on her first night to fend off the drunks alone! What the hell?"

Marisa's lips part, but she has no defense. "Sorry, Case. The place was mostly empty. I didn't think you'd have a problem."

"It's all right." Tiny divots deepen on either side of her cheeks as Casey's lips press into a thin line. She takes the shirt from my hand and jogs past her friend to the back room to change.

My eyes stay trained on Marisa in a stare down. My body is tense. More than it should be for the tiny infraction. It was just water, but for some reason, I'm furious about it.

"Lookin' good, Morello!" Marisa waggles her brows with a grin, ignoring my dirty look.

"Keep dreaming."

I drop onto the stool in front of me as Marisa sets a beer down on the sticky bar top. A peace offering. I inhale a deep breath and let it out, tipping the bottle to my lips. The frosty carbonation dances across my tongue as it slides down my dry throat. First beer of the night is always the best.

My heart's still racing from both my run-in with the drunk and the sight of the very wet and very hot bartender who was standing here just a minute ago. I stay hunched over; crossing my arms on the bar in front of me, I try my best to calm down.

The band loiters by the stage, talking to a couple of girls who are still hanging out. Usually, that's where I'd be. But for the first time since I started working here, I have zero interest in taking one of them home. I'm not exactly sure why that is, but I have a good suspicion it has something to do with the girl walking out of the backroom wearing my T-shirt.

Holy shit.

The sight is enough to make my mouth water. What is it about this girl? Her blue eyes sparkle as she comes around and sits on the stool next to me. One slender denim-covered leg crosses over the other, but I can't stop looking at her mouth.

Her lips are a plump little heart situated right under her tiny nose. Adrenaline continues to pump through my veins. Her sexy smile only adds to that aggression, making me want to own that sweet little mouth with my lips or my cock. Either will do. The thought not only arouses me, but it also makes me chuckle. Casey is the walking embodiment of The Girl Next Door. I bet those alluring little lips don't even curse, let alone slide over someone's hard-on.

She runs her hands through her damp hair, twisting it into a messy bun at the nape of her neck. Silky white wisps fall out around her face. She sweeps them away with her fingertips, closing her eyes for a second. "Thank you. I'll wash it and return it to you next week," she says, fidgeting with the collar.

"Keep it. Looks better on you, anyway." She grins and looks away, but I catch her looking back at me through her light lashes. "Anyone ever told you how pretty your smile is?"

Did I seriously just say that out loud?

"What?" When she giggles, I notice her dimples intensify as her smile widens.

"And don't take this the wrong way, but you have one of those smiles where it can be pretty, it could be cute, and it can be sexy. Not many people can pull off all three."

Dude. Stop talking.

"Oh, that's a line. Do you really say things like that to people?"

"Evidently."

I tip the bottle to my lips again, hoping to keep the word vomit at bay. My inner monologue must have gone on vacation. But if I'm rewarded with a smile like that for every cheesy pickup line, I'll blow out with a different one every night.

She giggles again. Betty Rubble has nothing on that sweet, melodic sound. If it's the last sound I hear for the rest of my life, I wouldn't even care.

"Have a beer with me."

"I think I've had enough action for the evenin'. I'm going home."

The point of her boot grazes my shin as she uncrosses her legs and hops off the stool. You don't see many cowgirl boots in New Jersey, at least not in this social circle, but Casey rocks them as if she's wearing Doc Martens.

"Thanks again for the shirt. See you at home, Miss."

As she walks away, she pulls my gaze along with her. The tee is tied in a knot at her side, leaving the tiniest strip of skin exposed. Heart-shaped rhinestones adorn the pockets of her skintight jeans. Much like her mouth, it's the perfect metaphor for her ass as a whole—a gorgeous, upside-down heart leading to legs that go on for days. What I wouldn't give to feel those long stems wrapped around me. Casey isn't just hot; she's spectacular.

A montage of filthy imagery rolls through my overactive brain. As my dick hardens, I have to consciously remind myself I'm not wearing a shirt to hide behind.

"Hey, Casanova, eyes off the goods."

Embarrassed at having been caught checking out her friend, I turn back toward Marisa. "What? A guy can look."

"Casey isn't a catch of the day. Don't fuck with her." Her eyes narrow, and her voice gets gruff.

"What is that supposed to mean?"

"You and I are the same, AJ. We both like chasing the strange, but Casey's different. She doesn't need another pretty face dragging her down."

"That's insulting. Maybe I'm looking for more than strange this time."

Her eyes dart toward the door. She props both elbows on the bar, leaning as close to me as she can get. "She's a special case, A."

The chick's a virgin. I knew it. "Special how?"

She rolls her eyes and blows out a strong breath. "She doesn't date. And she definitely doesn't date musicians."

"She doesn't date musicians," I mimic. "Why not?"

"Her reasons are hers to tell, not mine. Just tread lightly, okay?"

I nod and drain my beer. Casey's the first girl I've met in a long time who got my blood pumping like this. A few cryptic messages from her friend aren't enough to make me let that go. In fact, the challenge only makes me want her more.

Chapter 4

Casey

THE PIERCING BEEP of my alarm fills my tiny bed-room. I drag myself out of bed and make the trek to the dresser to clear it. Christ, it's already noon. I set the alarm on purpose to keep from sleeping the entire day away, which is also the reason I leave it on the other side of the room. A bartender's life is pretty much one long night with a few comatose hours of daylight in between. Sometimes, I feel like my life is nothing but darkness.

Yawning, I cross the living room to the kitchen in need of coffee. Calling it a kitchen is being kind. It's more of a kitch-enette, really. A small extension of the living room, it has a banquette of cabinets and a pub table with seating for two. Compared to my apartment in New York, though, this place feels like a palace.

Stepping off that bus the first day in the city, I was in awe of it. A stupid Texas-raised teenager, I'd never seen anything like it. The buildings, the lights, the hustle and bustle. It all seemed so magical. It was a bullshit illusion. New York is the worst, and I'm never going back.

"Coffee." Marisa zombie walks into the kitchen and plops

down at the table. Her hair is half a beehive now, all flat and hanging sadly to the side. Black mascara rings around each eye. She's so not a morning person. My alarm must have woken her.

"Good mornin' to you, too," I reply, setting a mug on the table in front of her. There's no use in talking to her until the cup is half empty. Her fingers slide across the sleek face of her phone as she takes a sip. Coffee and social media in silence. This is her daily routine.

"So what did you think of your first night at The Wreck?" Marisa asks, after returning to her human form.

"It's a job." I shrug.

My first night was interesting, to say the least. Most of it was business as usual, except for being doused in ice water. That kind of sucked.

"AJ's something to look at, huh?" She sucks in a slow breath, slicing her hands down her lower abdomen in a V formation.

I stir my coffee, averting her gaze. "I didn't notice."

I definitely noticed.

He's only about average height, but what he lacks in "tall" he more than makes up for in "dark and handsome." The Adonis belt was only part of it. He had it all. Thick biceps, broad shoulders, and abs that I could use to wash my laundry. He's ripped. Not in a "this guy goes to the gym every day" kind of way. No, he's more like a tough, blue collar, "you only get these kinds of muscles from hard work and sweat" kind of guy. The kind of sexy you see on the ranch back home. The memory of him ripping his shirt off and handing it to me ran through my mind all night in slow motion. It was like a scene from a movie.

So valiant.

So considerate.

So . . . hot.

Marisa laughs. "Yeah, sure you didn't. And you're not still wearing his T-shirt either."

"What? I like it. It's a nice shirt."

She quirks an eyebrow. "It says Orgasm Donor on it."

Unwilling to cave, I casually sip my coffee. The clean, masculine scent of this shirt is blowing my mind a little bit. It's been so long since I've been wrapped in something that smells this delicious that I'm in no rush to take it off. I may be celibate, but I'm not dead.

I jump off the stool to pour myself a second cup of coffee, although I don't need it. For some reason, I'm wired. My pulse is racing so fast it feels like I just ran a marathon. "You guys never . . . you know . . . did you?"

"No, we never hooked up."

Still facing the countertop, the breath I was holding slowly trickles out. Why do I care if they hooked up? I'm not planning to date him. It's not as if I dreamed about licking the sweat off his pecs all night. Nope. Not once did I imagine how his scruff would tickle my skin as his lips roamed my body. Nuh-uh. And by no means did I wake up thinking about his smoldering gray eyes and wide, sexy grin, either. Absolutely not.

Marisa saunters up next to me and leans on the countertop; her mug dangles from the crook of her index finger, waiting for a refill. "It's not from lack of trying, though. Believe me."

An unexpected pang of jealousy stabs me in the stomach. "He asked you out?"

"No." She snorts. "I've made a few innuendos; he turned me down, so I stopped. No use pumping a dry well, right? Besides, I think you're more his type."

"What makes you say that?"

"Honey, you're everybody's type. Besides, I caught him checking out your back end last night."

A flush creeps up my face so fast I feel it in my ears. As much as I'd love to deny it, AJ's gotten in my head. Something about the brooding, musical type sets my thighs on fire, but there's more to him than that. I can feel it. Unfortunately, the guys I'm into only end up breaking my heart. Sometimes worse.

★ ★ ★

I LEAN OVER the bar, wrenching my neck, trying to hear the guy in front of me shout out his order. Bar lights glint off the metal in his face, making it hard to concentrate on what he's saying. The distortion blasting from the stage is giving me a headache. It's so angry. How do people listen to this crap without completely losing their minds?

He shouts his order again, never taking his eyes off my breasts as he does so. My hand travels to the barely there neckline on my Wreck Me tank. Frankie D. presented me with a couple of new ones at the start of my shift. As far as this thing goes, I have two options: either pull the strings on the front super tight, which pushes my chest up and out, or leave them loose and expose more cleavage than I'm interested in showing at this stage of my life. Either way, I'm showing off the goods, and the metal heads are noticing.

The Wreck is slammed. Sweaty bodies press up against each other, writhing and smashing with wild delirium. I never realized how animated a rock crowd was. I grew up listening to country greats like Johnny Cash and Waylon Jennings with my gran. They crooned into their microphones, strumming their guitars and telling a story. Music shouldn't make you want to bang your head. It should uplift your soul.

"Thank you! Good night!" shouts the singer. He looks old and tired. As if he wasted his entire youth living the rock star fantasy only to end up in a crappy tribute band on a bar stage in New Jersey. Dressed in head-to-toe leather and studs, he looks like he belongs in a biker gang more than a rock group. Tonight's headliner called themselves Painkiller. I'm told they're a Judas Priest Tribute band. Whoever that is.

When the lights go on, everyone winces and shields their faces, dispersing into the dark night like vampires escaping the dawn. AJ rises from the board, scratching under his hat as he goes, leaving it slightly off kilter. He takes the seat behind the drum kit. Counting out beats with the shafts of his sticks . . . one, two, three, four . . . he crashes them down on the set around him. Even from here, in the dim light of the bar, I can see his eyes are closed. Sweat flies all over; biceps bulge under his skin with each slam of the sticks.

My knowledge of rock music isn't much, but what I do know is AJ commands that stage. He wails, fast and angry, not only controlling the band, but my heartbeat as well. I pause with an empty tray of glasses in my hands, body tingling as I watch. I'm stuck. Fixated on the beast beating the hell out of the kit and holding me hostage with his talent.

By the time he's finished, I can barely breathe. I'm supposed to hate musicians. The whole institution of show business is built on nothing but bullshit, but something about him captivates me. So much is hiding beneath the surface. He's shown me a little taste of what's deep inside, and now, I'm hungry for more.

A smile stretches across his face when he catches me watching. I drop my gaze and begin wiping the counter, but it's pointless. I've been caught. He moves from the drum kit and goes back to his work. His arms move fluidly, stretching out the power cables and then wrapping them into neat coils with his hands. It's a small, subtle movement, hardly one worth noticing. Something about the way they glide through his hands, like he takes so much pride in the littlest task. It's a rare trait for men these days.

A handful of women loiters about. Their over-the-top giggling bounces off the wooden walls and ceiling. They're trying like hell to get his attention, but his eyes focus on me. I don't have to look up to know. I can feel it. The weight of his stare gets heavier as he comes closer, and the air in the bar thickens.

"Can I get a beer?"

A tiny bead of sweat travels down his neck, and for a split second, I wonder what it would taste like on my tongue. His damp shirt clings to his frame just enough to remind me what's underneath and jack my pulse. This week, a cave man graces the front with the words 'I Swing Big Wood' written across his broad chest. I'm starting to notice a pattern.

"Nice shirt," I say, continuing to run the towel over the bar top. The corners of my mouth twist up in defiance of my brain. His vulgar collection of tees doesn't repulse me the way it should. It's almost as if he's overcompensating. Beneath that cocky attitude, something else is lurking. I see it inside his soulful eyes.

"You too. You look good dry."

He raises his hand to grab the bill of his ball cap with his thumb and pointer then uses the remaining fingers to scratch his scalp. A small jagged scar disappears into the thick mop of raven hair he'd been hiding underneath.

Dropping the hat back in place, he plops on the barstool at his feet. I set a beer down in front of him and try not to notice how utterly kissable his lips are as he brings the bottle to his mouth. "So what's a girl like you doing in a place like this?"

I arch a brow, waiting for the punch line. Did he seriously hit me with another cheesy pickup line? "You think you're pretty smooth, don't you?"

"Lil' bit." When he grins, I actually feel it slithering up the backs of my knees.

Do not let this guy under your skin, Case.

"What kind of girl am I?"

He leans over the bar and peers down at my feet. "The kind of girl who wears cowgirl boots and rhinestone jeans to a heavy metal club. You're too damn sweet to be around so much debauchery."

"Maybe I'm not as sweet as you think," I reply, re-wiping the already clean bar top. In addition to the black ball cap, he's still wearing the same perfect stubble as last weekend. Surrounded by all that darkness, his gray eyes stand out, capturing me like a fly in a web.

His fingers close around my wrist, bringing my incessant wiping to a halt. I'm certain he felt the jump in my pulse. "You're gonna clean a hole right through the counter, cowgirl."

I swallow hard. The intense beating of my heart could headline the next show. A burning tingle shoots up my bicep and spreads throughout my body, starting at the exact spot his rough hand remains clutching my arm. Whether it's from my attraction to him, or the fact that I haven't felt a man's touch in over five years, I can't say, but I suddenly have the same dizzy feeling you get when you stand up too fast after sitting for a while.

"It's late. I should get home." The quiver in my voice is a dead giveaway. My nerves are wound so tight I feel as if I'm about to burst. I can't remember the last time a man elicited this kind of reaction from me with just the touch of his hand, and it's only on my arm.

His grasp tightens as I turn to leave. As strong as he is, his grip, while firm, is still so gentle. He could easily squeeze hard, leaving a mark like a possessive alpha male, but he doesn't, and I know he won't.

"Or maybe it's early. Depends on how you look at it." When I meet his gaze, a touch of sadness behind his steel eyes stops my flight and keeps my feet rooted to the sticky floor.

Marisa crashes in through the doors from the back room. The blue neon lights from the bar catch her red hair, shrouding her in a purple glow. AJ's hand slides off my arm, but it doesn't matter. I still feel it there, scorching my skin and making it hard to breathe. *"Am I interrupting a moment?"*

"Nope." AJ brings the bottle to his lips again but stops just shy of them. *"Casey was just about to give me her phone number."*

"Was I." It's a statement, not a question. AJ's self-confidence is starting to crowd the empty room. This kind of bravado may work on the bar flies, but I know all about guys like him. Sexy and charming are a poisonous combination, the likes of which I am now immune.

AJ sets a single finger on the face of his phone and slides it to my side of the bar. His hand looks beat up, like an old saddle—not pretty to look at, but nothing feels as perfect between your legs. The thought of AJ's hands on my body instantly excites me. Judging by the crowd of women always around him, I have a hunch those hands are skilled in many ways.

I scowl at his phone as Missy scurries around me to start our side work for the night. I don't have time for this. I'm here to work, not give hot guys my number. *"See you next week, AJ."*

★ ★ ★

"NIGHT, FRANKIE; NIGHT, Bits."

I wave to the guys as I walk past, with my purse slung over my shoulder and my opposite hand mindlessly smoothing the ends of my hair. AJ left not long after I deflected his advance. It will be a whole week until I see him again. With any hope, that gives him time to move on and my libido a chance to mellow out. I don't know what's wrong with me. My taste in men has always been shit. If there's a loser within ten miles of me, that's the guy I want. I always did love a project.

I push the thought out of my head as I fling open the door and step out into the sultry spring night. The sky is so clear, lit up by a bright, full moon and millions of glittering stars overhead. This kind of night makes me long for the ranch, sitting on the porch drinking sweet tea with Austin. Sometimes, I sit out on the rickety fire escape, wishing I'd made better choices. That I'd never been swept up in Davis's promises of neon dreams and the thrill of the big city and had married Austin instead. He loved me, and I know he would have made sure we had a nice life together. Unfortunately, I just wasn't ready for it.

AJ leans against my car. Dressed in black from head to toe, he fades into the dark night. The tip of his cigarette glows bright orange when he brings it to his lips and inhales, before tipping his head back to blow the stream into the air. It curls around his lips as he watches me approach, gray eyes shining in the silver moonlight. "I'd offer you a cigarette, but you're already smokin' hot."

"Those things will kill you." I stop in front of him, resting my hand on my hip. My heart continues its relentless pounding, and his gaze drops to the open ties in the front of my tank.

He pulls the cigarette from his mouth with two fingers. I watch the ash whirl in the breeze before he drops it to the pavement and crushes it with the sole of his boot. "I've lived through worse."

"I'm sure you have. Good night."

AJ slides closer to the handle as I reach for it. "I don't bite. I only wanted your number." The familiar scent of detergent, smoke, and masculinity floats off him, making it hard to think. I wore his T-shirt so much this week, the smell of him has started to evaporate from its fibers, and I've actually started to miss it.

"What for?"

He shrugs. "What if I have an emergency rum and Coke situation?"

Don't you dare smile at him.

"If only there was a vast resource of information right at

our very fingertips," I chide, crossing my arms over my chest, holding back the smile threatening to crack my tough exterior. "Oh yeah, there is. It's called the Internet."

His hand smacks his chest as if he's been shot. "Beauty *and* brains? Looks like I hit the jackpot."

That line wins him a well-deserved eye roll. "What can I do to get you off my car?"

He digs his phone from his pocket again and holds it up. "Ten little digits, cowgirl. That's all I ask."

I can't believe I'm doing this.

I grab the phone from his hand, grazing his calloused fingertips in the process. *Lord have mercy, they're as rough as they look.* With trembling fingers, I type in my number and save it into his contacts. Getting involved with someone from work is a bad idea. My need for this job outweighs my need to know how those calloused fingers would feel trailing up my thigh.

He slides the phone out of my hand, gives the screen a few quick swipes, and then slips it back into his pocket. My purse chirps a second later. The moonlight catches on his gleaming white grin, and I notice a tooth off to the side that's slightly crooked. It's hardly noticeable. Something easily missed. But something about it still makes my heart jump. It makes him seem more real. Less perfect. It also makes him a little harder to resist.

Chapter 5

AJ

A ROLLING FOG of steam floats from the crack in my bathroom door so thick I can barely see as I enter. The moisture in the air is heavy, beading up on the mirror and turning my reflection into blobs of unrecognizable black and tan. I walk toward the sound of running water. It's so loud, pounding down on the tile like rain, beckoning to me, daring me to see who might be inside.

The walk seems endless. My bare feet slide on the dense layer of condensation built up on the warm ceramic tile, but the faint outline of a female body through the tempered-glass door stops me in my tracks. It's long and slender, a dancer's body. She moves and sways, lifting her arms above her head, letting the water roll over the delicate curves of her chest and hips. In one seamless movement, her hands glide through her wet hair, run over her breasts, and skim down her taut stomach.

I move in even closer, my need to see who the mystery woman in my shower is outweighing the blatant crossing of boundaries. A petite hand touches the glass. I lay my hand over it a split second before she pulls it away. The figure vanishes, replaced by a blinding light. I shield my face, but it's too late.

The door explodes. Shards of glass shatter all around me,

scratching my eyes and scattering in my hair. The force blows me off my feet. I open my mouth to scream for help, but it, too, fills with glass, tearing up my tongue and destroying my throat. I can't speak, I can't see, and the water continues to beat down on the ground fast and hard, echoing in my ears, making the pain in my head unbearable. My arm hangs uselessly at my side, unable to wipe away the blood I feel pouring over my face. Sirens and shouting, the deafening sound of metal tearing metal . . . then nothing but darkness.

I sit up in my bed, gasping for air. My fingers spring to my wet hair, tracing the scar that recedes into my hairline, but when I pull them back, it's only sweat. There's no blood. There's no glass. It was a dream.

With my heart still in my throat, I blink the remainder of the nightmare from my vision. The accident. Once upon a time, the nightmares were so vivid and frequent it was like re-living it. Constantly, night after night, long after I recovered and returned to my normal life. Well, the new version of my normal life.

But it was years ago. Six years, to be exact. I was a stupid kid, angry and bitter. I let that anger consume me until I was just a shell of my former self. That AJ Morello died on the road. Reborn in his place was a guy with an arm that never quite worked the same way again and nightmares that continued to torment me long after I wake each morning. They said I was lucky to be alive. Sometimes, I'm not so sure.

The chick in the shower is new, though no doubt influenced by a soaking wet cowgirl with killer legs and soft baby blues. I'd rather have that torturous cock-stiffening dream than the usual nightmare. Too many nights I've spent haunted by my baby sister's tears and apologies even though I was the one who fucked everything up.

The seductive woman in my dream was someone else alto-gether. She moved in the shower slow and deliberate as if her body was calling out to me. I swear I heard her whisper my name as she touched herself. Maybe I just need to get laid.

Too shaken to sleep, I light up a smoke and grab my phone. As memories of the dream start to subside, thoughts of Casey pop in front and center. Her heart-shaped lips, the way her eyes picked up the twinkle in the bar lights, and, for Christ's sake, those dimples. I never considered myself a smile guy, but damn. The girl lights up the room by merely walking into it. Marisa said she doesn't date, but I'm determined to put an end to that.

I open my inbox and type in quick text.

You must be exhausted from running through my mind all night.

Smoke pirouettes from the end of the cigarette hanging from my lips, forcing me to squint one eye. Someday, I'll live up to my promise to Jill and actually quit. But today isn't that day.

My heart jumps when my phone vibrates on my lap.

I'm exhausted because you woke me up.

I can almost hear the words dripping from her mouth in that sweet little twang of hers.

Since you're up, meet me for breakfast.

You don't give up, do you?

Nope. ;)

Can't do it, have errands to run today.

What errands?

Nosy, much? If you must know, I have laundry to wash and my car needs an oil change.

The smile that spreads across my face is so big it hurts. Casey obviously has no idea what I do for a living.

An oil change, huh? Meet me at Morello and Tate Restoration in an hour.

After sending off another quick text with the address, I jump out of bed, still laughing about her oil change comment and wondering if it was fate.

★ ★ ★

THE OLD, YELLOW building sits back along the edge of the highway, so bold and bright you can see it from a distance. That was my dad's grand marketing plan. Make it bright enough to notice from the road and ridiculous enough for the customers to remember when they need to come back. As absurd as it sounds, it actually works. Whenever I tell people who I am, commentary about the obnoxious yellow building is sure to follow. He was a crazy old man, but he knew what he was doing when it came to business strategies.

Back then, it was Morello and *Son's* Restoration. We changed it after Jillian got married and Jameson became our partner. He earned it. Our history is spotty, but after all is said and done, he's more than my brother-in-law. I give him a lot of shit, but that dude's my brother in every sense of the word.

It's not long before a Pontiac Grand Am pulls into the empty lot. The black paint glimmers in the sun, but nothing compares to the golden shine of Casey's hair as she emerges from the car.

For a brief moment, I feel like I'm still in a coma. All the blood leaves my brain as she sashays toward me. Her little beige dress flows in the gentle wind, floating around her bare legs. In the sunlight, I can just make out the outline of her body through the thin, almost see-through material. Brown cowboy boots match the braided leather belt cinched around her slim waist, and her hair blows wild and free as she moves. She's a country boy's wet dream. All she needs is a friggin' cowboy hat. I thought she was sexy in jeans, but Casey in a dress takes the cake, and my twitching dick approves.

"Well, you got me here. What's your plan?"

A slow smile spreads across my face as I extend my hand. "Anthony Morello Junior. Nice to make your acquaintance, ma'am," I quip in my best attempt at a Southern accent, tipping my hat.

"First of all, your Texas drawl sucks. Don't do it again. Second, you own this place?"

"That's my name on the sign, isn't it?"

The office door buzzes overhead as I push it open and usher her inside. A dozen donuts and two coffees sit on the monstrosity of a desk, waiting for her arrival. "I promised you breakfast, and I'm a man of my word."

"Well, aren't you just full of surprises?"

"You have no idea. Keys?"

The tinkling strips of metal dangle from her delicate fingers as she turns her palm toward the ceiling. I grab them with one hand and a glazed donut with the other. "Make yourself at home," I say, backing out of the office door.

Banjo playing blasts through her car speakers when I turn the key, followed by a drawling male voice. Casey's country roots run deep, right down to her taste in music. Never been a fan myself. It's not that I'm opposed to it; I just haven't been acquainted with it. I grew up on a steady diet of loud and brash rock 'n' roll from as far back as I can remember. My old man was as hardcore as they come. He was all about fast cars and fast music. It's no surprise Jill and I turned out the way we did. It's in our blood.

In no time, the car's jacked up and I'm in the zone. Oil changes are monotonous work. Lift the car, drain the oil, check the filter, and so on and so forth. It's mindless. A job any jackhole with half a brain could do, but nobody likes to get their hands dirty anymore. Not that I love what I do or anything, but it beats sitting in some stuffy office staring at a computer all day. I couldn't do that shit. Thankfully, Jill's good at it. She runs this office like a pro, and she's anal as hell. She has her system and doesn't allow anyone to mess with it. It's the reason she hasn't given in and hired someone to replace her now that she has Zakk. She can't give up control of the office. We're a great duo. Well, trio.

"How's it going out here?"

"All set."

Casey twirls a wavy tendril around her finger and leans against the wall as she sips her coffee. "So what do I owe you?"

I smack the button on the lift, and the car begins its slow descent to the ground. "Don't worry about it," I reply with a dismissive wave.

"You have to let me give you somethin'."

"Go out with me this week."

"Are you extorting a date out of me?"

"No. I'm asking you out. If you say no, it's still no charge." My boots scuff on the dirty concrete floor as I walk over to where she's standing. "But say yes, Case."

"What if I don't?"

"I'll just keep asking until you do."

Standing this close, I notice her blue eyes have flecks of topaz and sapphire in them. There's no usual green ring around her irises dulling their brilliant color. They size me up as if she's contemplating her answer. She wants to say yes, I can tell, but she's hesitating. This Tom and Jerry game excites her. The thrill of being hunted is what drives her. "You really interested in takin' me out, or you just hopin' to get your hands on my chassis?"

Car metaphors. I like this girl.

"These hands will stay in these pockets, I swear."

Her bottom lip disappears between her teeth and slides out slowly, leaving the tiniest bit of saliva on her plain pink lips. All it would take is one step forward to close the distance and press my mouth to hers. "Fine."

"Excuse me, what was that?" I say, cupping my hand around

my ear.

"You win, city boy. I'll go out with you. Afterward, you stop, okay? Stop askin' me out, stop with the pickup lines. Deal?"

"Sure, cowgirl. Whatever you want."

Chapter 6

Casey

"SO WHAT ARE you going to wear?"

Marisa lies sprawled out on my bed, watching me apply mascara. Two gigantic, messy buns flank each side of her head, like flames shooting out of her skull.

"Uh. This?" My usual wardrobe is jeans and a tank top, which is the exact outfit I'm wearing right now. I'll wear a skirt or the occasional dress, but it's best if I keep this casual. I don't want to give off the wrong impression.

She slides off the bed and pads to my closet. "Bor-ing," she singsongs, punctuating the syllables of the word. The hangers clang together as she pushes them across the bar in search of something better. "You have legs like a thoroughbred. Wear a skirt or something."

"Legs like a thoroughbred?" I laugh, pausing mid-mascara stroke.

"Yeah, you know. Strong, long, elegant. Thought you knew all about horses?"

"Ridin' them, not checkin' them out!"

A squeal echoes from the interior of the closet. "How about this?" A black strip of fabric—hanger and all—flies out and hits the floor with a thud. I turn and eye the satin garment on the ground as Marisa extracts herself from the closet and picks it up.

"That's a slip, Missy. Not a dress."

She looks at the slip then back at me with furrowed red brows. "So? It's hot. Give the stud horse a run for his money."

"Put it back," I say with a smile.

The old metal frame creaks under her weight after Marisa finishes her tour of my closet, and plops back down on my bed. "Show off a little skin, babe. That's all I'm saying."

Show off a little skin, she says. I'm half tempted to call this whole thing off and get back in my sweats. Butterflies flap inside my gut every time I think about AJ. Knowing he's on his way here has kicked the little suckers into high gear. "Am I makin' a mistake here?"

"I'd wear more eyeshadow, but that's just me."

"No, I mean goin' out with AJ."

In the mirror's reflection, I see Marisa pull herself to a sitting position. "No. You need to get out, Case. It's been long enough."

"I know you're right. It's just . . ."

"Listen." She slides to the edge of the bed as I turn to face her again. "I know you think God is smiting you or whatever, because of Austin, but that's crazy. You aren't meant to wander the Earth alone for all of eternity because you broke some good ol' boy's heart. It's just not logical."

"I did a little more than break his heart, Miss—"

The ringing doorbell cuts through my point. She doesn't get it. I broke a sacred oath. I promised my hand to a man fully knowing I never intended to deliver. I'm an awful human being and a poor excuse for a Christian.

"I'll get it." Marisa saunters out of my room, red buns bouncing as she goes. The word *Juicy* written across her slender backside sways with each step. Sometimes, I wish I had half her self-confidence. Everything about Marisa just screams, "Here I am! Love me or hate me, fuck you either way!"

Voices trickle in from the living room as I finish getting ready. Exhaling long and slow, I give myself one last look. *"The Lord is merciful and forgivin', even though we have rebelled against him. You can do this, Case."*

How did I get here? Back home, I felt like a big fish in a tiny pond. All that wide-open space was suffocating. I had plans. I was gonna be somebody. But who am I? A twenty-six-year-old bartender who's afraid of her own shadow and can't even stand her own reflection. Davis was supposed to save me, but he did the exact opposite.

Pushing off the dresser, I force myself through the door and out into the living room, where AJ leans against the arm of our ugly floral couch, talking to Marisa.

Holy hell.

He looks about as mouthwatering as a steak does. The graphic tee and black hat combo are nowhere in sight, replaced by a button-down shirt that hugs every curve of his torso. The light blue color is a perfect contrast to his olive skin and dark chin scruff. His hair is messy like he's a few days past a haircut, but it looks so dang good. I wouldn't doubt it's on purpose, much like the day-old stubble perpetually covering his jaw. When I first met AJ, I thought he was cute. The man standing in my living room is so far beyond cute it's scary. He looks good enough to eat, and I'm suddenly starving to death.

"You ready for me, cowgirl?" he says with a grin.

No, I'm definitely not ready for him. I expected to be going out with the goofy sound guy from The Wreck. The one with an easy smile who's full of jokes. But instead, I'm greeted at the door by a smoldering, sexy businessman with deliciously dirty hands who's looking at me like I'm a tall drink of water on a hot day. A far cry from the guy spouting pickup lines who literally gave me the shirt off his back last week. Underneath that cocky grin and stubble is more than meets the eye, and so far, I really like what I'm seeing.

The rocks in my stomach continue to tumble as we walk side by side through the parking lot. "This is your truck?" I ask, coming face to face with tires. The red pickup is lifted to a monolithic height; there are actually steps to get into it.

"Yup. I like to be in charge of the road, not the other way around."

AJ pulls the truck door open for me then grabs my hips to help me step inside. Warmth envelops my waist along with his hands and travels into all my limbs, before finding its home between my thighs. Being this close to him, I'm overcome by the strangest combination of feelings. Extreme anxiety with an acute sense of calm.

The bench seat in the Chevy is old, but the leather is soft and remains warm from the balmy spring day. The dashboard is sleek and shiny. There isn't a speck of dust inside this thing, which is shocking considering his profession. Most of the boys I knew back home had pickups that were filthy and full of dirt and hay and empty containers of Skoal.

"Where we headed?"

"A little place a few towns over called The Saloon. You'll like it." He moves the stick shift around with expert precision, letting his hand rest on the knob as he pulls out of the lot.

The Saloon, huh? I'm not sure if I should be flattered or offended, but I'm keeping an open mind.

The only sound on the way to the place is the low hum of rock music filtering out of the speakers of his truck. He doesn't say much, just concentrates on the road while tapping lightly on the steering wheel. AJ never stops moving. The constant bounce of his fingers and toes is a clear sign of the music in his head trying desperately to get out.

I reach over and switch the station on his radio. He glances in my direction for a split second and chucks me a lazy grin. "You're as bad as my sister is."

"Oh?" I reply, returning his smile.

"Yeah. She plays DJ every time she gets into anyone's car. Except for mine." He reaches out and taps the button on the radio back to where it was. "I'm the king of this castle on wheels."

"Who are you, Ralph Kramden?"

"Bang . . . zoom . . . ," AJ snaps, pointing at the moon. It surprises me. Very few people our age would understand a *Honeymooner's* reference, never mind being able to zing one back without thought. I guess I'm not the only one addicted to late-night television. "You really like this country shit, huh?"

"Yeah. Is it that bad?"

"The music's good, but I could do without all the religious undertones. There's too much Jesus talk."

"Some of it, sure. You got a problem with Jesus?"

"Never met the man." He glances in my direction with a cocky grin before turning his attention back on the road. "But I don't buy into this whole God and heaven stuff. Death is the end." The curt cut of his hand across his neck drives his point home.

That theory is too depressing to fathom. All my life, my faith has been what's gotten me through. I'm no religious zealot, but I hold strong to the idea of a higher power watching over us, aiding us as we make our way through life.

I flick the button again. The whining sound of the fiddle cries through the cab as Tim McGraw sings his homage to small town life. AJ looks my way again. The heel of one hand rests over the steering wheel, while the other continues to rest on the stick shift. "You're lucky you're cute."

"I love this song."

I ignore the compliment and hang on every word sung and every note played. Country music gets a bad rap. Most people think it's all depressing songs about lost loves, but it's not. It's deeper than that. It has a soul. It worms its way into your heart and stays there.

Unlike rock music that screams in your face—loud and relentless—country music comes together with a vibrant mix of instruments and sounds. It speaks to me in a beautiful, eloquent voice, whispering in my ear like a lost love. It takes me to another place, away from my problems, and somehow makes everything better.

Music, in general, has a power all its own. One single line or chord has the ability to change a person's entire outlook. It's magical, when you think about it.

Chapter 7

AJ

"**G**IMME THE BIGGEST margarita you got!" Casey shouts over the loud music in the bar.

"Budweiser," I add.

Her dimpled grin makes my insides tingle. "How the hell did you find a honky-tonk in New Jersey?"

"A wise woman once pointed out that I had a vast resource of information right at my fingertips."

I lean back on the bar with both elbows and bring the bottle to my lips. I've never seen so much concentrated plaid in my entire life. Hundreds of dudes in tight jeans and cowboy hats doing the two-step with girls in denim skirts. It's bizarre. This weird sense of displacement must be what Casey feels every time she goes to work.

The Saloon promised "Southern charm," and it seems to be holding up its end of the bargain. Not that I have any idea what I'm talking about, but the cavernous divots on Casey's cheeks tell me that even if it's all wrong, I've done something right. Making her smile is starting to become my number one goal. Her ass, tits, and legs are nothing short of perfection, but that smile blows them away. It blows *me* away.

"So what's it like in Texas?"

"Dry, hot . . . barren. You could see for miles in any direction." She takes a sip of her drink then flicks the tip of her tongue against the rim of the glass, picking up a few thick granules of salt. My dick perks up like a dog waiting for a treat. *Down, boy!*

"And your folks?" Small talk is not my specialty, but I can't get enough of the sound of her voice. It's like birds chirping outside your window. All sunny and pleasant and shit.

"I never knew my dad, and my mom was in and out. She was still in high school when I was born. My gran raised me."

"Is she still around?"

"Yeah, she's still kickin'. Gets up early, checks the horses. I grew up on a horse ranch in a tiny town most people have never heard of."

Thankfully, the music is loud enough that she can't hear me groan. *She rides horses.* As if the salt lick wasn't bad enough, all I can think about now is her riding me. Hard and fast, squeezing me to death with those long, tan legs of hers. I have to bite the inside of my cheek to keep from busting out of my jeans like a loser. At almost thirty, I should have more control over my body, but at this exact moment—hell, since the moment I met her—my junk is a puppet, and Casey is the one holding the strings.

"Ever ride a bull?" Casey turns to follow my gaze. In the corner of the bar, a mechanical bull spins lazily, waiting for its next rider. "Bet I can stay on it longer than you can." Just the very thought of her on top of that thing makes my dick press against my zipper so hard it's begging for salvation.

"You're on!"

Draining my beer, I grab her hand and drag her over to the bullpen. The sign near the gate says anyone who can stay on for thirty seconds gets a beer on the house. I chuckle. Thirty seconds is cake!

"You first," she says with a wry grin.

My bare feet sink into the thick padding as I walk through the pen and slide onto the headless replica of a bull. *How hard could this possibly be?*

It whizzes to life, slow at first. I hold on to the reins at the front of the saddle. The mischievous gleam in Casey's eyes matches her devious smile as she stands at the edge of the pen, crossing her arms over her chest.

The operator spins a dial, and the bull whips around in a full circle, catapulting me off its back. *What the hell just happened?* In the corner, Casey isn't just laughing. She's doubled over, holding her stomach and gasping for air. With bruised pride, I stand and brush myself off, trying to act cool, even though I feel like a dumbass.

"I wish I had that on film!" she spits out between sobs of laughter.

"Good luck, cowgirl. That shit is harder than it looks!"

She slides her boots off and pulls herself onto the saddle, nestling the bull between her thighs. *The lucky bastard.* With one hand wrapped securely around the rein, and the other wavering high in the air, she nods. The operator hits a button. The bull begins its slow movements but quickly picks up speed. Casey's thighs tighten around the fiberglass body. Her arm flies back and forth above her head, balancing herself on the massive contraption bucking between her powerful legs. It whips to the right. Then swings to the left. Casey moves with it, rolling her hips with each dip and turn. Inside, I'm dying. Woozy from lack of blood to the brain just watching the sensual way she rides.

The bull whips in a full circle, winning the war and knocking Casey off. Hollers erupt from the watching crowd as she pushes herself to her feet with a bow. That was, hands down, the hottest thirty-five seconds of my life.

"It ain't that hard," she quips as she walks past, sliding deeper into that slow Texas twang that turns my dick to steel.

An older dude in a bib shirt tips his cowboy hat and whistles as he passes. I pull Casey against me, keeping my arm secured around her waist as I whisper in her ear. "Is that what a real man looks like?"

I feel her smile on my cheek a second before her breathy giggle floats into my ear. The flowery scent of her hair mingles with the warmth of her hand on my chest while visions of her on that bull still burn into my memory. All of it overloads my senses and makes every outline in the dim bar fuzzy.

"Let's see if your dancin's better than your ridin'."

"I don't dance," I reply, but she continues forward, backing me onto the dance floor.

Casey's hip knocks against mine. I stand stock-still, unable to move even if I knew what to do. Her eyes lock on me as she dances. The beat booming overhead is a killer mash-up of cool country sounds with heavy hard rock guitar riffs, but I'm not paying attention. I'm too caught up in the way her body sways along with a smooth, seductive roll.

First, the bull and now, this. The woman oozes sex out of every single pore, yet still maintains such an air of elegance it knocks me on my ass. She's on fire. Stomping the floor with her boot and shimmying her hands up her body and into the air, she's dancing like she's the only person in the room.

I wasn't lying when I said I never dance, but for some reason, I find myself taking hold of her, spinning her around, and leading her along the dance floor as best I can. Golden strands of hair fly around her as she twirls. She laughs and spins and slides up against me, holding me close even though my two left feet have to be an atrocious embarrassment to her. I'm so far out of my element.

"I got you, city boy," she whispers in my ear.

If only she realized how true that statement really is. She's got me all right, in more ways than she even knows. If someone told me a month ago I'd be dancing in a country bar with a beautiful Southern belle, I'd have died of laughter. However, here I am doing the Boot Scootin' Boogie, and I don't give a crap about anything other than this moment right now.

I spin her to the edge of the dance floor, holding her body against mine. The tangy scent of limes lingers on her breath. Being with someone I like is alien territory. I don't know how to act around a girl like Casey. She's classy. Nothing like the girls who frequent The Wreck and my bed. I knew she was special from the second I saw her. Pickup lines and overconfidence may work on the masses, but I don't want to be that guy. I want Casey to see me as I am. A man. One who doesn't mince words and refuses to play games. Life's too damn short.

Casey shifts her stance, and her knee slides past mine. Inviting warmth radiates against my thigh, and the only thing I want to do right now is move my hand up her long ass leg and tear the jeans right off her.

Her fingers tangle in the ends of her hair, twisting around one way then the other. I want to know what she's thinking every time she twirls those beautiful strands of gold. I want to know what she's thinking in general. Her likes, her dislikes, and, most of all, how that tantalizing little twang sounds moaning my name.

There's something between us. Surely, she feels it too. Otherwise, she wouldn't be here. She wouldn't be holding me like this or watching me with fascinating eyes filled with a look that's anything but innocent. Casey is not the scared puppy I thought she was. No. She's a hellhound, and I'm definitely up for the challenge of taming the beast dying to break out of her.

Chapter 8

Casey

A STEAMING HOT mug of coffee weighs down each hand as I poke my head in Marisa's room. After last night's date, I could really use a little girl talk.

At noon, it's hardly early, but by Marisa's standards, it may as well be six a.m. To my chagrin, her bed is empty. "Dang it," I whisper, retreating to the kitchen. She must have stayed out last night.

Half the night, I spent awake, tossing and turning as I thought about my date with AJ. His dance moves are terrible, but that still didn't stop me from swooning every time he spun me around. Other than the overwhelming smack of desire I felt every time he put his arms around me, being with him was easy and effortless. Resisting his charms is no easy feat.

A musical jingle flows from my bedroom. I run to grab the phone, sure that it's going to be Marisa, but my elation over last night's date fades when I see the Texas area code.

Lord have mercy, something's happened to Mama.

The last time I received a call from an unknown Texas number, my mom needed me to wire her bail money. Mama's addictions have been a noose around all our necks for years. Every day, I wait for that phone call from Gran telling me she's gone. When that day comes, I wonder how I'll feel about it.

Back in her day, Loretta Grainger was something special. Blond and pretty, she was head cheerleader and pageant queen. She could have had her pick of any guy in town, but she wasn't interested in settling down. Mama always said trouble just had a way of finding her, but everybody knew she went out looking for it. She wanted danger, excitement. All she ended up with was me.

She tried for a little while, but she eventually left me with Gran to find herself a life. Every so often, she'd clean up her act and come home, swearing it was the last time and promising to make it up to me. I always believed her. But each time, without fail, she'd relapse and disappear, leaving Gran to pick up the pieces of my broken heart. I took it for granted, but Gran was always there. She was the one hosting the birthday parties and cheering me on in the stands. She even took a second job cleaning houses to buy me my first guitar for my fourteenth birthday. When push came to shove, Gran became the mother my own couldn't be.

I brace myself, anticipating a collect call from the Brewster County jail. "Hello?"

"Hi. Is a Miss Casey Grainger there, please?"

"This is Casey. Who's this?"

"Well, hey there, baby girl. I know it's been a long time, but I'm crushed you don't remember me."

The low sexy drawl on the other end is definitely not the sheriff. My old nickname punches me in the chest then sits in my stomach like a rock. It's a name from my past said in a voice I never thought I'd hear again.

"Austin?" I swallow hard, my heart racing greyhound fast. "You okay?" Beads of sweat form on my palms. The last time we spoke was on Gran's porch at graduation. When he proposed.

"Yep. Right as rain, just doin' my thing. You sound different. Hope big city living ain't changing ya too much."

I may sound different, but Austin's voice is exactly how I remember it. He speaks the way he makes love. Slow and deep. Hearing it after all these years is like coming home again. If I close my eyes, I can smell the hay in the stables, feel his dry, coarse hands on my body, and taste his sweat on my tongue. My body reacts. It's second nature. Austin made me feel things I'd never felt before—desired, lusted, loved, wanted. His scorching touch ignited a blaze in my heart and a firestorm down below.

Ghostly memories of us float around me. The polite way he used to smile when I tried to catch his attention, a stupid twelve-year-old trying too dang hard to impress the seventeen-year-old boy Gran hired to help on the ranch. He was always such a gentleman, though. He never treated me like a little kid, even though I'm sure my presence was more of a nuisance than anything. Austin Krehley is a good man, and I never deserved him.

"No, I'm still me."

A sad smile crosses my lips. As I grew up, our friendship evolved into something more. I was sixteen when he finally worked up the courage to ask Gran if he could take me out. He worried that being five years my senior would be a problem, but after four years on the ranch, Gran knew he was harmless. She saw the way he looked at me—with love instead of lust. His intentions were true from the start, and the years I spent with him were some of the happiest of my life. He was my best friend and my first love.

Until Davis Cole blew into town.

"Well, darlin', I hate to be the bearer of bad news, but this ain't a social call." Austin clears his throat and continues. "I know that mom o' yours ain't good for nothing, and you don't wanna hear from her anyway, so I'm calling you myself. Gran's passed on."

The phone slips from my hand and drops into my lap. I hear his distant voice say my name a second time, but I feel like I've been kicked by a mule. Gran can't be gone. I just talked to her last week. She sounded tired but good.

Goose bumps break out on my skin as I silently rehash our last conversation. *I miss ya something awful, but singing on the stage is what you left to do, and I'm damn proud of ya for living your dream.* Gran knew I worked in a club, but I didn't have the heart to tell her I was in the pit serving drinks instead of up in the spotlight where she claimed I belong. It was the last time I'll ever hear her voice, and it was all a lie.

"Casey Jane, did I lose you?"

Nausea twists in my gut. I lift the phone to my ear again, blinking back the tears. "What happened?"

"Heart attack."

The floodgates open, and fat giant tears roll down my cheeks, soaking my face with salty wetness. I should have been there. Married Austin and taken over the ranch the way Gran wanted. That was the plan, but I just wasn't ready. I was too young and naïve. I thought I had the rest of my life ahead of me. Now, I'll never see the ranch again. And I'll never see her again. She died alone, and it's all my fault.

"Where's Mama?" I choke out between sobs. The anger rises up my face just saying the title she never deserved.

"You know how your ma is. She dashed in for a second to sign some papers and split just as fast. Gran was cremated this morning."

All those years she stayed away, but the minute it came time to collect the deed to the ranch she came running. Of course. Anything for a buck. I wouldn't doubt if she's been on the phone with realtors all day trying to get it sold as fast as possible. Gran would be rolling over in her grave. That is if Loretta was warm-hearted enough to have given her one.

"Aww, baby girl. Hearin' you cry just breaks my heart," Austin goes on, killing me with the kindness ingrained in him from birth. How can he be so damn nice all the time? He should hate me for what I did. Lord knows I hate me. I told him I loved him, kissed him on the mouth, and then caught the midnight bus to the East Coast with a different man. I'm worse than dirt. I'm just like *her*.

"Look, I'm fixin' to finish up some stuff down at the stables. It's okay if I call on you again?" Austin never could stand being around a crying woman; I'm not surprised he wants off the phone the second my tears start.

"Yeah, of course. Thank you, Austin. For . . ." *the constant support, the tender care, taking control, staying to help Gran, and continuing to love me in spite of all I've done wrong,* "Everythin'."

"All right, darlin'. You take care of yourself."

I disconnect the call and curl into a sobbing ball on my bed, feeling so alone. I should have told Gran how much she meant to me. Now, she's gone, and I'll never get the chance. The sound of pride in her voice every time I lied about singing drives a stake through my wounded heart. I lied to an old woman, and I let it get so far out of hand.

When the phone rings again, I swipe the screen and answer without looking at the caller ID. "Austin?"

"Guess again, cowgirl. You okay?" AJ's Yankee tone sounds gruff compared to Austin's slow Texas style, but the concern in his voice is equal.

Immediately, I regret answering the phone. AJ and I have only scratched the surface of our relationship; I don't want him to hear me like this. Even still, I find myself answering his question with a brutal honesty that shocks me. "Not even a little bit," I sob. "My gran died."

"Oh shit. Do you have to go back for a funeral or something?"

Tears roll down my forearm when I wipe the back of my hand across my sopping cheek. I need to calm down. "No. She's already been cremated. There won't be any services."

"I'm really sorry, Case. Anything I can do?"

"Just . . . talk to me."

The line goes so quiet that I would have thought he hung up if not for the loud rock 'n' roll music blasting in the background. A few agonizing moments later, he starts talking again. "A woman wants to find a husband, so she puts out an ad. It says 'I'm looking for a man that won't hit me, won't run away, and can satisfy me.' A week later, she hears a very loud knock at the door. She answers it, and it's a man with no arms or legs. He says 'I can't beat you because I have no arms, and I can't run away because I have no legs.' The woman smiles and replies, 'How do I know you can satisfy me?' He grins and says 'How do you think I was knocking?'"

I furrow my brow for a split second before bursting into a strange mixture of cackling laughter and flowing tears. "You're disturbed."

"Maybe. But I got you laughing."

"You did," I say. The bing-bong sound of the doorbell rings through the apartment, breaking my train of thought. "Hold on a second. Someone's at my door."

Strolling past the mirror, I cringe at my own reflection. More so than usual. My eyes are swollen from crying, and my slept on hair looks like I've been through the wringer. I twist it into a quick ponytail and wipe my face. I can't do much about my puffy eyes, but at least whoever is on the other side won't have to worry about me trying to eat his brains. With the phone nestled snug between my ear and shoulder, I unlock the deadbolt and slide the door open.

"You sound like you need more than a dirty joke, cowgirl."

AJ's voice comes through in stereo. For the second time in less than twenty-four hours, I find myself falling into his arms and savoring the way they feel around me.

"I know how much it hurts, Casey." He steps into the room, closing the door behind him with his foot while his hand strokes my back. *"I'm not gonna lie and tell you the pain will go away. You'll always carry a piece of it with you because you'll never stop loving her, but I promise you, even though it doesn't seem like it now, one day you'll wake up, and it won't hurt as bad. You'll see something that reminds you of her, and instead of tears, you'll find joy in her memory."*

"This is all my fault. It broke her heart when I ran away."

Trying to be brave and strong flies right out the window as AJ holds me closer to his body. His scent is a mix of clean cotton, oil, and tobacco, mixed with the sweet spice of cologne, a fragrance that will make me think of him from this moment on. An unending river of tears flows from my eyes, soaking his 2112 shirt while we stand near the door in the living room.

"She gave me everythin', and I never had a chance to thank her for any of it. All I ever did was lie to her. I'm a huge disappointment. Just like my mother."

"Nothing you did caused this. I'm sure your grandmother was proud up until her last breath."

My knees give under the weight of my sorrow. AJ's arm hooks around them, lifting my feet off the floor. He settles on the couch, setting me on his lap. We stay like this, melting into each other's embrace, for what seems like an eternity. Until I'm completely empty inside.

"You know," he says after a while. *"Whenever I'm sad, I go in my garage and play the drums. I wail on the set until I'm so spent I no longer have the energy to be sad anymore, and I'm

cleansed of whatever is bothering me." He gently strokes the flyaway hairs back from my hairline and tucks them behind my ear. It's a simple touch, one meant to comfort me, I'm sure, but the tickling sensation from his fingertips sends a feeling of warmth settling in my stomach. "What helps take your mind off things?"

Sitting up, I wipe away the last of my sob-fest. I've never given it much thought. For the last few years, I've been in a permanent state of discontent and haven't really done much of anything. Except . . .

A lost memory hits me like a tidal wave. I was ten years old, and a boy at school was picking on me, saying having no parents makes me an orphan. All the way home from school, I cried, until I reached the ranch and ran into Gran's arms. She hugged me tight and said, "Don't cry about the past and don't worry about the future. Just live in the present and make it beautiful." We stayed in the kitchen, rolling dough and eating chocolate chips until I felt like I was ready to burst. Gran was good like that. She always knew what to say in any situation, and when in doubt, she always kept the pantry stocked with dessert ingredients.

"I bake."

AJ's brows crease. "You mean, like . . ." he starts, pressing his thumb and index finger together and bringing it to his lips.

"No, I don't *get* baked. I bake. Like cookies and stuff."

How does he do it? Even when I'm drowning in tears, AJ has the ability to make me laugh.

He rises from the couch, lifting me off his lap, and then sets my feet down gently on the floor. "I like cookies. Let's give it a shot."

Chapter 9

AJ

A LIGHT DUSTING of flour covers every surface of Casey's kitchen. It's like a scene from *Scarface* in here. Not that there are many surfaces to begin with—the room is the size of a matchbox. Almost as if the kitchen was an afterthought when they made this apartment.

Casey stands over a huge mixing bowl, humming along with the radio as she measures out a cup of sugar. I lean against the counter, one ankle crossed over the other just watching. Her hair is in a ponytail, she's not wearing a bit of makeup, and her Dallas Cowboys pajama pants do nothing for her figure, but I swear I've never seen her more beautiful. Standing at the oven, Casey seems completely at ease. She's baked two trays of cookies so far, all from memory, and not a single tear fell the whole time.

The earlier sadness in her voice tore me open. It was like reliving the death of my own parents again with every tear that fell from her giant blue eyes. Losing a loved one like that causes irreparable damage. I have an intense need to fix things. It's what I do when something is broken. I tinker with it until it's whole again. But this problem is unfixable. The only thing I can do is be a friend and keep her mind occupied.

When she pops the cookie sheet into the oven and turns, a wavy strand of gold falls over her face. *"Are you sure you don't have to go back to work? I feel bad keepin' you."* She pushes the strand away, leaving a small streak of flour in her hair. I reach for her, running my fingers through it and wiping it away.

"I think I'm entitled to one afternoon off. Besides, there's nowhere else I'd rather be than with you."

Casey's lashes are dark and stuck together from crying, tiny crowns gracing each lovely blue eye. Her tongue slips between her lips, moistening them as they part. It leaves a thin sheen of saliva that shines in the midday sunlight beaming through the small kitchen window. I lift the brim of my cap just long enough to scratch my head before plopping it back down—a nervous tic I've never been able to shake. Part of me wants to kiss her so badly it aches, but the logical part knows taking advantage of a vulnerable chick is a real douchey move. Still, I can't seem to tear myself away.

"You have a little chocolate here."

She swipes her fingertip over the corner of my mouth, letting it graze across my lips before slipping it between them. The taste of sugar explodes on my tongue, from both the cookies and what I'm sure is the natural flavor of Casey's skin. Everything about this is wrong. She spent the entire afternoon crying on my lap. She's confused and hurt, and I shouldn't want her this bad, but fuck, it's hard to control.

I reach up, closing my fingers around her wrist. *"What are you doing to me, Case?"* My voice is deep and husky, riddled with want I no longer care to hide. The look in her eyes and the smell of her skin turns me inside out. She knows what she's doing to me.

At the other end of the room, the doorknob jiggles. Casey jumps as Marisa comes bursting in. Her orange hair is wild, and huge silver earrings dance in the light as they dangle from her ears. I wouldn't be surprised if her panties were wadded up in a ball in her purse. She's the very poster child for the walk of shame. "Oh!" she says, hovering in the doorway, a sneaky smile spreading across her too-red lips. "Well, well, well. What's going on here?"

"Nothing," I reply, pushing off from the counter. "Just making some cookies."

Marisa looks at Casey, then back at me, with her Joker style grin. She probably thinks I slept here.

"Looks like a whole lot of nothing to me," she says, walking further into the room. "It's cool. I ain't here to judge." She saunters into her room and closes the door behind her.

I look back toward Casey while shoving my hands into my pockets to adjust myself with stealth. Marisa's sudden appearance threw water on my libido but not nearly enough. I need a cold shower and a cigarette. "I'm gonna take off for a bit and let you rest." I push her ponytail off her shoulder and run my fingers through it freely. "But I'll come back to pick you up tonight if you want."

"Can't wait." She lifts herself onto her toes and presses her lips against my cheek as I back away. "And AJ." I turn from the open doorway to face her. "Thanks."

★ ★ ★

THE SUN IS still high in the sky as I roll past Morello and Tate and into my sister's driveway. She's probably going to give me shit for never returning to work after lunch, but whatever.

As usual, music plays through the open windows, loud and brash. Geoff Tate screams in his high-pitched soprano, preaching about religion and sex ruling the world. Meanwhile, back at Casey's, some dude with two first names was prattling on about the power of prayer. The irony of the situation puts a smile on my face as I jump down from my truck and head for the door.

Not bothering to knock, because no one would hear me anyway, I let myself in and head for the kitchen. My sister is always cooking something. Whether it's a giant meal, a snack, or baby food, she lives in this kitchen. She's so much like our mother—it's scary sometimes.

"Don't you two have a room?" I grumble as I enter and find Jameson nuzzling her neck from behind while she stirs whatever it is she's cooking on the stove. He looks up, flashing me that stupid, lazy grin of his.

Originally, the idea of them together was enough to make me want to go on a murder spree. I actually went all alpha and forbade him from going near her, but I guess love has a way of conquering all the obstacles in its path. Fate will always intervene when it's meant to be. I sound like a chick, but it's true. Love will find a way. My father loved my mother so much he couldn't stand to be apart from her. Her death eventually killed him. It's hard to live with a heart that's so broken.

"It's my house, motherfucker. If I wanna bend my wife over the table and tap her ass in the dining room, I will." Jameson stands full height and steps away, punching my shoulder on his way to the fridge. "Again."

"You're late," Jillian jokes. She's so used to this routine between Jameson and me that it doesn't even faze her anymore.

She turns to give me a quick hug, and I panic. Usually, I change my shirt before coming over, but with everything that happened this afternoon I forgot. "And you smell like . . ." A sheen of sweat breaks out on my skin. Jillian may be the size of a large child, but you do not want to piss her off. The last time she caught me smoking, she lost her damn mind and went all Tasmanian devil on my ass. I wait for the inevitable shit storm, but instead, she pinches her brows together, and says

"Cookies?"

Why couldn't she just smell smoke?

"Oh. Yeah. I was with a friend."

A slow smile grows on her lips as she crosses her arms over her chest. "And you were baking? Would this be a female friend?"

"Yeah. What of it?"

"Look at his face! Holy shit!" Jameson bellows. It's not until he points it out that I realize I'm wearing the lamest grin of all time. I feel my face get hot. Thankfully, my skin is dark enough to hide that shit. Jillian got Mom's snow-white complexion, while I was blessed with an all-year tan like our father.

"Fuck you, dude!" I say, trying my best not to appear like a love-struck idiot in front of my brother-in-law. He'll never let me hear the end of it. Neither of them will. Ballbusters—both of them!

"Tell me everything," Jillian insists.

I should have just gone home. There's a reason I haven't mentioned my non-relationship with Casey. Because there's nothing to tell. We had one date. It's way too soon to be involving my crazy family. Especially Jillian.

When she was single, she didn't care what or who I was doing. Now that she's married, the topic of my love life is always front and center. Married people are cult leaders. They're always trying to recruit new members. If she thinks I have even the possibility of a girlfriend, she'll be naming my kids before I know it.

I bring a bottle of beer to my lips and hope my silence is enough of an indicator that I don't want to talk about it. Turns out, it's not. "At least tell me her name!" Jill begs.

"Casey. She works at The Wreck."

Jillian's absurdly large eyes grow as big as saucers. "Musician?"

If there's one person on this planet who loves rock 'n' roll as much, if not more, than I do, it's Jill. For me, it's always been about technique. The way the various pieces fit together seamlessly, each unique sound working together to create something majestic. Each player has his own voice; it's not just about the singer. Jill is different. She loves it as a whole. She feels it deep in her bones and uses it to control her moods and her feelings. The soundtrack to her life constantly plays wherever she is.

When we were kids, Jameson and I played music in the garage out back—me on the drums and him on guitar. Jill would sit there for hours just watching us. It didn't matter that we sucked, just hearing the music made her happy. The idea that I may be involved with a musician would be like completing the circle.

"Bartender."

Jill turns back to her pot and continues stirring. "Do I get to meet her?"

I take another swig of my bottle and change the subject. "Zakk sleeping?"

My nephew is the perfect segue out of any conversation. The second someone mentions his name, Jill gets all soft and pliable. It's ridiculous how something so small can have such an enormous impact. The second that little ass-kicker came flying out our family began breathing again.

"Nah," Jill says with an instant smile. "He's in his playpen in the other room. I have to feed him, though. You can go get him if you want."

Zakk's baby pen sits in the corner of the family room, facing the television. Bert and Ernie dance on the screen singing about ducks and shit, but Zakk looks too amused by the squishy ball in his lap to notice. Black hair pokes up on his head in every direction as he tries his best to shove the entire ball into his mouth.

"Hey, kid. You don't wanna eat that." I grab him from his mesh prison, making sure to avoid the V-shaped wet mark on his shirt. I'm told he's teething, which explains the drool always pouring out of his gummy smile. Wiping his face with a nearby cloth, I carry him into the kitchen where Jillian's already laid out a pureed feast.

"Thanks," she says, taking the baby and setting him in his high chair. He smacks the white tray in front of him and shouts, demanding food.

Jameson shoves a spoonful of vegetable mush into Zakk's waiting mouth. He swallows it down then yells until Jameson does it again. Seeing Jameson with his own kid is bizarre. When we were younger, I was the one on the straight and narrow, and he was the fuck up.

His home life was shit. He ran away at sixteen and didn't return for five whole years. Now, six years later, here he is, covered in tattoos, wearing a Quiet Riot T-shirt, and making silly faces at a baby who bears his eyes. If you had told me back then our lives would turn out this way, I never would have believed it. He should be the one coming to dinner at *my* house, envious of *my* awesome life, not the other way around.

★ ★ ★

A CURTAIN OF blond hair slides off Casey's shoulder as she leans forward in my truck. Above the hood, the diamond sparkle of a million stars glitter overhead and below us is a bird's-eye view of the tiny city I call home. This time of night most of the houses are dark, but the lights on the highway shine bright, as does the passing of each car racing to its next destination.

"What is this place?"

"When I was just a kid, my mom got cancer," I start, inhaling a deep breath and letting it out slowly. "She came into my room one day and told me she was dying and that, as the oldest child, it was my job to be strong for my sister. Jillian was only eleven at the time, so sweet and innocent. My mom made me promise to protect her, to be good to her, and to keep her safe. I said I would, and I never went back on that promise. Everywhere I went, Jill came along."

Secrets aren't something I keep. They fester inside your body like a spreading infection, turning everything sour as a result. I speak from experience. Nothing good comes from keeping shit inside. No, I wear it on my sleeve. If people don't like it, fuck 'em. No one has the right to judge me.

The death of my parents is hardly a secret, but discussing my feelings on the subject is rare. It's the one and only thing I continue to keep to myself, in spite of my open-door policy. But I need Casey to know that I understand how she feels. She's not alone in her grief. I feel my own every day. It's always there, hiding dormant and popping up at the worst times to say hello.

"I was thirteen when she died. My dad withdrew, my sister hid in her room and cried for days, and I was left to fend for myself. My dad had this old drum set and taking my aggression out on it really helped. When it got too late to play, I'd escape into the woods on those rare moments I was alone and just walk."

Now that I've started, I can't hold back the avalanche of words and feelings that seem to want to burst out of my chest and into the atmosphere. I've spent so long holding it in, unable to discuss it with Jill, not wanting to show my vulnerable side to Jameson, that now I can't control it.

"I found this place and, for some reason, being this far from the world made me feel closer to her. I'd just sit for hours until the sky began to change and the sun would rise before heading back to get Jill up for school. It was the only thing in the world that was mine and mine alone."

"You never brought anyone else up here?"

"There's never been anyone else, Case. I spent my life look-ing after Jillian, instead of building one for myself."

"What about your dad?"

"He was around for a while, but my mom took a piece of him with her when she died. He loved her so much." The lump in my throat is damn near suffocating. I swallow hard, blinking my emotion away. Men are supposed to be strong. Only pussies cry. "Anyway, he didn't last long. We lost him a few years later."

"Thank you for sharing it with me."

Casey's hand finds mine and, for the first time, I notice how filthy my hands look. Black stains from a lifetime of fixing cars have made their permanent home inside the cracks and crev-ices of my fingernails; no matter how hard I scrub, they never seem to get fully clean. I'm only twenty-seven, but my hands could tell the story of a fifty-year-old man.

The door of the old Chevy creaks as she pushes it open and jumps out. I follow suit, slipping down from the truck and meeting her in the front. The soft glow of the moon and stars is the only light, other than the twinkling of fireflies dancing around and the glimmer from the street lamps in the city below.

"Dance with me."

"But there's no music."

"We have all the music we need in here." She presses her hand to my chest before sliding it around my neck. I feel her heart beating fast as I hold her against me. The distant cars rushing down the highway and the chirp of a thousand crickets serve as the musical interlude to our dance that's hardly even a dance at all.

Her hands slip into the hair at the nape of my neck as she rests her head on my shoulder. The sweet smell of her skin rings around me. We're both alone in this world, needing some-one to lean on and coming up short. When everyone around me fell apart, I had to be the strong one, with no one to do the same for me. Casey and I share it, and together the burden isn't quite so heavy.

Warm breath fans across my mouth as she lifts her head and her lips come dangerously close to mine. She wears them natural. Not covered in the gunk girls wear around their mouths. They're petal pink and perfect, and I want nothing more right now than to make them mine.

"Casey." My whisper is hoarse as my index finger catches under her chin. Her blue eyes look black in the dim surroundings but shine as bright as the firefly glow around us. A gentle breeze sends golden tendrils across her forehead. I skim my fingertips across her skin, pushing the rogue strands behind her ear. The tongue sweeping across her lips is the sign I was looking for. My lips graze her cheek, leaving a tiny trail of kisses to her delectable mouth. Lightning flashes behind my eyes the second they meet.

It's a gentle caress, a whisper of a kiss, but her taste, her smell, the feel of her body pressed tightly against mine takes me over and makes me want more. I'm mindless with a need I've never had before. Her tongue skims mine with tentative little licks before allowing me to invade the sweet cavern of her mouth with my own.

When I pull away, her hooded eyes are glazed. My body reacts, knowing I'm the one who caused the lustful gaze staring back at me. It takes every ounce of restraint I have not to grab her again and kiss her lips raw. To push her against the truck, and guide every inch of my throbbing cock slowly inside her until she's begging for more. But she's a nice girl, and I don't want to push her too far.

"Come on, cowgirl. It's late. I'll take you home."

"Or maybe it's early. Depends on how you look at it."

Casey blinks her long lashes as she throws out the same line I fed to her just days ago. I feel her hands roaming my stomach as it twists with want. Is she giving me the green light?

We're all alone up here. I could throw her in the bed of my truck and fuck her mindless to the sounds of the cricket choir in the background, but as much as I want that, I just can't do it. For the first time in my life, I want to take this slow. I want to savor the moments I spend with her; bask in this untamed desire until neither of us can take it anymore, and we're forced to tear each other apart with primal need. I want her to want me so bad she can't take it. Because that's how I feel.

Chapter 10

Casey

THE PULSING VIBRATION against my butt cheek startles me.

You look really pretty tonight.

My gaze locks on AJ's from across the room. He's been texting me off and on throughout the show. Each line is cornier than the one before it, and I'm eating it up with a spoon.

Before I have time to respond, the phone vibrates a second time.

But you'd look beautiful in my arms.

"It must be incredibly hard to serve drinks when you can't take your eyes off the sound guy," Marisa chides.

Cringing, I slip my phone back in my pocket. "Sorry."

Even before he started texting, thoughts of AJ haven't left my mind all week. He seems to be all I can think about anymore. It also doesn't help that he looks downright edible tonight. I want to put him on a plate and sop him up with a biscuit.

When he walked in this evening, the tremor that rolled through my body would have tipped the Richter scale. He'd torn off the sleeves on his Zildjian tee, leaving the tiniest bit of his body on display. Judging by the way that the remaining fabric hugs his chest, I have no doubt he took them off simply because he couldn't fit them over his thick biceps. I've always been a sucker for a sexy set of arms.

Marisa glances toward AJ and back at me. "Oh, I get it. He's hot. But you're drooling into your tank top." She grins and pops the tops off two Coors Lights.

I look away, but when the phone pulsates again, I can't help but reach for it.

Did the sun come out, or is that you smiling at me?

He's watching me with his steely gaze, and I realize I'm grinning like a damn fool. His lines are getting to me, and he knows it. I must be really hard up.

AJ hangs back as Marisa and I finish our side work, but every so often, I see his gaze slide toward the bar. The night wears thin. I grab my stuff and say my goodbyes, but the hollow thumping of heavy boots stops me before I reach the door. "Case, wait up!" He jogs over to where I hover near the exit. "You forgot something."

"What?"

A devious smile rolls across his face. "Me."

"Do you just sit home and think of this stuff, or does it come to you on the fly?"

"Little of both." He falls in line next to me as we walk out into the parking lot. "Last night was fun."

AJ and I have seen each other almost every night for the last few weeks. Nothing crazy. Usually a movie or a trip to the diner. Yesterday, he picked me after work and took me bowling. His bowling is just as bad as his dancing, but the man has good form. That, of course, is code for he has a cute butt.

"Yeah. Puttin' up the bumpers really gave you an edge."

"Well, hardy har har," he jokes, leading me to his truck. "Here, get in."

"I have my own car, you realize." I cross my arms over my chest in a defiant stance. AJ never lets me drive. He has this thing about being the one in control behind the wheel. I'd be lying if I didn't admit to wondering if that need for control filters into other areas of his life. Like the bedroom.

Tonight, I plan to find out.

All week, he's been playing it cool. A sweet kiss, a gentle touch, a flirty grin. Building up the anticipation until I'm ready to crack and then leaving me wanting more. I'm so ready for more.

"Yeah. I'm familiar with your crappy Pontiac." He opens the passenger door and waits for me to enter. "Let's take a drive."

Randy Houser cries out of the speakers as he turns the key, and I smile. Usually, he listens to his iPod, but tonight, it's unplugged. He even set the country station as a preset on his truck's radio just for me. I've caught him tapping along with it when he doesn't think I'm paying attention. He would never admit it, but I think he's starting to like it.

"So where are we goin'?"

The crook of his finger beckons me closer. When I slide over, he slips his arm around me to pull me the rest of the way. His stubble scrapes against my throat as his lips find my neck.

"I've wanted to do that all night."

The tiny bit of contact singes my skin. I feel like I'm going to combust if he continues. "I think we should go back to your house." The sentence tumbles out of my mouth breathless and wanton. Five years is long enough. This ends now.

"Are you sure?"

"Drive, city boy."

"Yes, ma'am!" A slight Southern twang punctuates the words. Whether it's rubbed off from talking to me or all the country music I've been forcing down his throat, I don't know, but the sound makes my stomach curdle. I've grown used to hearing that phrase from another man.

A true Texas gentleman, Austin was always "yes, ma'am," "no, ma'am," and "thank ya, ma'am." It drove me nuts. I resented how polite he was all the damn time. Try as I might, I could never get a rise out of that man. There was no spark. No fire. He was always unrelentingly levelheaded to a fault.

"Don't say that." The lava creeping in my veins hardens into charcoal. I straighten up, untangling from his grasp and slide to my side of the truck.

He looks at me like I've lost my damn mind. "I'm sorry? What just happened?"

"Nothin'!"

I'm furious for no apparent reason. Austin's voice has seeped into my brain ever since we spoke last week. Memories I've long since forgotten float in and out of my mind like the ocean tide. The sound of my name on his lips, the way he breathes. Tiny things I loved so much yet forced from my mind the instant I turned the page and closed that chapter of my life. I don't need to hear it on the tongue of the man I'm planning to sleep with as well. Seven years and it still haunts me, refusing to allow me to move on. Why won't it just leave me alone? I've paid for my sins.

"Cowgirl, you're gonna have to give me some kind of clue."

"Enough with the cowgirl crap, too, all right? I ain't no friggin' cowgirl."

"What the fuck? You were normal five seconds ago! How do you go from wanting to fuck me to wanting to fight me in the blink of an eye?"

The incredulous look on AJ's face only pisses me off further. I'm just mad. Mad at my mom, at Austin, at Davis, at losing Gran . . .

"Is this why you don't date? Because you're bananas?"

My chin falls; a roiling boil sizzles up my cheeks and into

my ears. "You know what? You can just kiss my country ass!" Grasping for the handle, I swing the door open and jump out, stumbling on my boots and taking off for my own car. I don't need this shit. This is why I'm better off alone.

★ ★ ★

THE KNOCKING ON my front door is so quiet I wouldn't have heard it if I wasn't awake and stewing on the couch. My temper is the reason I've never been more popular. I can still hear Gran's voice telling me to cool my sass when I'd gotten too loud. However, once the bomb blows, I usually crumple along with the aftermath. AJ didn't deserve my wrath. It's not his fault.

The blanket draped across my lap falls on the floor as I stand from the couch. The Nash station on my television hums low in the background. Music has always had the ability to take me to another place. The song isn't important. Each one offers up a new feeling and a different outlook than the one before it. Tonight, though, I'm not finding the comfort I'm looking for.

I peek through the peephole, wondering who the early morning caller is. Usually, when someone knocks on our door at four a.m., it's either someone looking for Carlos, the guy who lived here before us, or it's Marisa, too drunk to get her key in the door. This time, it's neither.

"What the hell?" I whisper under my breath.

The force of AJ's lips against mine the minute I open the door knocks me off my feet. His tongue invades my mouth. I scramble backward, knocking his hat off and tearing at his shirt as I pull him toward my bedroom. He mumbles against my mouth, something about our fight, but doesn't stop kissing me hard until my legs hit the bed and I fall on my backside. I rip at his belt with trembling fingers. The shaking in my hands makes the buckle hard to manage. Or maybe it's just my haste.

Whatever it is, I can't get the damn thing undone fast enough.

"Slow down, baby. Where's the fire?"

"It's in me."

Whatever happened between us earlier is a distant memory. A freight train of untamed desire hits me head-on. Now that he's here, I can't think of anything other than feeling his body against mine. Moving inside me. Making me new again.

With a groan, AJ tugs my hand from his belt. "Wait. Wait. We should talk."

His mouth says talk, but the thick, hard ridge in his jeans says action. Still, I settle back on my bed, squeezing my thighs to smother the burning fire between them. "Okay."

The bed dips as he takes a seat next to me. "I'm sorry about earlier. I understand why you freaked out."

"You do?"

He nods and takes my hand. "Marisa warned me. You've never been with a guy before, and that's fine, Case. I don't want to rush you."

A nervous smile plays along my lips. The silly dates, and the hesitancy—it all makes sense now. AJ wasn't holding back on purpose. He was respecting my boundaries. What has Marisa been saying? "I'm not a virgin, AJ."

"You're not?"

"No."

"Then why don't you date?"

The way he looks at me, cocking his head with such wide-eyed interest, makes my insides seize. I don't want to talk about Austin. I don't want to think about him. I just want the memories of us to wash away instead of pulling me under their riptide every time I imagine his face, but AJ came here in the wee hours of the morning looking for answers. He deserves to know the truth. At least part of it. "I fall fast, and I love hard, and I end up getting hurt."

Or hurting someone in the process.

He doesn't respond, but his slow nod tells me he understands. At least somewhat. "I was engaged real young, but it didn't work out. The relationship that followed was a nightmare. I started to wonder if I was cursed. Figured maybe I'm meant to be alone. So, for the past five years, I have been."

Everything Davis did to me I deserved. Every smack, every nasty word. He hurt me in so many ways, and every single time, I took it without a fight. It was my price to pay for my sin. I swallow past the lump that's found itself lodged in my throat. "But I'm ready to start over, AJ. If you'll have me."

Messy hat hair curls around his fingers as he scratches at his scalp. "I'm really into you, Case." Resting his hand on my cheek, he leans in closer. His breath tickles my lips as they part, waiting for him to claim them. "And I really want you. But I'm not breaking a five-year dry spell at four in the morning." Feather soft kisses flutter against my mouth. "I'm going to take my time"—they skim across my jaw—"and taste every"—down my neck—"square"—over my collarbone—"inch of you."

The throbbing pulse between my legs beats as his mouth glides up my throat. My panties are past damp. He hasn't even touched me, yet I'm so wet my thighs are sticky. It only takes being near him for my body to respond this way, but his lips on my skin and his masculine scent this close up adds a slick layer of want on top of my already raging case of need.

Taking his hand in mine, I slip it between my thighs. "Do you feel what you do to me?"

His thumb moves in a slow circle over the flimsy piece of soaking cotton making me gasp. "I feel it," he whispers against my skin, increasing the pressure with his hand; tight little circles that concentrate on the tiny nub beneath the fabric of my underwear.

The rock-solid ridge in his jeans jumps at the touch of my

hand, and a groan vibrates against my neck. When his lips find mine, he uses his body to lower me back to the bed. His tongue plunges into my mouth, teasing mine with its delightful twirl. A series of slow, sensual caresses that only serves to reignite my already flaming desire.

Catching the light from the living room, his gray eyes sparkle in the dark. He pushes my hair back, dropping kisses to my forehead, cheeks, and nose before sitting up. "Good night, cowgirl."

I squeeze his forearm as he tries to get up. "Will you stay until I fall asleep?"

Dang, Case. Desperate much?

"Do you want me to?" I nod. It's a loaded statement. I kind of want him to stay forever. "All right. Scooch over."

The lower half of his face is all I can see from the corner of my eye as he settles in, allowing me to cuddle into his shoulder. "You ever think about going back to Texas?"

"Sometimes." His grip tightens. "I never really felt at home here, you know? Then again, I don't know if I really fit in down there, either."

His hand comes up, sweeping the hair off my temple and circles around my ear. The lightness of his rugged touch sends a shiver across my skin. "You fit perfect right here."

With the room so dark, everything seems magnified. His heartbeat drums a gentle rhythm against my cheek, his breath, so deep and calm, washes over me, comforting me in a way I can't remember ever feeling. The rich sound of his voice soothes my weary soul. Together, all the sounds that make up AJ Morello lull me into a cozy cocoon of warmth I wish could last forever.

Chapter 11

AJ

"AJ!" MY EYES drift open, still glazed over from the nightmare attacking my subconscious. "Are you okay? You're screamin' in your sleep."

Casey's eyes are as crisp and clear as the afternoon sky outside her bedroom window. Just staring into them fills me with an instant sense of calm. "Yeah. Bad dream."

The nightmares have started up again, as fresh and vibrant as ever. Every time I close my eyes, all I see is wreckage. The taunting sounds of sirens and screams fill my ears. I hear Jillian crying my name, but I can't find her. My arms and legs are concrete. No matter how many times I try to move, I'm stuck.

Concern crosses Casey's beautiful face, a look I inadvertently put there. Punishment for mistakes I've made and can't undo. I finger the scar in my hairline. The puckered flesh is a visual reminder of the damage still lingering inside.

Casey's fingertips follow mine, tracing the Frankenstein mark on my forehead, proof of how broken I once was. "Tell me about this."

I pull a Marlboro Red from the box and hold it up between my fingers. "You mind?"

"Nah. Go ahead."

Lighting my cig, I take a long drag, holding the sweet smoke in my lungs before letting it out. Casey rests on my shoulder, extending two fingers and taking the cigarette from my hand. I watch the orange glow on the cherry as she places it to her lips and takes a hit before handing it back. She exhales slowly, letting the smoke billow out of her gorgeous mouth.

"I was in a car wreck," I say, flicking my ashes into a half-empty Solo cup on the table.

"A bad one?"

"Bad enough. But the accident isn't the worst part. It's what happened before it that haunts me." I pause to take a drag on my cigarette, summoning the memory that won't leave me alone.

"I found my sister in bed with my best friend. Shit got ugly." I slip the cigarette between my lips and pull before handing it back to Casey a second time. "I wasn't too keen on the idea of them together. I guess I wasn't too keen on the idea of anyone touching my little sister."

"Overprotective brother syndrome." Smoke curls around Casey's lips when she talks.

"Yeah, I guess. Some words were said, some punches were thrown. I got in my car, just to blow off some steam, ya know? Next thing I know, I'm in the hospital hooked up to all kinds of machines and shit. Jillian's crying at my bedside. I lost two weeks of my life asleep."

The butt sizzles as it hits the water in the cup, and I continue. "My mother's dying wish was for me to watch out for my sister, and I accepted the task so literally that I almost killed myself in the process. I'll never forgive myself for what I put Jillian through."

Emotion stings my eyes as I remember how small and meek Jill looked in the chair next to me. She didn't leave my side.

Even in the coma, I was aware of what was going on around me. They aren't real memories, though. More like faded dream sequences that come and go in waves. It was hard to tell the difference between fantasy and reality. I'd hear a voice and imagine it elsewhere. I'd hear music and think I was at a concert. It all seemed so real. The power of the brain is an amazing thing, but the only constant in every dream I had was Jillian.

My insides shriek with remorse, but my exterior remains stoic as usual. I don't cry. Even when my mother died, not one tear fell from my eyes. My father sobbed, the emptiness he felt losing his soul mate filling him to the point of agony; Jillian wailed like a dying animal, but my eyes were dry as a bone through the entire service and beyond. I'm the strength when everyone around me falls apart. It's my cross to bear.

"But it was an accident. You didn't do it on purpose."

I detach from her embrace and climb out of bed. My blood feels stagnant lying in this spot, and I need to move to get it pumping again. Casey just sits, watching me stalk the room as memories threaten to drown me. "I wished for a way out, Case. I was a young guy saddled with more responsibility than I was ready for. I hated my life, and I resented my parents for dying and forcing me to finish what they created. I was twenty years old, and every dream I ever had was burned to ash along with my father."

"What would you be doin' if things were different?" Petite fingers close around my wrist, stopping my pacing.

"Honestly?" A sad smile grows on my face as I sit back on the bed next to her. "I'd be doing exactly what I'm doing now. Fixing cars is what I know. I'm good at it. My dad built this shop with the intentions of passing it down. I never would have left it. I just didn't realize that until it was too late."

I pull her against my chest, not wanting her to see the hairline cracks in my façade. "I was only starting to become a man.

I still had so much to learn from him, but he left me too soon."

"What was he like?"

Explaining Anthony Morello Senior is like trying to smell the color nine. Those of us who had the honor of knowing him knew what an amazing person he was. He wasn't just some dumb mechanic. He was so much more than that. "He was a goofball, a romantic, a natural leader, musical genius, and a born family man. He had funny nicknames for everyone; his smile never faltered."

My fingers run through Casey's hair, trying to control the trembling that's taken them over. "He taught me about music and carburetors, and a basic knowledge of business that carries me through. Family is number one. He reminded me of that fact repeatedly until the very end. You never turn your back on your loved ones. No matter what."

"He sounds wonderful. I'm sorry you lost him."

Still losing my hands in her hair, I nod because the lump in my throat is too large to get around. My father was more important to me than anyone was. The morning I found him in his bed was the moment my life turned to shit. It ruined me, and I can never get that image out of my head no matter how hard I try.

Jillian had already gone off to the shop that morning, but I was dragging my ass, too tired from staying up late trying to impress some random chick with my musical prowess. Getting laid and playing music were all I cared to do. Fixing cars seemed beneath me. I was born for better things than that. I was sure of it.

I was dressed and ready to head down when I noticed my father's bedroom door was closed. It was after nine o'clock. The old man was never late for work. The pounding of my heart drowned out the creaking of the ancient floorboards as I walked to his room. I knocked at first, calling for him and praying he'd answer. But he didn't.

"Dad?" I said again, turning the knob with shaking hands. A

tense knot formed in my stomach; my palms were clammy, but my mind was still in denial. It didn't want to admit to what my body already knew. Something wasn't right.

He was in his bed, lying on his back. The grayish blue hue of his skin stood out against all the white in the room. I ran to his bed, but it was too late. He was stiff and so cold; I felt like my fingers would freeze just from touching him.

Stumbling back, I searched my pockets for my phone to call 911. I didn't know what else to do. When the operator came on the line, I couldn't say the words out loud. I didn't want them in the atmosphere; I didn't want to believe it. The only thing I could think about was my sister. How the fuck was I going to explain this to Jillian?

A second death.

Another lost parent.

The end of life as we knew it.

I settle back in bed taking Casey beneath me. Her slender body molds against mine the moment our lips touch. Her legs hook around my waist, encasing me in warmth. It's so intimate. Just holding her in my arms, surrounded by her sweet scent, is enough to make me happy.

For the first time in my life, my brain isn't screaming at me. It's not telling me I'm the family fuck up, and it's not shouting at me to do something worthwhile with my life. The degrading voices have stopped, leaving me with nothing but peaceful quiet and a sense of contentment I've never felt before. It's because of her. She's the missing piece. The one I've needed all along.

Chapter 12

Casey

AJ PUSHES THE stick shift as he puts the massive truck in gear. This time, instead of leaving his hand on the knob, he rests it on my knee. When I grin, he responds with a flirty little squeeze. As comfortable as the touch of his hand is, it doesn't stop the bout of nervousness threatening to eat me alive. Meeting his sister is a big deal.

Using one hand, he cuts the wheel and swings into the parking lot of the bright yellow building where he works. Hidden behind it, a blue-gray house sits among the trees. A garden of pink and red pansies flanks the stone walkway leading up to the tall colonial with black shutters and a black front door. A lovely little dollhouse sitting alone back here in the middle of the woods, private and secluded from the busy street.

"Your sister lives behind the shop?"

"Yeah."

AJ grins, and my eyes focus on the crooked tooth that can only be seen when his smile is this wide. It's so insignificant, but something about it drives me nuts. That tiny bit of imperfection on an otherwise perfect specimen that reminds me that he's a real person. Reality trumps fantasy, always.

"This was my parents' house. We grew up here."

He jumps down from the truck and comes around to my side then opens the door for me. I'm fully capable of climbing down myself, but he's always there to help me. Taking my hand or guiding my waist. Little things like that make it hard not to fall for him.

"What's up, dick? What are you knocking for? Just come in."

The guy in the doorway must be the brother-in-law. He's tall, light, and has the greenest eyes I've ever seen on a human being, but the tattoos are a bit much. So much ink covers each arm it takes away from the size of them. I've never understood why someone would go through all that pain just for something that only fades over time. There are so many places to find art. Permanently embedding it into your skin seems like an unnecessary practice. AJ's body, what I've seen of it, is smooth and flawless. Just the way I like it.

"I don't want to walk in on you salivating all over my sister again, ass!" AJ threads his fingers with mine as we walk into the foyer together. "Jameson, this is Casey."

A screech comes from deep within the bowels of the house. From upstairs, a squeaky voice bellows for her husband over the loud shriek of rock music. "Welcome to the nut house, Casey," Jameson says turning toward the stairs, before addressing AJ again. "Zakk's in the kitchen. You'd think the kid hasn't eaten in days. Let me see what Jill wants."

"My nephew is like a bear. Come between him and his meal and he'll bite your damn arm off."

Zakk sits in his highchair, trying like hell to get a Cheerio into his mouth but failing miserably. His lips pinch together in a pout, but his face lights up the minute he sees AJ. He pumps his little fists in the air, reaching toward him as AJ picks up the O-shaped cereal and lifts it to Zakk's open mouth. "Miss Casey, meet Zakk Anthony Tate."

Oversized green eyes blink at me as Zakk chucks me a tooth-less grin. They are the only evidence that ties him to Jameson. The thick black hair, smooth olive skin, and plump little lips are all too familiar. Zakk is a dead ringer for AJ.

As I watch him feed Cheerios one by one to the chubby ver-sion of himself, I'm so overloaded with cuteness that my ova-ries quiver. I always thought nothing was sexier than a blue-col-lar guy, but I was wrong. Watching that same rough, blue-collar man fawning over a baby? That's a box-clencher.

"Hey, little guy," I croon, squatting down to his level and holding the edge of the high chair for support. "You're a little heartbreaker, ain't ya?"

"He's handsome like his uncle," AJ says with a sly grin.

Zakk smacks the tray again, making the Cheerios jump. He looks down at them in awe as if they are magic, having no idea that he was the one who made it happen in the first place.

"That he is." I tap the tray with my fingernail. Zakk watch-es then repeats the action, making the tiny O's jump again. "Smart too."

"Yeah, he's a keeper."

Zakk opens his mouth, shaking his head back and forth try-ing to get the Cheerio resting atop AJ's fingertip. A trickle of drool dribbles down his chin. AJ catches it with his hand, wipes it on his pants, and then goes about his business shoveling more food into the baby's waiting mouth. It's so natural. As if he's done this a hundred times and can do it in his sleep. The ad-oration reflected in AJ's eyes when he looks at his nephew is almost that of a parent rather than an uncle. He and Zakk have something special.

Footsteps shuffle in the hall. The tiniest, most badass look-ing woman I've ever seen comes through the doorway. A stud-ded belt cinches her tiny waist, and a cutoff tee says *Megadeth* across her large chest. Jameson's outfit is freakishly similar.

"S'up, bro?" She wraps her arms around AJ's waist and presses her cheek to his chest.

"S'up, sis?" AJ replies, returning her embrace with a kiss on her head. "Casey, this is my sister, Jillian."

"Hi, Casey! So glad you could come!" The faint smell of oranges lifts off her hair when she greets me with a less affectionate hug.

"It's great to finally meet you! I've heard so much about you."

"Funny. I've heard very little about you." She wears a sarcastic smirk as her gaze falls on AJ.

AJ rolls his eyes. "You're so dramatic." He pulls two beers from the fridge and opens mine before handing it to me.

"Thanks for havin' me, y'all. Smells delicious in here."

"Compliment my sister's food and she'll love you forever."

"If she puts up with your shit, I love her already." Jill opens the oven door a crack to peek in then goes about stirring a pot of potatoes as Jameson starts laying out plates on the table.

"Let me help with that." I take the silverware from his hand and make quick work of setting it all out.

"So, Casey. You're from the South," Jillian says with a matter-of-fact tone.

"No, ma'am. I'm from Texas."

Three sets of eyes turn to look at me as if I've lost my mind. Texas is a whole world of its own. So much so, that it actually wanted to secede from the United States and become its own damn country. To say Texans are proud folk is an understatement. "Texas isn't Southern. Texas is Texas."

"What the hell are you doing in New Jersey?" She wrinkles hcr nosc whcn shc says the state as if it feels funny rolling off her tongue. She's so dang cute, I kind of want to squeeze her. I'm not a big woman, maybe five-foot-five, but AJ's sister is so little, I could put her in my pocket. With her deep brown cow eyes and fair skin, I never would have guessed she and AJ were related. Except for the smile—they both have the same wide, infectious grin that takes up half their face.

I feel AJ's eyes on me and wonder what I should say. Lying to AJ's family isn't the best way to start on the right foot, but I don't want to get into that mess about Davis and Austin either. Now is not the time to be letting out the skeletons I've kept well hidden in my closet. "My boyfriend at the time came for work. I followed."

"Ah, yes. What is it about men that makes us willing to drop everything for them?" Jillian turns to face me, but her gaze lands elsewhere. The fire in her eyes burns fierce and bright. I follow it and see she's looking at Jameson.

"For you, it was greasy hands and a cool car. I didn't even have to try," he says with a lopsided grin.

"What can I say? I like them kind of dirty." Jillian shrugs.

"Aw, heck yeah. I'm so down with that," I drawl, giggling along with Jillian.

"Two peas in a friggin' pod over here," AJ mumbles with a roll of his eyes.

"Zip it, peanut gallery." Jill opens the oven and carefully removes the roast with her oven-mitted hands. "Everybody sit. Time to eat."

She and her husband aren't what I expected. They're both so hardcore in their metal tees, him with his tats and her with her nose ring, but they're both so friendly and welcoming. It goes to show you can't judge a book by its cover.

★ ★ ★

"THANKS SO MUCH for dinner, guys. Everything was great."

"Our pleasure." Jill smiles.

"Don't lump me in with that. Jill bought it. Jill cooked it. All I did was eat it," Jameson adds. "Beautiful and a good cook. I'm a lucky man." He drops a kiss on his wife's upturned face as he carries their plates to the sink.

"Y'all are too dang cute for words."

AJ snorts, and Jill shoots daggers at him. "All right, guys, scoot. Casey and I can't talk about you if you're sitting right there."

"You all right?" AJ mouths to me from across the room. I smile and nod. He knows how nervous I was. His family is so important to him, and I worried I wouldn't fit in, but Jill and Jameson are great. I feel completely at ease in their company.

"Come on, Zakky. Let's find some trouble." Jameson pulls Zakk from his chair and disappears into the living room with AJ following close behind.

The sound of running water fills the kitchen as I stand next to Jillian at the sink, towel in hand. "So . . . you and my brother, huh?" she asks, handing me a freshly washed dish.

I dry it off and set it on the counter. "It's lookin' that way."

"I'm glad. He's been alone way too long."

"What about you and Jameson? How long have y'all been together?"

"About six years now. Damn, it feels like a lifetime. But we grew up together, so I guess it kind of was."

I do some quick math in my head. AJ was twenty-one when he had the accident. Suddenly, his grumbling and snarky behavior whenever Jameson and Jill show a little affection makes sense. "Jameson was the secret boyfriend?" It flies out faster than it takes my brain to tell my mouth to quiet down. *Damn, my loose lips.*

Jillian snickers. "He told you about that, huh? Shocker."

"I'm sorry. I didn't mean to overstep."

"No," Jill says, with a dismissive wave. "No trouble on my end. I'm just surprised is all. He's got a sweet, gooey center, but it's well hidden under a thick, candy shell."

I open a random cabinet trying to figure out where to put away the stack of clean dishes piling up in front of me. "What do you mean?"

"He's not real big on feelings." She points to the cabinet I'm looking for. "He's like Robocop. Never shows emotion. Never talks about anything serious. Even when our folks died, he was so blank-faced. I don't even think he cried."

Now that she mentions it, I have noticed his tendency to turn to stone at the drop of a hat. He's funny and sarcastic, with an easy smile when we're playing, but the minute he starts talking about anything serious, he clams up quick. A mask falls over his face. Deep down, he feels so much. I can see it every time he looks at me. However, for some reason, he's chosen to box it up and hide it from sight.

It's the same thing with his Chevy. On the outside, he appears to be all big and bad with his monster truck, but it's obvious he only drives that beast because he's afraid. If he's the biggest thing on the road, nothing can hurt him.

Jillian and I finish the dishes and meet the boys in the living room. Mechanical music plays in the background as AJ smacks the mini bongo drum in front of Zakk, baiting him to hit it. He looks up at me from the floor, and all I want to do is wrap my arms around him. His confidence comes and goes in crushing waves of disappointment clearly visible in his sad eyes. I know how he feels. Both of us are stuck in this life, unhappy and unfulfilled. Maybe together we can each find the inner peace we need.

Chapter 13

AJ

"YOUR FAMILY'S REALLY great, AJ. I loved meeting them."

Casey sits next to me on the bench seat, twirling her hair around her finger. She's given up on the passenger side of the bench, claiming the center as her seat, and I'm not complaining.

My hand rests on her thigh. I move it to shift gears, and then set it right back where it belongs. On her. Not touching her is an impossible feat. The light pink color of her tank top blends in so damn perfect with the peachy glow of her skin that I'm having trouble controlling the semi I've been toting around all night. Her light hair is curled at the ends, just as it was the day we met, flowing over each shoulder and down her back to the waistband of her jeans.

"They seemed to love you too. Then again, what's not to love?"

I glance in her direction before locking my gaze back on the road. A shy smile tugs at the corners of her mouth. I want to pull this truck over and run my lips over her flushed skin, kiss the adorable pink circles on her cheeks, and lick down her chest to see how far it goes, but I already know that gorgeous shade of pink is everywhere. It blooms on her skin, darkening the more excited she gets.

The sign for Route 3 breezes past. "You missed my exit."

"I know that."

My gaze flickers in her direction again, and just as I anticipated, the flush deepens. Last night's little make-out session was just a taste. An appetizer. A tiny little nibble compared to the way I intend to feast on her tonight. She's perfection in every way; I knew it the day we met, but seeing her with my family sealed the deal. Not that I ever had any doubt. Jillian would love whoever I love. She's not a stubborn ass like I am.

I pull into the driveway and cut the engine. Casey looks at me wide-eyed. "Is this your house?"

"Yep. Come on. I'll give you the tour."

She follows me inside as I open the door and flick the switch, bathing the open floor plan in yellow light. The house is small and sparse, but it's mine. At least, it will be after three hundred and twenty-four more payments. I pull her to the center and point out each room as if she can't deduce what everything is for herself. "Living room, kitchen, dining room . . ."

I turn and lead her down the short, narrow hall next. The only room I really wanted to show her. "Bedroom." The clean scent of her hair and flowery fragrance of her perfume assault my senses as I back her against the wall, tasting her neck like I wanted to in the truck.

"Does this conclude the tour?" Her voice is breathless as she kicks off her boots and socks.

"Not for me."

Her pulse beats against my tongue as it trails along her skin, wanting to sample every inch of her. My dick pushes against my fly, begging for freedom. He's been furious at me since last night, but tonight, nothing is stopping us. I'm a man of my word, and I'm going to savor this moment.

My lips sweep across her collarbone, pulling away only to lift her shirt over her head before snapping right back. I'm drawn to her. Enveloped by her. She consumes me—mind, body, and soul.

Casey unhooks her bra, letting it fall to the floor. An open invitation to her luscious tits. Loud moans fill the quiet room as I take my time, flicking each pebbled pink nipple with my tongue until her head falls back against the wall.

A fiery heat burns between her legs as I open her jeans and push them down. Crystal blue eyes lock on mine. I kneel before her on the floor, worshipping her body like a deity. "Do you have any idea how sexy you are?" Blond hair swings around her face with her gentle head shake. "Well, you should. Your body is a song." I sound like a love-struck dope, but it's the truth. Her skin is like lyrics, her moans the chorus, and together, we're the beat. It moves me like nothing else, holding me hostage with its melody.

My eyes stay fixed on hers as I smooth my hands up her legs and hook my thumbs into the elastic of her panties. Lavender lace. A tiny strip that barely covers anything yet still hides too much. Slowly, I slip them over the slender curve of her ass, down her thighs, and wait as she steps out of them, one dainty bare foot at a time.

"Everything about you is fucking beautiful," I groan. "Even this."

A breathy hiss slips through her teeth as I skim my fingertip over the soft peach fuzz trimmed down to supple skin. The sweet scent of her desire wafts off her, fogging my brain with its heady brand and begging me to taste it. I want to take this slow. Drag it out. Hold off until she wants it so bad she can no longer stand from the weight of her need pushing down on her.

The husky sound of her whimpers undoes me as I kiss an

open-mouthed trail from hipbone to hipbone. Watching her squirm is so fucking hot. My dick throbs harder with each desperate moan. I part her legs, giving her what she wants. What we both want.

The minute my tongue passes her slit, her knees buckle. She drapes her leg over my shoulder, opening herself to me fully while her hands fist my hair.

Palming her ass, I knead with tight fingers and pull her closer, diving into the warm, wet spot between her thighs. I always suspected, but now, I'm sure. Heaven isn't above us. It's right here on Earth. Casey's creamy legs are the Pearly Gates. And this succulent mound of flesh against my tongue? This is the Promised Land.

When I slide two fingers knuckle deep, her hips roll, grating her clit against my eager tongue. She's so tight, clamping down as I play her body with the strong, slow rhythm of a power ballad. The heat begins to build, and I feel her muscles dancing to the beat I set. I'm in control. Working her into a frenzy with my hand and my mouth, I twirl her swollen clit until she cries aloud. Sugary fluid bursts in my mouth, sweet honey dripping off my lips and sliding down my throat.

Hot cum shines on her thighs as I pull away and use my shirt as a towel. She's wrecked. Destroyed. Sliding down the wall on shaky legs. I catch her in my arms and carry her to my bed.

Her breathing is spastic as I shed my clothes and sheath myself with a condom. My cock is steel, pulsing with need, aching to fill the perfect hole that's glistening and ready for more. Just seeing her splayed out on my bed, naked and waiting, is better than any fantasy. It's fucking ecstasy.

Casey trembles beneath me. Her mouth's as hot and wet as the spot between her legs. And just as sweet. I tongue it with the same attentiveness. Exploring it. Claiming it. Mangling her lips until her slick body curls up to meet mine.

The need I have for her is primal. I've never wanted anything this much in my life. It's not enough to have her; I need to own her. Possess her the way she's possessed me. How the fuck I fell this hard, I have no idea. She's like Mayberry and white bread: good, wholesome, and clean.

And I'm about to make her very, very dirty.

Her back bows as I push into her in one steady thrust. My groan vibrates against her lips. All her muscles clamp around me. Fingers bite my back; long legs encase me. I rock into her slowly, pulling out and slamming back into her needy hole.

"Oh, God . . . you feel so good." The words rush out on a shallow breath as her head digs into my pillow.

"It's *my* cock you feel buried inside that pretty pussy. The only name I want to hear falling from your lips is mine."

When my teeth sink into her shoulder, the moan that tumbles from her mouth catches me by surprise. Casey's a little bit of a freak. I bite her again; leaving tiny marks up the side of her neck, I feel her cunt vibrate harder with each one.

Husky moans play on her lips; her insides flutter. Wrapped around me, her body quivers so hard, she can't get my full name out. Just, "A . . . A . . . A . . ." as she shatters.

The knowledge that I'm the only man in five years to make her feel this way has my ego soaring. It feels so good I don't want to finish. I want to pound into her all night. Ride her through orgasm after orgasm until my mattress is soaked clear through. I'm drunk on lust, high on Casey, and I don't ever want to come down.

Beads of sweat roll between my shoulder blades. I brace myself on my arms, using my stomach muscles to piston into her as she squirms and writhes beneath me. Another orgasm crests over her, dragging me along with it. "Fuck," I grind out.

Casey's inner walls clench around me, still quivering with waves of unbridled pleasure. My balls tighten to a fist, and my own cum shoots out hard and fast.

"Fuck," I spit out again. I've never been especially eloquent, but it seems to be the only word I can say right now. My brain is numb, but a sudden moment of clarity hits when her lips find mine again. She was made for me.

★ ★ ★

CASEY'S SPRAWLED OUT on her stomach, naked as a jay-bird. Blond hair fans out like spun gold against my black sheets. The graceful curve of her slender back leads down to where her tight ass hides beneath the blanket. An ass that rode me hard as hell well into the night. I'm exhausted, but it was so worth it.

Yawning and stretching, I slip out of bed, wondering how the hell I'm going to take a piss with the massive hard-on hanging between my legs. Leaving Casey in bed while I go to work is physically painful. It took all my willpower not to roll her over and have my way with her before I go. Even my icy shower doesn't squelch it completely, leaving me with a semi that only grows again when I find her awake and waiting for me.

"Give me a sec. I'll get dressed and call Missy for a ride." She climbs out of bed, but I gently push her back down. A smile crosses my lips looking down at the messy glam rock video mop on her head. *This babe rocks my world.*

"No, stay. I want you here when I get home."

"But I don't even have any clean clothes."

"So stay naked," I reply with a salacious grin. The thought of Casey waiting here for me, naked and ready, makes me want to get to work so I can hurry up and come back home. I'm already pondering the various ways I plan to make her come the second I step foot in my house this afternoon.

"Or you can call out sick and come back to bed."

I'm so damned tempted to take her up on that—I am the boss, after all—but I can't. Unfortunately, responsibilities come first, fun second. Being an adult is so lame. "Can't, babe. I have to go."

Still wearing nothing but a smile, she crawls across the bed on all fours like a cat approaching a plaything. My eyes burn into her from my position at the dresser. She falls onto her stomach, squeezing her amazing tits together with her arms while her crossed ankles move with a frisky sway. The suggestive crook of her finger requests my presence. All the blood drains from the rational parts of my brain and collects in an area I hope she intends to unwrap the minute I get over there.

I drop the shirt in my hand and walk to the edge of the bed. She slinks my way, pushing herself onto her knees when she reaches the edge. Lips of sugar land on mine then move down my neck, slow and controlled, taking charge like the little freak she is.

Using the heels of her palms, she pushes my pants down, and my rock hard erection springs free. She gasps at first, and then her lips curl into a wicked grin. "I thought you said you had to go?" she simpers, giving the shaft a placid tug.

"Baby, you're impossible to resist."

She watches me with her smoldering baby blues as her fist pumps harder and faster. It jumpstarts my heartbeat, making my breath ragged and forced. Then she puts her mouth on me.

The soft, wet feel of her tongue sliding across my balls sends an electric current firing through me. It follows her path as she slithers up the base and spirals around the tip. Licking, flicking, and teasing me with her lips before swallowing me whole.

"Fuuuuuck . . ." I groan, my hand disappearing in the hair at the nape of her neck. Whenever she touches me, I turn into a cave dweller and lose all capability of speech. I'm going to be so late for work, but screw it. I've fantasized about Casey's plump lips on my dick from day one, but even the hottest dreams don't come close to the real thing.

Her hair falls around her face, teasing the bare skin on my thighs. Taking it in my fist, I guide her with my other hand. When I feel myself hit the back of her throat, my head falls back. She gives the base a light squeeze with her hand, jerking in a fluid carousel motion that knocks me on my ass. Side to side. Up and down. Sucking the very soul from my body through the tip of my cock.

Looking down at her kneeling on my bed, I admire her perfect curves, thanking a God I didn't believe existed until right this second. Guess it's true. No one's an atheist thirty seconds before an orgasm.

The polite thing to do would be to tap out and let her know I'm about to finish, but the sight of her ocean eyes looking up at me from beyond light blond lashes unleashes an animal within me. She's my angel with dirty wings. *Mine*. And I want to fill her. Own her. Plant my seed inside her any way I can.

Spasms wrack my body as I blow down her throat. She doesn't even flinch. Just swallows my cum with her mouth still clamped around me, then slides me out slowly, suckling the last of my climax from the tip and letting go with a bowing string of saliva still clinging between us.

I fall forward, bracing myself with my hand, my mouth forming a circle as I exhale hard. Casey jumps off the bed and trots to the bathroom, while I sit on the edge with my pants still around my ankles, reeling and dizzy from quite possibly the best blowjob of my life.

Casey is a rare find. A good girl when she has to be and a bad one when she wants to be. And she's all mine. I have no idea how the hell I found her, but I'm never letting go.

Chapter 14

Casey

AJ'S BACHELOR PAD makes me grin. Actually, I'm grinning anyway. Amazing sex does that to a girl. All morning, I found myself losing whole chunks of time just daydreaming about him. The way his gray eyes churn with raw, erotic desire. A look that leaves my breath choppy and my panties wet with each passing gaze.

Alone with my thoughts, I walk through the quiet house just taking it all in. He lives like a refugee. The only furniture in the living room is a couch; a crazy sound system and a movie theater-sized television hang on the plain white wall. There are no tables, no color, and nothing on the windows but stark white mini blinds. It's almost as if he moved in but never bothered to settle. The apartment Missy and I share is so full of personal artifacts, it's stuffed to the gills, but AJ has nothing but the barest necessities. I guess it's a guy thing.

The kitchen is just as empty. The cabinets house service for two—two mugs, two plates, and two bowls—and the fridge is full of take-out containers, condiments, rolls, and a single onion. On the front, a lone photograph dangles from a piece of Scotch tape. A couple looking at each other with love so fierce I can almost feel it vibrating off the faded photo paper. Two little kids with dark hair and goofy faces hug their legs. A portrait of a loving family. So innocent. The woman is beautiful, and the kids are cute, but the man in the photo steals my breath. Much like Zakk, the resemblance to AJ is uncanny except for the eyes. The jovial twinkle in them is proof that he has everything he's ever wanted.

When the phone rings, my silly grin returns, but I'm shocked to see it's not AJ calling. It's Austin.

"Hey, baby girl. Just makin' sure you're all right." The sound of his voice makes my heart beat in my ears. Last time he called, it was to tell me Gran was gone.

"Hi, Austin. I'm fine." I wait for his response, but he doesn't say anything else. "Is that all?"

"Yeah . . ." The silence hanging between is odd. He sounds so vulnerable. I'm pacing the floor in small tight circles, waiting for him to drop another bomb. Momma died . . . the ranch was sold . . . Surely, something scream-worthy is about to hurtle from his lips. I brace myself for the impact of a tornado, but all that comes is a gentle wind. Regardless, it knocks me over just the same. "Well, nah. That ain't the whole truth. I kinda just wanted to hear your voice again."

The beating of my heart gets louder. "Why?"

"'Cause it's the prettiest sound I've ever heard. Maybe some-day, I'll be lucky enough to see the pretty face that goes with it."

I swallow hard, pulling a lonely glass from the cabinet and filling it with water to quench my dry throat. Wrapped in AJ's shirt, his scent surrounds me. The apex of my thighs still tin-gles from his recent presence there, yet the baritone of Austin's drawl is like a hug from far away. "Thanks for checkin' in, Austin. I appreciate it from the bottom of my heart."

"It ain't nothin'. Just thinkin' about you is all. I'll talk to you soon. Bye, baby."

My body shakes from inside its core. After all these years, why now? I'm finally starting to feel happy. Things with AJ are going well. Why, after I've finally moved past my emotional baggage, does God push Austin Krehley back into my life? I'll never understand. But the clock on the stove flashes 5:00, and AJ will be home soon. I can't worry about it now.

I manage to find a brick of ground beef in the back of the freezer and chuck it in the microwave to thaw. Bright sunlight peeks through the closed vertical blinds covering the sliding glass door in the back of the kitchen. I walk around opening the windows and blinds, cranking up the stereo. Birds jump around the backyard through the bay window near the sink. The promise of summer lies ahead in the bright sunshine gleaming on the lawn. Another summer in a stretch of many; another chance to start anew.

I'm starting over. AJ and I—together.

The microwave beeps as the front door creaks open. All thoughts of Austin dissolve as AJ comes in, deliciously dirty and happy as a clam. Black stains litter his coveralls, and his red trucker cap looks a little worse for wear. Thick cardboard peeps out beyond the tattered fabric on the cracked brim. Across the front reads *Morello and Son's*. Even covered in dirt, grease, and that destroyed hat of his, he still looks so damn good that everything dampens in response. My palms, my mouth, and the spot between my legs that's suddenly pounding with persistent need.

"That is a nice shirt," he beams. "But I think it would look way nicer on the floor."

"What, this old thing?" I answer, with a curtsy.

After my shower this morning, I threw on a tee from AJ's dresser. The words *Ozzy for President* stand out across my chest on the threadbare shirt that hangs down to my thighs. I look ridiculous.

"I'm fixin' to get supper on the table. Go get washed up."

The sound of Gran's voice coming out of my mouth startles me. Every evening as a kid, I'd run through the house after being down at the stables at the exact moment Gran was getting dinner on the table. It's such an insignificant part of one's childhood, but for some reason, it's a distinct moment I can't forget. Over a decade later, I can still smell the scent of the soap in her kitchen. A mix of aloe and honeysuckle. A fragrance that will forever remind me of her.

"Aww, baby. You're cooking for me?"

"A man's got to eat, right?"

The scorching look in his eyes, coupled with his mischievous grin, makes my body react. I did want to eat. Now, I want to rip those coveralls off and make him dirtier.

"I'll be out of the shower in five." He walks past, leaving a chaste kiss on my lips on his way to the bathroom.

Slow country croons out of the stereo. My hips sway to the sexy sound of Jason Aldean as I press the meat and chopped onion together into patties. Lost in my own head, I don't hear AJ approaching until his fingers tangle in my ponytail. His thumb hooks the neck of my shirt, tugging gently as his lips sear my neck. He nibbles me like a savory snack and then glides his tongue across my shoulder.

"Dinner's gonna burn," I mumble, but food is the last thing on my mind. Every touch of his hand and scrape of his teeth strikes my nerves like lightning.

"I'm not hungry for food."

Stubble scuffs along my skin as he slowly kisses, licks, and bites his way from shoulder to shoulder, fisting my hair with one hand while palming my breast with the other. I turn my head to catch his lips. He grants me one wet, smoldering kiss before yanking his fist to expose more of my throat to his hungry mouth.

His dominance overwhelms me. I'm flying high, tipsy from the soft caress of his lips on my skin, and drowning in need as his hand slips beneath the waistband of my panties. My mind is racing a mile a minute. The world goes silent. Nothing can stop the desire spiraling around me the second his naughty fingers find what they're looking for.

"I thought about this pretty pussy all day," he groans against my hair as his calloused fingertips tickle my damp flesh. "So hot." Two thick fingers inch between my lower lips. "So wet." I moan, feeling the stretch as they plunge into my depths. "And so, so fucking tight."

Freshly showered, he smells crisp and clean, but the lingering odor of oil clings to his skin, permeating my nostrils and making me dizzy. AJ's a gentleman in public, but a man in private. He knows how to give and when to take and doesn't hesitate to do either.

A sigh floats to the sky as his teeth squeeze the delicate skin on the back of my neck, and his free hand snakes around, joining its rough twin. He's magic. All sleight of hand, tricks, and illusion, he fills me with one hand while circling my swollen clit with the other. He plays me like a hi-hat. Keeping the beat as a cry tears from my throat that's part porn flick, part horror movie.

The force knocks me backward. He slips his hands from between my legs and locks them around my waist, holding me upright while I pant and whimper my way back to life. "Burnin' It Down" still murmurs in the background. AJ's lips brush against my ear. "Goddamn, baby," he growls, letting my earlobe slide between his teeth. "That was so hot; I'm tempted to fuck you right here."

I arch my back, pressing my backside against him. A hard

ridge rises beneath the heavy denim of his jeans. When my center heats a second time, I silently pray that he makes good on his threat. "What's stoppin' you?"

He turns me around to face him, still nipping at my neck, but doesn't give in to the need that has my body crying out for him. "I want you to stay with me."

"I wasn't plannin' on runnin' away."

"No." He lightly shakes his head, running his thumb across my cheek. "I want you to stay here, in my house. Move in with me."

"But you hardly know me."

"I know you're the one I want. Life's too damn short, Casey. I don't want to waste any more time."

When shit with Davis hit the fan, I knew I deserved it because of the way I left things with Austin. Eye for an eye. But I'll never know what I did in my life to deserve AJ. The magnetic connection I've felt from day one is unexplainable and unavoidable. It scares the bejesus out of me. Every time I look at him, my heart wants to burst from my chest and jump right into his hand. I spent five years alone, never coming close to meeting anyone who makes me feel the way AJ does. Every look owns me, every touch overwhelms me, and every smile makes my heart smile just as wide.

It can't last. It's just too perfect. Disaster looms on the horizon.

I can feel it.

Chapter 15

AJ

C ASEY SITS SO close to me at the kitchen table that our thighs brush together as we eat. Or, rather, I eat. She nibbled the edges of her burger and declared herself full. Now, it's getting cold on her plate while I wolf down my third. They're burned to hell on one side, a result of our little rendezvous at the counter, but hell if I care. I'm just happy to be fed. And the beautiful girl in my T-shirt doing the cooking was the perfect appetizer.

"Why don't you park the truck in the garage?

"I can't." I stuff the last of my burger in my mouth. Ketchup clings to the corner of my lips. I wipe it away and bring our plates to the sink. She cooked, so I'll do the dishes. Eventually.

"Why not? You got some kind of tricked out muscle car in there?"

A loud bubble of laughter bursts from my chest. "Jill is the car fanatic of the family. I just fix them." Her gaze darts to the door in the kitchen and back to me. In her eyes, I can see my cryptic answer burning a hole in her brain. "That's where I keep the victims!" I say with evil laughter.

"Nuh-uh!" She laughs, but there's a nervous edge to it. As if there's a slight possibility that I might actually have a room in my house with bodies piled up to the ceiling.

"Come on. I'll show you." I extend my hand, but she only looks at it. "I'm not a murderer, Case." I chuckle. "I promise."

She slips her petite hand in mine, letting me pull her off the chair. The garage door hides in a little mudroom right off the kitchen where I keep my washer and dryer. The naked light bulbs flicker to life as we enter, and Casey's eyes gleam when she sees what's inside.

"This is my studio."

Thick foam panels cover each wall, the ceiling, and garage door. They are meant to absorb the sound, so I don't bother my neighbor when I play my drums. I can't park my truck in here because it's sealed shut.

She walks farther into the room, taking it all in. Her hand grazes over the mixing board against the wall. It's similar to the one I use at The Wreck but has far fewer knobs and faders. This one is for personal use. My little toy to play with when I feel like laying something down.

"Do you know how to play this?"

With dancing blue eyes, she ogles my collection. Hanging on the wall is a Jackson V guitar. The deep onyx finish gleams in the sporadically placed recessed lighting. The corner is nicked, but that's fine with me. It went for a bargain at a closeout sale, and I couldn't resist. It's just like the one Randy Rhoades himself played. Jameson was jealous as hell when I came home with it. He's the guitar player in the family, and my collection blows his away.

Next to it hangs a Gibson Les Paul. The bright yellow center fades to a dark orange hue around the edges in a beautiful sunburst paint job. It glimmers with a faint glittery finish that picks up every shaft of light that filters into the room. Another amazing yard sale find I couldn't pass up. This would be why I have nothing in my house. Musical hobbies are expensive.

With both of those two electric beauties hanging side-by-side, Casey still stops in front of an old acoustic in the corner. A vintage Gibson sits in a rack all by itself. A relic collecting dust that no one's even looked at in I don't know how long. Every dent and scratch in the old worn wood tell a different story from my childhood. I can still hear my dad plucking the strings singing "Dust in the Wind" while my mother hummed along. Of all the things in this house, that's the only thing that means anything to me. That and the photo on my fridge.

"I can play a little."

I gently lift the Gibson from the rack. Sitting on a stool, balancing it on my knee, I'm ten years old again. My father is sitting on the couch next to me. The huge, clunky guitar takes up the majority of my lap and the space between the frets is too wide for my little fingers, but my old man is patient as I try my best to play the song he's attempting to teach me. The only song I had learned to play from beginning to end before the drums caught my eye and I gave up strumming for banging.

Trying to remember the chords in my head, I place my fingers on the frets and play. I close my eyes and let the sound take over. The simple notes of Tesla's famous love song fill the garage. It transports me back in time. It's not perfect, but it's there. Every note. Every chord. Just the way my dad taught it to me.

"That was beautiful."

"I'm not much of a guitar player, and I'm definitely not a ballad guy," I reply, placing the Gibson back in its spot.

"What kind of guy are you?" Her playful tone makes my dick jump. The smirk etched in her face sets a mosaic of dirty thoughts spiraling through my mind, including, but not limited to, setting her on top of the monstrosity of a kit in the center of the room and banging her like a floor tom.

"I like my music like I like my women—loud and dirty."

I return her smirk with one of my own as I squeeze through a small open space and sit upon my throne like the king I am when I'm surrounded by this much awesomeness.

Hi-hats, splashes, rides, crashes, bass drums, toms, snares—they all sit in a systematically placed circle with a swivel stool in the middle. A low-key re-creation of Neil Peart's Time Machine setup. Well, as best I could get it anyway.

"This is my baby," I say with a grin. A combination of acoustics and electronics, it's much larger than your standard percussion kit. It has twenty individual drums, eighteen cymbals, and a jungle of hardware to navigate around the setup. It's a beast, and I'm hella proud of it.

This is my church. I don't need a higher power. I don't need prayer books, hymnals, or the blood of Christ on my tongue. This is where I feel holy.

"It looks complicated."

I drag Casey through an opening in the kit and set her down on the stool between my legs. The clean, floral fragrance of her skin hits my nostrils and travels straight to my dick, which I'm positive she can feel growing along her backside. "Here," I murmur, slipping a stick into each hand. "Now cross your arms like this."

With both our hands on the sticks, I cross our arms over her body. "This stick hits the hi-hat . . ." A tinny *ting-ting-ting* sound fills the room as I tap the stick on the hats "And this one hits the snare." A *ratta-tat-tat* snaps to my right as I let the stick bounce against the skin.

Together, we do a standard jazz beat, nothing fancy, but she laughs with that amazing giggle that tickles my spine every time I hear it. "See? Easy."

"Mmmhmm. Sure it is, drummer boy. Bet I know how to make it hard for you." She wiggles her ass into my crotch a little before standing up and shimmying out from the set. Not only did she throw down a challenge, but she also left me with a massive hard-on.

Behind my kit, the world melts away. All my shit dissolves into the atmosphere as I wail away with all my might. It takes me to another place. One where I'm the master of my fate. The captain of my soul. Nothing matters. Nothing hurts. The beat takes over, and I'm untouchable.

In my mind, the sound of Alex Lifeson's guitar riffs and Geddy Lee's bass line brings me home as I add the fills and rolls, going off on my own tangents and inserting my own flair to the song in my head. No one can hear it but me, but that's fine. I'm the only one who counts, and I know it's epic.

My eyelids crack open, and I see her sitting on the edge of her seat, lips parted, eyes wide as she anxiously watches. This is everything. My woman, my drums, my house. All I've ever wanted in one place. If I was an emotional man, I might just shed a tear, but that Y chromosome keeps me from being a total pussy.

We lock eyes as my abuse on the kit continues. She stands, fingering the hem of her Ozzy tee—*my* Ozzy tee—letting her tongue graze along her lower lip.

Smash! Crash! Bang! Bang! Bang!

My feet pound the pedals, my arms flail, and the cymbals crash all around me. Crossing her arms over her body, she lifts the hem of the shirt. Slowly. She cocks her head to the side, watching me with her fiery blue gaze as the shirt rises past her taut stomach.

Adrenaline shoots through my overheated blood. Even the dull sting in my shoulder doesn't calm my racing pulse. I'm amped. On fire. Both in my arms and in my pants. One turquoise eye peeks over the hem of the shirt, disappearing behind it altogether as the tee leaves her body and wisps to the floor.

I'm still going. Sweat pours down my face. My gaze burns into her exposed flesh in front of me. Little pink nipples stand at attention in the cool room, begging my mouth to warm them. I have no idea what I'm even playing at this point; I'm just banging everything in sight until this game is over and I reap my reward.

A dimpled smirk grows on her face. Her eyes gleam with mischief as her thumbs hook into the lacy strings of underwear around her slender hips.

Crack!

The snapping sound of wood echoes through the room. Chunks of the splintered drumstick fly everywhere; I look down in awe at the mangled stick in my hand and then back up at her. "You're evil."

"Me?" Lashes flutter above her innocent, girl-next-door grin, dimples and all. Casey's arms fly at her sides as she does a twirl and heads for the door.

I jump up from the throne and scurry between the massive floor toms, trying my best not to knock everything over in my haste as Casey runs from the room. "You'd better run!"

Her giggling echoes through the empty house, bouncing off the plain white walls, followed by the pitter-patter of bare feet on the hardwood floors. The house isn't that big. She doesn't get far before I'm right behind her. "Gotcha!" I hook my arm around her middle and pull her against me.

Golden tendrils hang wildly over her face as she turns to face me. "You got me, AJ. What do you intend to do with me?"

Her breath fans across my lips as I tuck the strands of hair behind her ear. "I'm gonna keep you. Forever and ever, cow-girl," I whisper, walking her into my bedroom and closing the door behind us.

Chapter 16

Casey

"GREETINGS, GUYS AND gals!" Marisa slurs as I open the door to our apartment. The sun is still in the sky, and she's already half in the bag.

"Ooh, you have the glow of a woman who's just been gloriously fucked!" She tips the bottle of booze to her crimson lips, swallowing down a swig of straight whiskey. "And the limp," she adds with a snort. The bold green shadow swept over her lids makes her eyes pop against the vibrant red bangs cut straight across them. All dressed up and nowhere to go.

The strange man sitting next to her on our couch offers me a rotten smile as I enter. A spider tattoo creeps along his lanky neck. Every guy she comes home with looks pretty much just like this. The ladies are buxom, but the guys are foul. To each his own, I guess.

"You wanna join?" he asks, adding the emphasis on the last word. At least, I think that's what he asks. The thick Scottish accent and the half-empty bottle of Jack between them make him hard to understand. This guy is her spirit animal.

"No, she doesn't." AJ stomps through the door and drapes a possessive arm over my shoulders.

"Relax! Lee's just kidding. Ain't ya, baby?" Marisa coos, fingering the bullring in Lee's nose. If this guy adds one more piece of metal to his face, he's going to pierce himself shut.

He mumbles something incoherent then pulls her by the ears and fuses his thin lips to hers.

"You got some mail on the table," she warbles around his grimy mouth. Staying at AJ's is looking more and more like the best decision for all of us. I don't know if I can handle another one of Missy's get-togethers where I'm stuck in my room while she makes it impossible for me to ever want to sit on my own couch again.

"Classy as ever, huh, Miss?" AJ says, following me into the kitchen, but Missy's long ago stopped paying attention. The guy's already on top of her, grinding her into the sofa cushions as we speak.

A small pile sits on our tiny pub table. I go through the envelopes until one catches my eye. A certified letter from Texas. The fancy stamp in the corner says *The Law Office of Roger Dixon*. "It's from Gran's lawyer," I say to no one in particular, tearing the letter open.

"Holy Jesus H. Christ!" My hand flies to my heart as I fall back into the chair behind me. I have to read the letter again to make sure I'm not hallucinating.

"What is it, babe?" For a second, I forgot AJ was even there. I forgot about Marisa and her beau, regardless of the moans traveling from the couch twenty feet away. Hell, I almost forgot to breathe.

"Gran had a will." I'm determined to force my heartbeat to slow down to a manageable pace, but it doesn't seem to want to listen. "She left me everything . . ." As the words leave my mouth, the lights in the room appear to dim before my very eyes. If I don't relax, I'm going to pass out right here on this stool. "Including the ranch."

There has to be some mistake. Mama is Gran's direct kin, not me. Grainger Ranch has been in our family for generations. Why on God's green earth would she leave it to me? If anyone deserves it, it's Austin. He's the one who's still there after all these years, the one who was with Gran on her last days, taking care of things when her wayward girls took flight.

My gran was full of piss and vinegar on her best day and stung like a hornet on her worst. She had a head for business better than any man I'd ever known. Me, on the other hand? All I know is how to strum a guitar and mix drinks.

"Okay," AJ starts. "What's the next move then?"

I look up from the paper into AJ's steel gaze. He's flipped again. My funny, sexy man is hiding behind an emotionless shield. He's seen this scenario play out already. In his own life.

"I don't know. I guess I have to go to Texas."

Nausea hits hard when I think about going back there without Gran. My choices are limited, though. Gran trusted me, so I can't let her down. This is my chance to make everything right.

"It's the right thing to do." He nods, trying to keep his face unreadable, but his feelings show through the cracks. He takes a step forward, entering my personal space. "You gonna come back to me, cowgirl?" His knuckles graze my cheek.

The tenderness reflected in his gaze is enough to break me. I knew this would happen. I just knew the minute I opened myself to another person fate would intervene. Karma is a cold-hearted bitch, that's for damn sure. "I'll try."

I'd love to give him a definitive yes, but I have no idea how long I'll be gone or what's waiting for me out there. Texas is my home. Grainger Ranch is my birthright. I just didn't expect it this soon.

I fold the letter and slip it back into the envelope before going to tell Marisa the news. The last thing I want to do is get in the middle of her action, but I'd also like to get my stuff and get out of here before atomic punk starts shedding his clothes.

"Miss," I whisper, approaching the couch. "Hold up a sec."

Lee raises his pockmarked face with a creepy grin. "Change your mind, then?"

"Settle down, killer." Marisa slides out from under him and pushes herself to a sitting position. "What's up?"

"I'm going back to Texas for a while. I have to settle Gran's estate."

Her orange-red brows shoot up to her hairline, and her bold green eyes get wide. "You're leaving me?"

Marisa has her puppy dog pout down to a science. We've been roommates for five years. Missy was the first friend I made when I moved to New York. She may be flighty, but she's been with me through it all. She knows all my secrets, even the ones I swore I'd never tell. Leaving her breaks my heart, but I have to do what's right. Whatever happens, we'll always be besties.

"Just for a while. I'll send you some money as soon as I can to cover my half of the rent."

"You sure this is just about the ranch?"

"What else would it be about?"

Marisa's thickly lined cat eyes roll toward the kitchen before settling back on me. "Uhh, Austin?"

A feeling of dread comes over me just hearing his name out loud. The thought of coming face to face with Austin again makes the bile rise in my throat. I turn my head, hoping AJ's not within earshot, and turn back when I see him on the phone facing the corner. "I doubt I'll see him. Gran's been gone a few weeks now. I'm sure he packed up shop and split." My wishful thinking is just that. Wishful. I know he'll be there. He'd never leave the horses unattended, and he'd never let the ranch fall to hell. It's too important to him.

The oldest of eight kids, Austin comes from a huge family. His father's a preacher, and his mother's a homemaker. They barely had enough money to scrape by. It's how Austin ended up on our ranch to begin with. It started with him just wanting to bring some money to his family and ended with him becoming a part of ours. Half the time, I'd find him sleeping in the stables instead of going home. I finally begged Gran to make up a space for him in the house. She traded part of his salary for room and board, and from then on, he was ours twenty-four hours a day. A live-in ranch hand at our disposal.

"How much does AJ know about him?"

"Enough."

My history with Austin is about as ancient as scripture and as dead as the Latin it's written in. AJ knows I was engaged. He doesn't need the whole nasty story.

"You're gonna break the little drummer boy's heart, aren't you?"

"Of course not! There is nothin' between Austin and me anymore. That ship sailed a long time ago."

Am I trying to convince her or myself? Hearing his voice was like a trigger. Something in my chest blossomed the minute that slow drawl seeped into my ear. It seeped into my heart. I'm sure it's just homesickness, but leaving him has been a decision I've regretted since day one. I can't deny that.

I glance back at AJ, who's still on the phone. A small smile grows on his lips when he catches my eye. We haven't known each other long, but there's something about him I can't quite shake. He, too, has found his way into my heart. However, I can't have them both.

★ ★ ★

BRIGHT PINK SPLASHES streak the sky as the sun begins to set over Jill and Jameson's house. The new life that's been thrust upon me weighs heavily on my shoulders as I hop down from the truck. The crooked set of AJ's hat is a sign of his equaled discontent. That letter was a bomb that blew up in our faces, eliminating everyone's joy.

I force a smile on my face as the front door opens wide. "Hi!" Jillian singsongs. "Thank you so much, guys! We really appreciate this."

AJ takes the baby from his sister's arms as we enter. She adjusts the fallen strap on her little black dress and continues rattling off information. "Jameson already fed Zakk and put him in his jammies, so all you guys really have to do is hang out with him then put him to bed . . ."

Jameson comes down the stairs, dapper in a button-down shirt and jeans.

Date night. How adorable?

"You have my number and Jameson's number. I made up some bottles and left out some snacks just in case. Oh, and don't forget—he can't sleep without his monkey. And leave the nightlight on so I can check on him when I get home—"

"All right, Jill!" AJ snaps. "Go out already. I'll take care of the kid."

Jameson snorts and leads his wife toward the door. "First night away. She's freaking out a little," he whispers.

"You know I can hear you," Jill adds.

Jameson rolls his eyes with a grin. "Thanks, guys. Have fun."

"You too," I reply, as they walk outside.

The door clicks closed, and AJ just looks at me. Behind his eyes, a layer of melancholy settles over his normally smoldering gaze. Bubbles of spit form in the corners of Zakk's mouth. He screeches and kicks his feet, trying to get down. I follow AJ into the family room and sit, while he drops to the floor, setting Zakk down in front of him.

"I'm sorry your last night in New Jersey is spent like this," he murmurs.

I sit down next to him and take his hand in mine. "It doesn't matter. If I'm with you, I'm happy."

Cartoon cats count to ten on the television set, but the silence in the room is deafening. It's our last night together, so we need to make this count. The moment is heavy as we sit in silence, both of us fixated on Zakk. "Look," AJ starts. "Why don't you grab a bottle while I order us a pizza or something? We'll put Zakk to bed and just chill."

"You're hungry again?" This time, my smile is genuine.

"I have to keep up my energy. Satisfying you is hard work!" he jokes, returning my grin with one of his own.

I push to my feet and go to the kitchen. A cold blast of air bursts from the fridge when I open it in search of a prepared bottle. Everything in here has a specific place. Clear bins labeled with care, organized down to the very last strawberry. Mini jars of what look like baby food are stacked in neat rows next to a line of bottles on the side. I grab the first one and pull off the attached sticky note, reading Jillian's big loopy handwriting.

Run bottle under hot water for about five minutes until warm. Do not microwave!

Taking a quick survey of the kitchen, I notice sticky notes in several places. Small neon squares with instructions in the same messy script, while others are love notes in neat tiny print. I didn't notice them the last time I was here, but now that I see them, they make me smile.

I warm the bottle as instructed and bring it back to the family room where Zakk waits on AJ's lap. "Your sister likes things a certain way, huh?"

AJ chuckles. "That she does. Here, take Zakk. I'm going to order the food." He stands, resting the baby on my lap.

The minute he sees the bottle, Zakk opens his mouth then sucks down the milk with the fervor of a starving man. "Slow down, lil' guy. You'll get a belly ache." His jaw clamps tight as I give the bottle a light tug.

The bottle is almost empty by the time AJ is finished with his call. "He's drinking that bottle way too fast . . ." he starts, but before he has time to finish, milk erupts from Zakk's mouth in a volcanic stream, covering us both in warm, opaque fluid.

"Gross!" I whine.

AJ just laughs. "Go get cleaned up. I'll take care of Zakk."

Covered in a mix of vomit and spit, I jog to the kitchen while AJ takes the baby upstairs. My shirt is soaked—there's no saving it. I pull the milk-stained garment off my body and wipe the remaining mess off my skin with a paper towel. The sound of running water flows from upstairs. I follow it, hoping to borrow AJ's tee, but his gentle voice slows my pace.

"That wasn't nice, Shredder. Look at you. All covered in milk."

I peek through the crack between the door and the frame as AJ sets Zakk in the tub. He washes him with care, using a tender voice I've never heard before. The minute he thinks no one's watching he drops the tough-guy routine. But *I'm* watching. And my heart melts when he pulls Zakk from the tub and wraps him in a towel, cradling him against his burly chest.

Zakk cuddles into him, and AJ drops a kiss to his towel covered head. "Tired, huh, kid? Let's get some new jammies and get you to bed," he coos again.

I back up and move toward the stairs as swiftly as I can before he catches me watching. The reality of it makes my head spin. AJ wants a family. He's not just looking for a girlfriend; he's looking for a future. There's only one problem . . . I'm not sure I'm cut out for that.

Austin always talked about children. He wanted a big family, but the word "kids" falling off his lips was enough to make my skin crawl. I have no positive parental role models—I can't even keep a Chia Pet alive. How am I supposed to raise a litter of babies?

Yet seeing AJ with Zakk filled my inside with warmth. He would be an excellent father. The kind of dad who throws the ball around and helps with homework. The kind of dad any kid would be lucky to have.

Curiosity grabs hold again, and I sneak up the stairs. Zakk is dressed in clean pajamas, and his head rests on AJ's shoulder as his uncle rocks from foot to foot, quietly humming a soft lullaby. The moment steals the breath from my lungs. There are many facets to AJ Morello. He's rough and tumble, full of jokes and attitude, passionate and lewd. They're all things I love about him, but the side he keeps hidden away might be my favorite one of all: the sentimental side. The kind and softhearted piece he buries away. The part that turns him from a guy to a man. The real AJ.

Chapter 17

AJ

DAY BREAKS OVER the horizon as I load Casey's bags in the truck. The sky is purple, and the streets are silent. I love this time of morning. When the Earth's still sleeping and no one is around to disturb the scenery.

It's one of the reasons I chose this house. It sits at the end of a dead end street, across the way from undeveloped, county-owned property. Only one house is next to mine, and a woman who's about two hundred years old owns it. She never comes outside. Every so often, I'll see a delivery guy bringing in groceries, but that's the extent of it. My own quiet oasis from the commotion of life.

It's not that noise bothers me. I am a drummer, after all. It's just that sometimes it's nice to be able to shut the world out. Close the door and bask in the silence for a minute.

The slam of the storm door echoes through the quiet neighborhood as Casey comes out of the house. It's June, but already far too hot by New Jersey standards. Her shorts barely cover her, making her shapely legs go on and on without end. She's graceful, like a dancer. Slender and long. I watch her come toward me, taking the last of her things from her hands when she gets here. The only thing I want to do is drag her back inside the house and take those shorts back off her, but our time together has run out.

"We should get going if you want to make your flight. You ready?"

"Ready as I'll ever be." She sighs.

We haven't even gotten on the road yet, and she already looks tired. She didn't sleep well. She tossed and turned, flipping her pillows and fiddling with the blankets. Something about going home has her on edge. Casey shouldn't have to do this alone. I wish I could go with her, but I can't. Jill needs me. "Oh, I think I left my phone plugged in on the counter."

She turns back toward the house, but I stop her. "You go ahead in the truck. I got it."

I jog back to the house to grab the pink camouflage Samsung and smile when I see my picture as her background. She took this photo just the other day. I was lying in my bed, wrapped in crisp black sheets, hugging my pillow under my arm. She whispered, "Wake up, sleepyhead," and the moment my eye cracked open, she snapped it.

Casey's already settled in the truck when I emerge. Her golden head shines in the sunlight as she sings along to whatever's playing on the radio. Pink lips move without a care in the world. She's always so shy about singing along. I watch her when she thinks I'm not paying attention. She mouths the words silently to herself, but alone in my truck, she lets it all out. It's damn hot.

Carrie Underwood belts out of my speakers at a shockingly loud decibel as I pull open the door. She startles, and a sad smile leaks across her face. My fingers catch under her chin, lifting it to meet my gaze. "Why so sad, cowgirl?"

"I only just found you. I'm not ready to let you go."

"A little distance isn't going to change anything. We'll make it work."

It's more than a little distance. Texas and New Jersey aren't even in the same time zone. She might as well be going to Mars. Truthfully, I have no idea what this means for Casey and me. All I know is that my feelings for her aren't geographical. This isn't a smash and dash situation. I can't give her up that easily.

"You seem so sure." Her light touch caresses my face. "How do I know you aren't going to find someone else?"

My fingers gently close around her wrist. "I waited twenty-seven years for *you*."

With a swift tug, I pull her closer, take her in my arms, and press my lips against hers. I allow myself to get lost in her for just a moment, soaking in the taste of her mouth and her flower fragrance before forcing myself away. My dick is already twitching in my jeans from this tiny amount of contact. We'll never get to the airport if I don't stop now.

Casey steals the hat from my head as I ease onto the highway and pulls the brim low over her eyes. Blond waves fall out from underneath, flying around in the wind and rushing through the open window at her side. Iron Maiden rocks the speakers. Bruce Dickinson cries aloud with all his might, screaming over the nasty sounds of heavy riffs. The heels of my palms press against the steering wheel, while my thumbs tap out the beat. It takes my mind off the fact that we're saying goodbye for an undetermined length of time. Usually, I'm fine with her constant country caterwauling—I've even started to like it—but today, I need something louder. Casey's about to be schooled in Metal 101.

"Your music is so angry." She pushes up the hat's bill with one finger; her eyes are as bright as the sky as she looks my way.

"Some of it, but this one is different." I turn the volume up so she can hear it better. "You need to listen beyond the distortion and wailing drum beats. The words hold more power than the music behind it."

Lyrics don't usually matter to me, but every so often, a song will come along that speaks directly to my soul. This is one of them. A song about a man in his dying hour, full of regrets and lamenting about the things he hasn't achieved yet.

The maniacal music in the background is the only sound as we drive to the airport. The weight we both carry on our hearts is a heavy burden to hold. Yesterday, I had everything I ever wanted nestled in the palm of my hand, but today, it's all falling to hell. It's my shit luck coming back to bite me in the ass. My gift from the universe for being an asshole. I'm given the tiniest taste of something real, only to have it jerked from my grasp. It's not fair.

Even in the wee hours of the morning, the airport bustles with life. Commuters, travelers, and airport workers move about with the rolling sounds of luggage following close behind them. Casey stands at the entrance of the airport looking sad and afraid. Two feelings I'm on board with, even though I refuse to let it show. I've always been the strong one, and now is no different.

"Call me as soon as you get in so I know you got there safely."

Still wearing my hat, she takes the carry-on from my hand before setting it on the ground and wrapping her arms around my neck. "I will. I promise."

Her body is warm, her skin sweet. I don't want to let her go, but I pull away just enough to look in her hypnotic eyes one more time, touch her face, and feel her lips. It's not the last time I'll ever see her, but I feel like it is.

"Hey, AJ." She sucks her bottom lip between her teeth, letting the corners of her mouth turn up, teasing me with those damn dimples I love so much. "Can I borrow a kiss? I promise I'll return it when I get back."

"Damn, baby. You stole my heart and my lines."

A giggle floats from her mouth, embedding itself in my chest and threatening to cave it in. Her laugh is still one of the best sounds I've ever heard, coming in a close second to her sexy twang moaning my name. I drop my lips to hers, savoring the taste and the softness of her mouth against mine. "We'll see each other soon."

I watch her walk away until she disappears from sight. I feel like my heart's been crushed to dust. I should have known better than to open myself up to someone like this. Everyone I love just leaves me eventually.

★ ★ ★

JILLIAN'S ALREADY AT the shop when I arrive, which means Jameson isn't far behind. She's always the first one on the scene, opening the office and making coffee. It's a routine she's so used to, I bet she can do it in her sleep by now. Zakk's playpen is perched in the corner under a Budweiser clock with a naked woman on it. The phrase *Future Headbanger* sits over the flaming guitar on his miniature Pantera tee. The Morello family is a classy bunch.

"Estranged" emanates quietly from the huge desk in the center. Normally, I love this song, but I'm in no mood for it today. "Turn that shit off."

"It's not GNR's best album, but I wouldn't call it shit," Jillian argues but complies anyway, before walking to the percolator to pour me a coffee. I've told her a hundred times that I'm capable of making it myself, but she insists. "What's wrong with you?"

I take the coffee from her hand and blow on the hot liquid before taking a tiny test sip. Her hard gaze bores a hole through me. Jill knows me better than I know myself. We've spent so much time together that we don't even need words to communicate. The problem is, she likes to talk about shit, and I don't. "Nothing. I'm fine."

"Whatever, dude. You look like you're ready to Hulk out and kill us all."

The door buzzes overhead as Jameson walks in. Like clockwork, Jill hands him a cup of coffee, and he drops a peck on her lips. Their open affection is a hot poker jabbing me in the gut. I've seen this every day for the past six years, but for some reason, I can't handle it right now. My jealous fist closes on the Styrofoam cup in my hand, cracking it. Scorching black coffee runs all over my hand and coveralls. "Shit!" The cup makes a hollow sound as it bounces off the floor and lands in the dark brown puddle at my feet.

I'm a mess, both literally and figuratively. Watching Casey walk away was so much harder than I anticipated. I assured her that we could make the long distance work, but I don't want that. I want her here so I can kiss her whenever the mood strikes.

"Yeah, sure, you're fine," Jill quips, grabbing the mop from the bathroom as I try to dry myself with a nearby red rag.

"Sorry," I grumble walking through the shop door. I have to put some space between Jill and me. It's too damn easy to take my shit out on her. Her love for me is unconditional, and I don't want to take that for granted. I've been that guy already, and he sucks. I just have to get through the day, and then I can bang my aggression out on my kit at home.

In my empty house.

Alone.

"Everything cool with you and Casey, dude?" Jameson's voice cuts through my solitary moment of self-loathing. I really need some new people in my life. Preferably, ones who can't read me like an open book. "I know that look. Hell, I've had that look. What's going on?"

I love the guy, but my brother-in-law is such a monumental pussy. He was always a little on the soft side, but after Jill and Zakk got their hands on him, he might as well be a woman himself.

"Casey went back to Texas." Just saying it adds to the pressure sitting on my chest.

Jameson runs his hand through his sandy hair, pushing it behind his ear. "Just out of the blue?"

"She has some family shit to take care of. Don't know when or if she'll be back."

I feel my face get hot and turn toward the tool bench. Jameson's been my best friend since we were kids. Whenever he's had a problem, I was the one he turned to. I'm usually the fixer, but now, those roles are reversed. He has everything figured out, and I'm the one floundering around, living my life in limbo. It's embarrassing, and I don't want him to see me like this.

"Why aren't you with her?"

The corner of my mouth curls up with a "what the hell" expression. Lover boy's lost his mind. "I got work to do, bro."

Jameson grabs my bicep as I try to move past him. "You love her?"

Well, isn't that the million-dollar question? Having never been in love before, I have no idea what the answer is. I definitely like her. A lot. When I think about the possibility of never seeing Casey again, my chest burns, and I can't catch my breath. Even now, I can feel the distance between us as if something's missing. If that's not love, I'm not sure what is. "I guess?"

Jameson closes his eyes, shaking his head with a snort. "If you love her, you should be with her. Nothing is more important."

He releases his grip and steps under the Nissan on the lift. Our uncomfortable conversation is over, but instead of feeling relief, I'm more worked up than I was before. It's so easy for him to say. He came into his relationship with nothing to lose. No family, no livelihood. He blew in with the wind and never left. His choices were easy. I have responsibilities. I can't chase a girl I've only known a few weeks across the country. No matter how bad it hurts to let her go.

Chapter 18

Casey

I'M OVERDOSING ON nostalgia as I stop in front of my childhood home for the first time in seven years. Standing on the worn wooden planks of the wraparound porch, I can almost hear Gran humming through the window and smell the fresh cornbread baking. I should have come back sooner.

I slide my old key into the lock; shocked it still works, I'm greeted by Gran's wall of Casey as I push open the door. A school photo for every year hangs in a circle, showing my various stages of life. The center spot is empty. Gran was saving it for my wedding photo. In every one, my hair is neat, and my clothes are pressed—a perfect, smiling girl with child-like dimples and a plain face—but the wild child hidden inside shows through in my devilish blue eyes. I put Gran through so much heartache.

The sunshine yellow kitchen calls to me from the foyer. This was always my favorite room in the house. When the school bus dropped me at the gate, I'd run up the trail and burst through the door. Gran would be waiting for me, snack in hand, ready to hear about my day. Playing at her feet on this old linoleum floor is one of my earliest memories.

Emotion chokes me as I run my hands over the ancient wall-paper. Once white with bold sunflowers, it's faded to a dingy bone color, but it's still lovely nonetheless. I feel her. Smell her. Hear her voice and see her delicate hands rolling out dough. If she were here right now, she'd look at me with tear-filled eyes and wrap her slender arms around me. *Welcome home, Casey Jane.*

But it's too late. I don't have the right to cry. I made my bed, and now, I have to lie in it.

A few deep breaths later, I find myself on the porch out back. Gran's rocking chair sits motionless, facing the pasture where the horses run. When the day was over, and the work finished, this is where she'd be. Watching her beloved horses.

"Can I help you?" A deep, slow drawl rumbles from my right far out by the stables. I turn toward the direction of the voice, and my legs turn to jelly. The Earth spins too fast. I lose my balance and fall onto the warm, white wood.

When my eyes open again, I'm cradled in strong arms and staring into the warmest brown eyes I've ever seen. "You all right, baby girl? You gave this ol' boy a fright the way you hit the deck like that."

Dazed and confused, I blink my lashes, trying to remember. The recollection hit hard and fast, goring me like an angry bull. The horses, the barn . . . Austin. It was all too much.

"Yeah, I'm fine. Just haven't eaten all day, is all." I struggle to my feet, breaking loose from his strong grasp.

"Well then, let's get some food in ya." Austin pushes himself to his feet, smacking his big hands against his well-worn jeans. A little *too* well worn. They hang on his hips, dirty and tattered, defining every tendon in his muscular thighs. "C'mon. I'll get washed up."

He pushes his way into the house, and I watch him disap-pear inside. Austin was twenty-three when I left, all lean muscle, wiry and thin. Now, at thirty, he's filled out. He's brawny and wide, tan and tall. With a voice that apparently still brings me to my knees. Literally.

I join him in the kitchen, dropping down at the large oak table, and watch him move about. His brown hair is much shorter than it used to be, and his face, once so young and boyish, is chiseled and mature.

"I was wonderin' when you'd come home." He sets a plate down and sits across from me at the table. After all these years, he still remembers I eat pickles on a turkey sub.

"I'm sure you heard. I'm the new owner of Grainger Ranch." My insides somersault at the thought. *I own a ranch. I'm not prepared for this.*

"Yup. Your ma was madder than a hornet in a beer can when she found out. She came out here cussin' and yellin'. I told her, 'I didn't do it. I just work here.'" A small grin curls his lips, and his eyes crinkle in the corners. "But I'm glad you're home."

When his warm hand settles over mine, my eyes drop to his bare ring finger. I let it remain there for just a moment before pulling away. Austin is a friend now, nothing more, yet the look on his face when I slip my hand from his slices a wound in my chest.

"Thanks for the sandwich." I take a bite, although I'm not all that hungry anymore. I just need a distraction from the heavy moment. "Are you still livin' here?"

His handsome face is tired and sad. "Where else am I gonna go, Casey Jane? This ranch has been my life for more than ten years. Just because Gran's gone . . ." Silence fills the room, and pangs of guilt stab me in the gut. Gran was a mother to us both.

"Gran always said you were a blessin' sent from heaven. She'd appreciate all you've done."

He smiles and nods, his warm brown eyes searching my

face. Quiet falls between us again. I want him to yell at me. Tell me I broke his heart; say I'm not welcome, that he can't stand the sight of me. Anything other than this sullen lack of speech. But Austin was never one with words. He's a man of action, who proved himself to me in ways other than talk. "What'd he do to you, Casey?"

"What you mean?"

"You ain't the same. You talk different; you look different. Where's the girl I knew? Surely, she's still in there."

The sandwich is a rock in my stomach. "I'm still her." My voice comes out meek and strained. Off and on, I'd practiced what I'd say to Austin should we ever be face to face again, but no amount of mental notes could have prepared me for the way it feels to stare into the face of the man I've wronged and still see love in his eyes.

"Nah. My sweet girl wouldn't have stayed away so long."

The wooden legs of the chair squeak on the linoleum as Austin rises and walks to the screen door. Staring out into the yard, he's quiet for a moment before adding, "Maybe while you're here, I can help you can find her."

★ ★ ★

RISE AND SHINE, cowgirl.

The text message makes me smile. It's five a.m., which means it's six o'clock in New Jersey. AJ's been my wake-up call every morning, even though he doesn't have to be at work until nine. It's my favorite part of the day, but fondling my phone isn't quite the same as waking up in his arms. He's the first person I hear when I wake up, and the last voice I hear before bed. The hours in the middle I spend going over the books, cleaning out the house, and working down at the stables. I have aches in places I didn't know could ache. My years in the city have made me soft.

Typing in a quick "good morning" response, I hit send and place the phone back down where it was. Sleeping in my old room is still strange, even though it's changed a bit since I've been gone. Gran ditched the old blue bed linens and added a bold floral pattern to the bed and windows. It's sunnier in here than I remember, but it could just be my mind playing tricks on me.

The smell of coffee wafts up from the kitchen. My conversations with Austin have been mostly about business, but every now and again, I see the craving swirling in his eyes. I feel it radiating from him, the same way I did all those years ago before he finally gave in and made me his.

Austin never rushed me. He was patient and compassionate. We'd already been dating a year, but he would have gladly waited a lifetime for me.

Once I knew Gran was asleep, I snuck down to his room off the foyer. I watched his shadow pass through the light peeking out from under the door before letting myself in. He looked at me with heated desire, his eyes leaving mine for only the short moment it took me to close the door and turn the latch, locking us in together.

"You need somethin', baby girl?"

"Yes."

I wanted to be brave, but my whole body quivered when I dropped my robe. He swallowed hard, his Adam's apple bobbing as his eyes raked over the satin and lace nightie I wore. Up until then, we'd only kissed, but I wanted more. I was seventeen. Still a girl, but head over heels in love with a man I was anxious to please.

"You put this on for me?"

I took a deep breath and nodded before taking a step further. His hand skimmed over my hip and slipped underneath the sheer fabric. "Is this for me, too?" A sharp breath hit my lungs when his fingertip ran across the obvious wet spot in my matching panties.

"If you want it."

My heart thundered, and my pulse pounded. It was awkward at first. I laid on the bed with damp palms and damp panties, while his gentle kisses covered my body, and his hands roamed to places nobody had ever touched before. The anticipation was killing me. He took his time exploring me, murmuring sweet words in my ear and making sure I really wanted this. It was exhilarating and scary, and I wanted nothing more than for him to hurry up and get started.

"I love you, baby girl. I'm gonna marry you one day," he whispered as his body invaded mine, slow and deep. Those two adjectives always come to mind when describing Austin. They are fitting in every possible way. His moves, his voice, the way he loves, the way he fucks. Slowly, deeply, with so much power and conviction that it took me over from day one.

"Mornin'."

Dressed and ready to start the day, I traipse into the kitchen, struck by his size for the fifth morning that week. The flannel shirt sitting pretty on his six-foot frame does nothing to hide the massive homegrown muscle hiding underneath. He doesn't say anything; just slides a mug of fresh, hot coffee in front of me and stares out the window with his own mug braced between his long fingers. Having lived with Marisa for five years, silent mornings are common for me, but standing next to Austin, the air is thick and heavy, and the quiet is excruciating.

"Whatcha got going on today?" I ask, dragging the conversation out of him.

"Truck ain't kickin' over. I gotta do some maintenance on it." He sips his coffee, still looking out at the pasture as if there's something interesting to see besides grass.

"I'll do the mornin' feedin' then."

I drain my mug and rinse it in the sink. Heat hits my back. Flannel tickles my bare shoulder as Austin leans over and drops his cup in front of me, lingering longer than he should. "Somethin' about the way you smell, baby girl, it's. . . ." His smooth face brushes over my hair as an 'mmm' sound completes his statement, then he's gone. I'm left at the sink with the same damp palms I had so long ago, missing his warmth and watching the languid way he moves toward the barn.

Once my breath returns to normal, I head out to the stable to water the horses and get them fed. Each horse gets two hay flakes in their feeder, and then I start mixing up the feed. Lined up along the wall of the stable are three thirty-two gallon garbage drums, each one containing a different type. I measure out the powdered bran mash and sweet feed with a three-quart scoop then sprinkle on some Safe Choice supplement, topping it off with a splash of corn oil to keep their coats shiny.

It's amazing how certain things stick in your mind. I can't remember the piano lessons I took as a kid and do not remember how to bake a pecan pie without a recipe, but caring for these horses is second nature regardless of my time away.

They whinny and neigh as I fill their troughs with water and pet their soft manes with love. Way back when, we had double what we have now. Gran stopped breeding shortly after Grandpa passed and concentrated on riding lessons and performance training. In order to do that, she also supplemented the income by boarding. Taking care of other people's horses is a hell of a responsibility, but Gran loved them as if they were her own. She was good like that.

The days are busy, and when I'm not filling them with work, I'm thinking about AJ. I miss his easy smile, his smoky gray eyes, and the way he kisses me. AJ's adamant about making this work, and I'm giving it a fair shake, but the more I look at Austin, the more at home I feel. He's more than my ex-lover—he's a part of my family. A part of me. Being here and working side by side, I'm getting a glimpse of what my life may have been like had I stayed.

I don't hate it.

"Can I get in there?"

Jamming out to Eric Church on the radio, I turn and see Austin standing the kitchen. A flannel shirt drapes over one broad shoulder, allowing me to see his smooth sun-kissed body. Thick black grease tracks slither up each forearm, and every inch of him glistens with sweat. My breath catches as he comes closer to where I'm standing. My lips part and I realize a split second too late that he's talking about the sink. He wants to wash up.

"Yeah. Knock yourself out," I say, swallowing my tongue and smacking the handle on the faucet. Water rushes out, fast and angry, equal to the way my heart beats in my chest.

Turning away, I guzzle my sweet tea, trying to quench the sudden desert in my throat. "How's the truck?"

"Ain't lookin' good. Still can't get the damn thing to kick over."

Gray water swirls down the drain as he scrubs his hands clean with Lava soap. He dries them with a length of paper towel then sweeps it over his face and around the back of his hot neck. "So, uh . . . I'm fixin' to head into town tonight. What's say you get cleaned up and come on with me?"

He leans his hip against the sink, catching me in his warm brown gaze. Other than our little chat over my turkey sub, this is more talking than Austin has done all week. I don't know what to say, but when I don't answer fast enough, he pushes a little harder. "C'mon, baby girl. Live a little."

His choice of phrases strikes me as funny, and I smile. The irony of Austin telling me to live a little is a bit much. Trying to have a life was what brought us here in the first place. "Where ya headed?"

"Thought we'd jump the county line and hit up Rocky's."

My stomach growls at the thought. Rocky's has the best barbecue this side of Texas. The majority of the meals I had in

Jersey were from either a sack or a box. Cowboy-style brisket sounds like heaven right about now. "Yeah, all right."

Austin smiles as I walk past him to the stairs.

What are you doing? Tell Austin you changed your mind. Lock the door. Call AJ.

I ignore the thoughts running through my head and pull the blue floral dress from my closet. *It's just two friends hanging out like old times.* If that were the truth, then why am I stricken with sudden feelings of betrayal?

At the bottom of the stairs, Austin waits for me with a Stetson in one hand and a fist full of wildflowers in the other. The hard lines of his body are obvious under his pressed shirt and clean jeans. He looks good. *Too good.*

"Damn, baby. I reckon you're as pretty as a bluebonnet."

The airy material of my dress floats around my knees as I descend the steps, and Austin's eyes glitter as he watches. I try to smile, but my lips are dry. It's as if all the moisture in my body has flowed between my legs, leaving everything else as arid as the grass outside my window. I remind myself again that this isn't a date, but my body and my head are in disagreement.

Rocky's is hoppin' this time of night, but we end up finding a small table near the edge of the patio. "I'll go up. You want the usual?"

I can't help but smile. Austin and I have spent so much time together, it all blurs into one big pile of years. But it just dawned on me right this second that our first official date was here. I'd ask if he realized that, but the look on his face tells me the answer is yes. Every time we came, I'd get the same thing: brisket, potato salad, and a sweet tea. It tastes so good; I never felt the need to try anything else. If only my love life was as simple as my appetite.

Austin rambles to the counter, dragging my wandering eyes along with him. I shouldn't be looking at him so hard, and I shouldn't be enjoying our quiet moments alone this much. But so many snapshots of us are glued to the scrapbook pages of my mind, and it's making them difficult to turn. They say our memories are more closely linked to our sense of smell than anything else is. Certain aromas have the ability to evoke particular memories. Sitting here, surrounded by the smoky scents of burning mesquite and charred beef, I believe it.

I remember as if it were yesterday. *A faded Bruce Springsteen tee tightly covered his slender frame, but I couldn't stop looking at the hole in his jeans. It wasn't big, no larger than a dime, but every time he shifted in his seat, a tiny flash of skin would show through. I imagined sticking my finger in the little gap, so I could feel the manly swatch of hair that I knew covered his leg.*

That day, when he returned to the table, he sat on the same side as me, not opposite as he is right now. When I questioned him about it, he said, "This way I know you ain't gonna run away." He meant it as a joke. We laughed. No one's laughing anymore.

"What's on your mind, baby girl? You look a million miles away."

I look up from my lap and find Austin's jovial gaze staring at me. The wounded look in his eyes is falling away, leaving nothing in them but hope. I don't want to lead him on. "Just thinking."

"About anythin' good?"

"I don't know. I haven't really decided yet."

"Well, when you figure it out, you be sure to let this ol' boy know." He winks and pushes the plate closer to me. "Go on now. Eat up." He sticks a fork into the blackened beef and offers me the first bite. My lips part; the flavor melts on my tongue and a small moan escapes. My fingertips spring to my wicked mouth. Austin lowers his head, pretending he didn't notice the unintentionally erotic sound, but I catch him looking up at me through dark lashes with an impish grin.

The rest of dinner is light and fun. Austin tells me all about his family and fills me in on everything I missed. I listen, loving the sound of his voice and watching the crooked way his mouth moves. His top lip lifts just slightly higher on the left than on the right when he speaks. It was always my favorite. I find myself hanging on his words, relishing his company, and not wanting the night to end. However, the sweet smell of tobacco from a nearby table sends a crushing blow to my blissful high. *AJ.*

This is wrong. We need to go.

"You almost ready to head out?" I ask.

Want flashes in Austin's eyes for a brief moment before he composes himself and stands from the table. We drive home in silence, but the energy between us reels me in. I'm fighting it as hard as I can, but the set of his jaw tells me he feels it too.

I walk briskly from the car to the safety of the house, but the tip of my boot catches on the threshold of the kitchen door. Austin catches me when I stumble. The warmth of his body against mine sends a bubble of nervous laughter popping from my chest. "There she is," he drawls, running his fingertip across my jaw. "I knew I'd find her."

The tiny touch shoots shivers down my arms. He's close. If I wanted to, I could reach out and pull him against me, cement our lips together, and have him take me right here. Do I want that? I'm buried under a mountain of confusion, fueled by lust and my own guilt for having hurt a man I still have feelings for.

My skin tingles from his touch, but AJ's face is the one I see when my eyes flutter closed. "I'm seein' someone."

His hand drops to his side, but he remains rooted to the floor in front of me. "*Him?*"

"No. Someone new."

Austin nods slowly, his lips pressed into a thin line. "You run from him too?"

The jagged teeth slice me deeper as Austin twists the knife a little further into my gut. "That's not fair."

"Neither is you runnin' out on me!" The harsh sound of his voice makes me jump. Austin has never used that tone with me before. He's always so even-tempered and mild-mannered. "Goddammit!" His fist connects with the counter before he turns, shoving his hands through his short, dark hair. I watch him become unhinged, stalking the kitchen, inwardly talking himself off the ledge.

"You don't understand!" My voice hitches, and my eyes grow wet. "You were already a grown man ready to start your life. I was only eighteen! Suffocating under the weight of the commitment you needed from me." Salty tears leak out of my both my eyes, staining my face and falling onto my chest. "I loved you, Austin. But I couldn't resign myself to this life without seein' what else was out there!"

"And whaddya find, Case? Somethin' good out there, worth breakin' my heart over?"

Goose bumps break out on my flesh. Backed into a corner, I feel like a feral cat ready to pounce. "What do you want me to say, Austin? That I regret it? That I hate my life? That I never should have left, to try to succeed?"

"If you were that unhappy, you should have told me. I'd have waited. Hell, I've been waitin'." He squats down, hanging his head in hands for just a moment before returning to his normal calm state. "I can't unlove you, Casey Jane. No matter how hard I try."

Without looking at me again, he rises to his feet and walks away.

Chapter 19

AJ

"HI, BABY. DID I wake you?"

"I was dozin', but I was waitin' for your call. How was work tonight?" Casey's sleepy voice dulls the ringing in my ears usually caused by a night at The Wreck.

"Fight broke out. Pretty sure Bits lost his last remaining tooth in battle."

Her face comes to mind as her giggle chimes through the phone like bells. I see eyes, bright and blue as the summer sky, dimples adorning smooth, creamy skin, and pink lips as plump and sweet as strawberries. I reach into my boxers to adjust the growing erection I get just thinking about her, but my hand lingers. Girl's got me wound so tight, I'm ready to snap. This long distance shit really puts a damper on a guy's sex life. I've spent far too many nights this month with Rosie Palm and her five sisters.

"You lonely there without me?"

"I wish you could be here."

"Close your eyes and pretend I'm there. What are you wearing?"

"AJ Morello, you talkin' dirty to me?"

"Come on, baby, I'm dying over here. Tell me."

"A tank top and panties."

My dick twitches in my palm. "What color?"

"Pink," she purrs, pausing for effect. "Just like the rest of me."

Every nerve in my body vibrates. Visions of Casey spread out before me wearing nothing but a rosy flush on her perfect skin assault my mind as my hand squeezes the base of my cock. "Take them off."

She hesitates. "I don't do . . . that . . . very often."

She's so fucking sweet and innocent I can't help but grin. "Just close your eyes and pretend it's me." I hear the rustling of sheets as she shuffles in her bed, carrying out my order. "Now, wet your fingers, baby. I know that pretty pussy is dripping for me."

The faint sounds of shallow breath waft into my ear. "It is."

"That's my girl."

Images swim beneath my pinched eyelids. Casey on her back, her unending legs sprawled wide on either side of me. Her back arched, and her head pressed into the pillow while my greedy hands roam every inch of her. That gorgeous, glistening cunt waiting, wanting. It's a view I'll remember until my dying breath. That and the taste of her on my tongue as I lick her into a wild, wet frenzy.

A moan floats into my ear when I tell her in detail the exact picture in my head. "Do you feel me touching you?" Another breathy whimper fucks my eardrum, and my hand picks up the pace. "Do you feel my face buried deep between those sexy thighs? Tonguing the shit out of you?"

Panting. Whimpering. Sighing.

"AJ . . . Oh, shit . . . I wish you were here."

"I am, baby. I am. Come with me."

Yelping. Mewling. Moaning.

"Fuck, fuck, fuck . . ."

Catching my wad in my hand, I lie comatose for a second while my brain short circuits. Heavy breathing is all I hear on the other end of the phone. I can visualize her face, and the satisfied, bewildered look that crosses over it moments after she comes, just before her eyes refocus.

The line goes quiet for a moment, and I worry that I lost her. "Case?" Her whimpers continue, but they're not the same erotic, throaty moans I heard a few moments ago. Her cries of pleasure have turned to sad sobbing. "Baby, what's wrong?"

"This is so hard."

"I know. It's hard for me, too." I sit up in bed, wiping my soiled hands on my discarded T-shirt.

"It's not just us. It's . . . everything. I have no idea what I'm doin'. I'm gonna fail, AJ."

"Listen to me, Casey. You're not going to fail. Everything you're feeling, I've felt it too."

When my dad died, he left me with a mountain of paperwork to go through. Deeds, contracts, bank statements, you name it. Hours and hours, I pored over paperwork I'd never seen and wasn't quite sure how to even read. It took time, a ton of energy, and more sleepless nights than I ever imagined. At one point, it seemed impossible. I had zero knowledge about running a business, and even less interest, but I not only did it, but I also did it well. Business is thriving, and my old man would be proud.

"It's scary, and it's hard, but you can do this. I know it, and your gran knew it."

Not being able to hold her is killing me slowly. I want to take her in my arms, absorb her pain, and make it better, but I'm stuck here, and she's there, and it sucks ass. There has to be a better way.

★ ★ ★

THE BAND TONIGHT is on fire. The lead singer of The Blackout belts out the lyrics to "No One Like You" as if he were Klaus Meine himself. It's impressive, and I'm not that easily impressed.

Bits pokes his head in from the door, checking Marisa every ten minutes or so. She's alone behind the bar, and he worries. Frankie D. has yet to find a replacement for Casey. She wasn't here that long, but The Wreck isn't the same without her. Even after all these weeks, my eye still travels to the bar expecting to see the neon blue lights shining against her golden hair, and I'm stabbed by a sharp twinge of sadness when I remember she's not there.

"Thank you! Good night!"

The band starts breaking down their equipment as I begin pulling the cords from the amplifiers. The crowd thins, but as usual, a few stragglers hang around, finishing their drinks and waiting to be noticed. The smell of perfume wafts around me, followed by the sound of someone clearing her throat. Here we go.

Behind me, a cute little brunette sways on her feet. "Hey there," she slurs. She walks slowly to the stage in front of me, and then slides her ass onto it. She's hot—very hot—and very drunk. The old me would defile this chick six ways to Sunday, and something tells me that's exactly what she's hoping. It's not going to happen.

Marisa watches me from across the room, making sure I'm on the up and up. She's already told me that if I break Casey's heart while she's away, she'll ship my balls down to Texas in a Mason jar. I don't doubt for a second that she wouldn't make good on that promise. She's a crazy bitch.

"I've seen you play the drums here before. You're really good."

"Thanks," I grumble, shuffling around her as I finish my work. I don't want to be rude, but I also don't want to give her any indication that I'm interested.

The cable in my hand pulls back. I look up and find Drunk Girl's combat boot on top of it. "Where are you headed after this?" As she twirls one of the white streaks in her hair, I'm immediately reminded of Casey.

"Home."

"You want some company?" Her back arches as she flicks the hair off her shoulders, purposely shoving her rack in my face. Yeah, I notice. Having a girlfriend doesn't stop me from being a guy, after all, and hers are on full display. Nice and big, rising out of her low cut tank as if she's a walking advertisement for free motor boating.

A set of footsteps clacks on the wooden floor behind me, taking Drunk Chick's attention off me for a split second. "Becky, we're ready to go. Are you coming or what?"

Brown eyes lock on mine, as she slips off the stage and saunters my way. "I don't know," she says with a pout. "*Am* I gonna come? Or what?"

Ignoring her advance, I turn to face both her and her friend before walking away. "Careful getting home, ladies."

Marisa sets out a beer as I approach the bar. Bits hovers behind it, secretly sniffing the air around her as she finishes her side work. This guy's in sad shape. I wouldn't be surprised if he had a shrine devoted to her in his house somewhere. He should just tell her how he feels. What does he have to lose? Bits is a good man, and Marisa could do a lot worse.

I throw my phone on the bar as I take a seat, trying not to make it obvious that I'm checking it for the hundredth time, but the looks on their faces tell me I'm as transparent as cellophane. The last message I got from Casey was a response to my good morning text. She's told me before that she keeps her phone in the house during the day because having it on her is too much of a distraction. Still, I miss her angelic voice almost as much as I miss seeing her face.

"You heard from Casey recently?"

Marisa squints, staring up into nothing. "I called her the other day, but she and Austin were bathing one of the foals or some shit. I dunno. They're always busy whenever I call."

"Austin?" I feel the crease between my brows deepen, and Marisa's already pale complexion turns a shade of freckly chalk dust I've never quite seen on a human before. "Who's Austin?"

A distant memory flies into my head. Something I disregarded at the time, which now sits front and center in my mind. The day she found out about her grandma, she answered the phone expecting him.

Green eyes flicker toward Bits, who turns away from me, suddenly super interested in collecting glasses from the other end of the bar. "O-oh! He's the ranch hand. You know, the guy that, like, helps with the horses and forks hay. I don't know exactly what he does, but he works there." Marisa's nervous rambling assures me there's more than meets the eye on this. Something's rotten in Jersey.

"Out with it, Marisa. Is Casey screwing some other guy?"

"No! No, definitely not!" Her earrings swing along with the violent shake of her head. "What they had is totally over. He only works there now. That's all."

Totally over! When did it start?

"Okay. I'm heading out. Night guys." Grabbing my phone off the bar, I keep it in my fist while I decide whether I should call and ask her myself. Something about Marisa's reaction to this Austin guy docsn't sit well with me. I make a snap decision and dial her number.

"Hello?"

"Who's Austin?" I blurt out more stern than I intend to.

"What?" Casey's groggy voice sounds like she's still in dreamland.

I take a deep breath, trying to calm myself down. I'm getting all worked up before knowing the details. That's been a problem of mine my whole life. "Austin. You have something to tell me?"

The pause before answering is far too long for my liking. "He's our ranch hand. Why?"

"You sleeping with him?"

Through the phone, I hear fabric rustling and the click of a lamp switch. "Why would you ask me somethin' like that?"

"Marisa said what you had is totally over? What exactly did you have? Why am I just hearing about this now?"

"I told you I was engaged once. You never asked for more information."

"Whoa, whoa!" I clip, pacing next to my truck, brimming with testosterone-fueled fire. "You were engaged to this guy?" The only response I get is sniffling. "Tell me you don't still have feelings for him."

"AJ . . ."

"Well, that's just perfect, isn't it?"

"But it doesn't change the way I feel about *you!*"

Sweat drips off every part of me. My fingers wrap so tightly around the phone, I worry I might crush it in my hand. When I open my mouth, my jaw hurts from clenching it. Hostility has taken me over, turning me into the asshole I try so hard not to be. "But in the meantime, you're getting cozy on the ranch with someone else."

"Nothin's happened between us. But it's hard," she sobs. "I'm here and you're there and there's all this history–"

"Save it. I don't need you to tell me how hard it is! You think it's not hard on me? Well, things are about to get real fucking easy for both of us. Go do what you want, because I don't want anything to do with you." I hit end and shove the phone in my pocket.

At this point, I'd rather her just go at me with a baseball bat. The bruises would eventually heal, but this ache in my chest is never going to fade. The pain is heavy, constricting my lungs and making it hard to breathe. Hard to think.

The voices in my head won't stop yammering for a second no matter how much I yell at them to stop. It's Jillian's voice nagging in my ear.

You love her. Stop being an asshole.

She lied to me.

She didn't lie, she just omitted one tiny detail. Kind of how you omitted having slept with half the Tri-State Area, you hypocrite.

That's not even close to the same thing.

Isn't it? You're overreacting. Stop with your stubborn male bullshit and go there. Claim what's yours.

I shove a knuckle in both my eyes to control the overwhelming burn that arises out of nowhere. My heart hurts. My head hurts. I'm leaned against my truck, willing them both to work together instead of fighting for control. The logical part of my brain is telling me there must be an explanation for why she never told me about this, but the hothead in me wants to fuck the first thing it sees to get even.

A Mazda peeling through the parking lot makes my decision for me. "Thought you were going home?" Drunk Chick calls through the open window. What was her name? Beth or something. It doesn't matter. There's only one thing I need from her, and her name isn't it.

Pulling the pack of Reds from my pocket, I bring it to my mouth, and slide a cigarette out with my teeth. The end crackles as I light it and take a huge calming drag. "Heading there now. Where you ladies going?"

"Wherever you're going," Beth or Betsy or whatever her

name replies.

I take another pull of my cig and blow rings of smoke into the night sky. *"You live around here?"*

"Not far."

"Hold up. I'll follow you."

As I climb into my truck, the same voice in my head begins yelling, telling me this is a bad idea, but I stomp it out just like my cigarette butt. Screw it. I'm too full of blind anger to care right now. I'm here in New Jersey waiting for her, pining for her, carrying my heart in my hands, and she's over in Texas with someone else.

I follow the Mazda to a run-down building on the far side of town. When what's-her-name gets out, I half-wonder if she's going to rob me. Ghetto is an understatement. There's a dope-head passed out on the stoop of her complex, and all of the windows have bars on them. The first thing that rolls through my mind is we're not in Kansas anymore. The second is, I hope my truck doesn't get stolen and shredded for parts.

My date for the night (Belinda?) leads me up a disheveled stairwell, past broken doors and cracked walls—and a few crackheads for that matter—to a door with so many locks, I'm worried what she's hiding inside. Turns out, there's nothing of value in there. Just a shitty couch, an old box television, and a kitchen table with a broken leg. The whole place smells like spoiled milk and sadness.

Now that I'm here, I just want to get this over with. I grab her by the waist and smash her against me. The stink of booze and cheap perfume is nauseating. At the bar, she was a hot little number, but here in the crack house of shame, she just looks skanky.

What am I doing? This isn't going to make me feel better. It's only making me feel worse. I can't just fuck Casey out of my system. My feelings for her are deeper than that. She's who I want. Not another one-night stand. Casey. My beautiful, homegrown, Texas bombshell. But she broke my heart, and I don't know how to handle it.

A sudden attack of conscience pummels me as Bella starts to work my fly. "I'm sorry, I can't do this. I gotta go."

Chapter 20

Casey

THE SUMMER HEAT is oppressive, even as the sun goes down. It's too hot to be outside but too tense to be inside. It's been two weeks since our fight, and Austin hasn't brought it up again, but its lingering presence makes the air around us heavy whenever he enters a room. Much like he is now.

The floorboards creak under his weight as he sits next to me on the porch. The smells of soap and clean laundry enter my personal space. "What are ya doing out here?"

I've taken to spending my time in Gran's chair, watching the fireflies dance in the evening sky. Every day when I'm finished with work, I come out here with a beer, listen to music, and think. AJ hasn't returned any of my calls. It's been a week since I've heard from him, and I miss him so much my whole body aches.

"Just enjoyin' the quiet."

At least, I was.

"Seein' your face the other month was like waking up from a nightmare, but every mornin' since, I relive it. I can't do it again, Casey Jane, so I'm askin' you point blank. You stickin' around this time?"

I shrug as I bring the cold beer to my mouth, wetting my dry lips. Might as well. AJ is the only thing I have to go back to, but a woman can only try so hard before taking the hint. If he doesn't want me anymore, I have no reason to return.

"S'pose so."

He tips his bottle in the same fashion, following my gaze out into the grassy pasture that stretches out in front of us. "Then I reckon a truce is in order."

His warm gaze falls on me, but I continue looking out into nothing and sipping my beer as if I don't feel it melting the skin off my bones. He holds out his large hand, watching and waiting for me to take it. I do, but he doesn't shake it, just holds it like it breathes new life back into his hollow shell.

I sure made a mess of everything. Wrecked it up good. My life, my relationships, all of it doomed to fail from the start. The only thing I have is this ranch, and considering the mountain of paperwork on Gran's desk, I'm not sure that I'll have it much longer. She was organized, and I'm lucky in that regard, but she was also behind on everything. She wasn't charging nearly enough for her boarding services, and the riding lessons dwindled down to practically nothing after I left. Fate really knows how to kick a gal while she's down.

"So what now?"

My head falls back as the remainder of my beer slides down my throat. "Another one of these." I hand him the empty bottle, and he grins, taking it from my hand before going into the house for another.

The chirping of crickets, the crooning voice of Dierks Bentley, and the occasional creaking of the rockers are the only sounds heard while Austin and I sit watching the remainder of the sun as it disappears beyond the horizon. The pile of empty bottles on the counter has doubled in size, and my vision swims in front of me. I lost count of how many I've had, but I'm pretty sure most of them are mine.

"You remember how many times you snuck outta this ol' house to meet me down at the pond?" Austin asks after a while.

"Sure do. I don't know if I can call it sneakin', though. Fairly certain Gran knew all about it."

"Shit. Ol' lady knew everything that went on around here." His snicker echoes into the half-empty beer bottle near his lips. The moonlight casts shards of gray light onto the porch, highlighting his profile. I watch the way his head tilts back, the way his throat moves. It's weird how he can be so different yet still be the same old Austin I always knew.

"We weren't doin' wrong. Just swimmin'."

Austin's fist bounces on his knee. "I kissed you for the first time durin' one of them swims."

"You did. I remember."

It wasn't just our first kiss. It was my first kiss. The first of many. The November night had a slight chill in the air. I had snuck out the back door and ran to the pond, excited to find Austin waiting for me. His hair was longer then, his face round, his body slim. A late blooming twenty-one-year-old, adorable in every conceivable way. I had blossomed that summer. Changed from a girl to a young woman, and he finally began to notice.

"What would you do if I jumped in?" I asked, jutting my chin toward the pond.

"Well, I guess I'd have to jump in there and save you. But you ain't gonna jump in."

"You don't think I'll do it?"

"I dare ya."

Never one to turn down a challenge, I stripped down to my bra and panties and dove in. The cold water prickled my skin. A splash burst in the water above me. I felt his body next to mine, taking me in his arms to pull me to the surface and drag me out. He ripped the blanket off the ground and wrapped it around my shoulders, rubbing his hands up and down my arms, warming them with his touch. "You're gonna be the death of me, crazy girl."

I put my arms around his back, covering both our wet bodies with the blanket. He smiled down at me. Pond water dripped off his nose and landed on mine. He lifted his hand and wiped it away, letting his knuckle graze down my cheek.

Hesitancy spun in his eyes. Our five-year age difference, while nothing right now, was huge back then. He was a man, holding a wet, half-naked teenage girl in his arms. "You wanna kiss me, Austin?"

"More than anythin', baby girl." His normally smooth voice was raspy and tense. His grip on me tightened, and the hand on my jaw slid to the nape of my neck to pull me closer.

The second his lips met mine, a breathless moan left my lungs. They never moved from my mouth, yet I still felt them everywhere. In my mind, they roamed over every bit of my skin, making me his. I was so sure that Austin was my forever. Little did either of us know, forever would only last the next couple of years.

Standing from the rocker, he offers me his hand. "Walk with me."

I slip my hand into his, allowing him to pull me from the chair and off the porch. The world spins, and my body sways. The evening grass is damp beneath my bare toes as we wander through the yard. The smell of hay gives way to the scent of the soggy earth as we near the pond, and the occasional burp of a random bullfrog fights over the constant chirp of crickets. The familiarity of it all astounds me. It's as if I never left.

Austin stops to face me and threads our fingers. "I used to sit out by this ol' pond at night, half expectin' you to show. I never gave up hope that you'd come back to me." When his gaze lands on mine, I see it. Relief. Austin's spent so much time waiting for me to be ready; I don't know why I thought now would be any different. He'll always wait for me.

Between the pond, the night, and Austin's warm hands in mine, everything makes sense. This is where I belong. The pond is like this Texas town. It seems so small to the outside eye, but only a select few of us know how deep it really goes. My roots run all over these grounds, and embedded within them, now and always, is Austin.

Nevertheless, AJ is the one in my dreams at night. His haunted gaze and sexy smile still flash behind my lids every time I close my eyes. Being with him was the first time I ever felt like I belonged, but then I come down here, and this feels right too.

Two completely different men both hold two completely different pieces of my heart. My past has caught up to my present, making it impossible to move forward. It's not fair. Not to me, and not to Austin. I can't move on because I still want AJ.

"I thought about it a thousand times, baby girl. Now, here you are."

"I'm here, but I'm not. A part of me still exists up north, Austin. I'm not ready to let it go yet."

"When you're ready, I'll be waiting. Always."

Chapter 21

AJ

BLOODCURDLING SCREAMS TEAR *through my eardrums. I'm running, trying to find her, but the fog is so thick, and the night is so black, I can barely see my hands out in front of me. "Where are you?" I call, but the shrieks continue as if they're coming from all directions.*

Bright light beams out of nowhere, blinding me. Crunching gravel, shattering glass, and those ear-piercing screams that just won't stop. My feet leave the ground. Am I being pulled? I don't know, but I'm moving. Backward. A gravitational feeling sits in my gut. My back hits the cold pavement. The smell of wet blacktop fills my nose. No, it's not blacktop. It's . . . dirt. Clean, fresh soil. It's all around me.

Sudden silence then the sound of digging. Through the black, I see her, though she has no face. Just golden rays of sunshine yellow hair blowing in the night. I can't move. Piles of dirt fall on my legs, my stomach, my chest. She's burying me alive. Or maybe I'm dead.

The desperate wails begin again, louder and more shrill. I want to move, but I can't. I open my mouth, but no sound comes out. Another pile lands on my face, but this time, it's glass. So much glass, twinkling as it cascades down on me in slow motion.

"AJ!" The voice saying my name is haunted and hollow as if

coming through a tunnel.

"AJ!" I want to go toward it. I move and fight and claw my way through the wreckage.

"AJ!" Silken strands of hair crumple in my fists. My eyes pop open, but all I see is darkness.

My eyes focus. There's no dirt, no glass, no fog. I'm safe and sound, lying in my bed alone and mangling the sheets with my hands. The dreams have not only increased in frequency, but they have also gotten much more intense ever since she left. Even after I'm awake, they continue to torment me until I can't stand to be in my bed anymore.

Letting Casey go out there alone was a stupid mistake. I should have gone with her, supported her. Now, I'm sitting around my lonely house worrying that I ruined what we had forever. Had I known our goodbye at the airport was the last time I'd see her, I would have held her tighter. Kissed her longer. Our romance was a whirlwind, but it was real. At least to me. Whoever made up that "it's better to have loved and lost" bullshit is an idiot. I'd give anything not to feel this soul crushing weight that sits upon my chest and doesn't seem to want to go away.

Knowing I'll never be able to sleep, I swipe my phone from the side table and sweep my thumb across the smooth glass front. It comes to life, a tiny sliver of light highlighting the gorgeous ocean eyes of the most beautiful girl in the world sitting as my background image. The need to see her hits me like a bucket of water. The tip of my finger traces the outline of her face as if I'm Gollum fondling the ring whispering, "My precious." If I don't do something soon, I'm going to end up in the friggin' loony bin.

I light up a smoke, contemplating my next move. It curls around my phone as I begin searching for the next available flight. I should have done this from day one. My job, my house,

my life in New Jersey . . . none of it matters. Nothing is as important as she is. I just hope she still wants me when I get there.

★ ★ ★

CASEY SAID TEXAS was barren, but I wasn't prepared for the
full brunt of that statement. New Jersey is rich with trees and
mountains, buildings and construction. There's always a view
and something to see on the horizon, whether it's thick, dense
woods or the New York City skyline. A state that was once
nothing but farmland built up into an industrial wasteland.
Congested and overcrowded.

The state is loud, even in the suburbs. Our home may have
been alone on a wooded lot, but behind that lot is a strip mall,
and beyond that, a highway. Late at night, eighteen-wheelers
would thunder down the road, bumping and rumbling as they
passed. The Doppler Effect sound of motorcycles racing at high
speed would pollute the airwaves. I've gotten so used to it that I
don't even notice it anymore. It's part of the background noise
of my life.

Out here, everything is flat. The deserted land strings for
miles with no end in sight. I've never seen anything like it before. It's almost as if I can see to the ends of the Earth. The
highway stretches out in front of me, a long line disappearing
into a never-ending V with no other cars on it. It's eerie.

Off the highway stands a small sign post with the name
Grainger burned into the worn wooden plaque. Gravel crunches under my tires as I veer up the winding dirt road under a
freestanding log structure announcing that Grainger Ranch is
up ahead between the endless trails of white washed picket
fencing on either side.

It's a little greener over here and slightly less desolate. In
the far-off distance, mountains stand proud against the evening
sky. It's beautiful. Another world. No construction, no trash, no

cursing commuters veering in and out of lanes—just acres and acres of undeveloped land, pristine, untouched, and very, very dry.

It's so quiet you can hear a pin drop. If I strain hard enough, I can hear the sleepy sounds of toads croaking by the pond or the occasional neigh of a horse somewhere on the property, but even that's so far off it's hardly noticeable.

Casey and I are from two very different worlds. I finally see it firsthand. Mine is a fast frenzy of loud, brash rock 'n' roll, while hers is a slower, simpler kind of life. One that strums a quiet tune on your heartstrings.

While hopping on the next plane to Texas wasn't my initial plan, I am a little excited to see where Casey comes from and feel her familial roots in the place that raised her. You can learn so much from a person that way. Humans have a tendency to adapt to their surroundings, but try as they might, they can never shed where they came from. It's an integral part of a person's history. The biggest piece of who they are.

I park the only available rental car they had, a hideous school bus yellow Kia Soul, next to the pond down a ways from the house. It's dusk, but it's so hot I can barely breathe as I follow the path to Casey's new home. With its lemonade porch and beautiful bay windows, the quaint farmhouse is something out of a storybook. There's even a porch swing rocking in the gentle breeze passing under the overhang.

One lone light in the house is on, but no one answers when I knock on the front door. I follow the porch around, hoping to find her home, but what I find stops me in my tracks. The rhythmic *clop-clop-clop* of hooves echoes between the house and the barn. A majestic, black horse jogs around the track, guided by the angel sitting on his back. The ends of her blond hair carry on the wind as she makes her way around the track, but the black ball cap shielding her eyes hides most of it from sight.

The milky skin I see every time I close my eyes is bronze now and shines in the soft sunlight still peeking out from behind the mountains.

From the porch, I watch the way she holds the reins and squeezes her legs, commanding the beast to move faster or slower at her will. She captivates me. Owns me. I may as well sleep in the stable with the rest of the animals she controls.

Casey steers the horse toward the stable, dismounts, and disappears inside. My feet propel me forward. Hay crunches underfoot as I step lightly into the stable. "I don't mean to stare, but you look an awful lot like this girl I used to know."

She jumps, gasping at the sound of my voice, and turns toward me. "AJ," she whispers. The blood drains from her face. "What are you doing here?"

How is it possible that she's more beautiful now than she was at the beginning of the summer? I don't even care what happened. The call, Austin, it all flew into the atmosphere the second I laid eyes on her again. The only phrase that runs through my head is I love you, but those three little words could make or break me if she doesn't feel the same way.

"Saying I'm sorry just didn't seem like enough."

A lock of hair twirls around her finger, one way then the other, surrounding me in its flowery scent as she steps closer. Horses huff and puff in their stalls waiting to be tended to, but her eyes are locked on me. "So you came all the way out here?"

"Of course." I pluck the Zildjian cap off her head and slip it onto mine. "How else was I gonna get my hat back?"

She rolls her eyes, flipping the lock of hair over her shoulder in a huff. My jokes aren't going to cut it this time. If I want back in her good graces, I'm going to have to grovel a bit. "I'm an asshole, Case. I lost my cool, and I really am sorry. You still my girl?"

"I haven't heard from you in a week. I thought you were

done with me, and now you're standing here expectin' me to jump right back in your arms? Not quite, city boy. You need to work for it."

Her glittering eyes, her quivering lips—I can see she's not nearly as angry as she's letting on. "A little hard work never bothered me."

Overcome with want, I fuse my lips to hers. The sweet taste of her mouth kick starts my pulse, now pounding with possessive need. I have to have her. The sexy way she breathes my name already echoes in my mind. I need to bury myself so deep inside her that it makes up for these last few months apart and soothes the trembling desire radiating from her until I know she's mine.

"You think . . . a few . . . sultry little kisses . . . are gonna . . . make it all better?" she whispers defiantly against my mouth, but her hungry lips devour mine as her nails rake across my back. The fiery inferno inside her burns hot; I can feel it seeping through her clothes.

"The first thing I plan to work on is getting you out of these shorts."

Chapter 22

Casey

HAVING AJ IN my room makes me feel naughty. I've never had a boy in this bedroom before. Not even Austin. "No boys upstairs" was a hard and fast rule. One Gran wasn't about to bend on. A girl's room is a private place. However, right now, all my private places are open for business as AJ's mouth treks across my skin with a luscious mix of nips and kisses. His tongue runs over every freckle and every pore until the throbbing in my core is unbearable.

The bedroom door sits open a crack. Footsteps pad across the flattened area rug, but I'm too enthralled with AJ's mouth to care. Austin stands at the foot of my bed. He doesn't yell. Doesn't freak. Just stays there watching as AJ continues to tease my body manic.

Still on my knees, I fall limp, resting on my hands, as I bask in the feeling of AJ's lips sliding over every inch of exposed skin. My head falls back between my shoulder blades, and my eyes lock on Austin's. The way he watches, ravaging me with his gaze, unleashes a demon inside. One that seems to reach out and pull him onto the bed with us. With a slow, sensual crawl, he slinks up behind me.

"Austin . . ."

"No more talkin', baby girl. From here on out, I only want to hear *you moan."*

One pair of hands slides my bra off my shoulders, while another unhooks the back. I'm sandwiched between two warm bodies, feasted on by two scalding mouths, and driven mad by the sound of two men growling my name in unison, as they push my panties off my hips.

My head feels fogged, clouded over with lust and confusion. "I can't have you both," I whisper, but the feeling of dual erections pressing against my bare flesh makes it hard to want anything else.

AJ's gray gaze flits up and down my naked body with carnal hunger. He blows out a long, slow breath across my dampened skin, hardening my nipples into stiff peaks. "But you want us both." Two calloused fingers trail up my thigh. "You want me here . . ." They slip inside me, as Austin's hands come from behind and glide up my throat to finger my mouth. "In this wet little pussy."

Austin pulls his fingers from my mouth and slides them over the curve of my rear. "While I fuck you here . . ." His saliva covered finger slips between my cheeks and pushes into my backside, stretching the taut flesh where no one's ever been before. "In your tight little asshole."

"Is this what you want, cowgirl? You ride my cock while Austin rides your ass?"

They work me over with their hands, making it impossible to think straight enough to answer. I'm lost in the mindless pleasure of the two men who hold my heart filling me completely. Rough and rhythmic in the front, slow and steady from behind, they're total opposites yet share one common ground. They don't just want to fuck me; they want to own me. Swallow my broken pieces inside themselves then spit me out whole again—shiny, new, and theirs, to do with what they please. Fighting this aching desire is pointless. They're right. I want them to own me. Both of them.

I'm reduced to a gyrating pile of whimpers and whines. Their stimulating hands keep me from falling over as the storm begins to brew.

"Come for us, cowgirl."

The buildup swirls in my tailbone, twisting around, roiling through my gut until I feel like I'm about to unravel. I fuse my mouth to AJ's, filling it with the keening cry that tears from my lungs as I come apart, still riding both their hands for dear life.

I sit up with a gasp, soaked in sweat, alone in my bed. The area between my thighs is slick and pounding. "Holy hell!" I catch my reflection in the mirror ahead. An aroused flush mars my cheeks, but the bite marks on my neck are a reminder that not all of it was a dream. AJ did show up here unannounced. What started in the stable, ended in my bed, and I didn't get the chance to introduce him and Austin properly.

I need to find him.

Before Austin does.

But I'm too late. Voices bark at each other from downstairs. The words muffle through my bedroom door, but the tension seeps under the crack.

The voices get louder as I race down the stairs. An irate Rebel and a smart-ass Yankee go head to head in Gran's kitchen. AJ and Austin ram into one another like goats locking horns, but I'm too stunned by the sight of them to move at first. Just like my dream, they're shirtless in jeans. Two bare chests, each puffed out, overexerting dominance that unleashes so much pure testosterone into the space that I'm chewing on it.

Trying my best to ignore the awkward uprising of hormones threatening to burn me to soot, I run toward both men and push them apart.

"This guy claims he's a friend of yours. That true?" The divot between Austin's eyebrows is so deep I could fit my pinky in it. This is bad. Add a check in the box marked *Poor Decision Skills* and add it to the pile. A blind man could have seen this coming. Why didn't I?

"He is, Austin."

"*You're* Austin?" AJ pushes the thick swatch of raven hair

from his forehead with both hands and holds it there while the wheels in his head turn at a furious pace.

Something somehow got lost in translation. Judging by AJ's reaction, he was picturing some toothless yokel, not a tall thirty-year-old man with dark brown hair and flawless abs.

"Oh, you've heard of me? Nice to know she's talked to someone about somethin'!"

"That's not true. I told you I was seein' someone. I never lied to you about that."

"But I thought you were done sowin' your wild oats when you came back! How long am I supposed to wait, Casey Jane?" I've never seen Austin's eyes this wild and manic. Foaming at the mouth, he's lost all semblance of self-control. I don't know how to fix this. "Did you ever love me at all?"

I keep my eyes trained on Austin, too terrified to see the expression I can only imagine is on AJ's face. This isn't how this was supposed to go down, but the lid has popped off the box, and since I can't shove it all back in, I may as well empty it for good. Put on some music; let the skeletons dance right out of my closet for all to see.

"I loved you so much I couldn't stand it, but I couldn't be your wife, Austin! I'm not the kind of girl you're lookin' for." A river of tears leak down each cheek, one after the other, until the hurt on Austin's face is nothing but a blur in front of me. "Raising a hundred kids on a farm was your dream, not mine. Davis made me an offer, and I took it!"

A bang thunders through the room as Austin's fists come down on the kitchen table. "Don't you fuckin' say his name in this house!" Austin's furious outburst makes me jump. He's never cussed at me. Not one time in all the years I've known him. "Second thought? Nah. Call him up; go ahead. We can have a reunion tour of all the guys you've fucked behind my back."

The serrated edge of his hateful words cut jagged pieces of my heart off in bite-sized pieces. *You're not allowed to be angry, Casey. You did this. Deal with it. Take the backlash; you deserve it.*

"How many more times can I apologize? I can't take it back, Austin. And I wouldn't want to. Davis was a bastard on wheels, but he's a part of my past, just like you are."

"I'm not sticking around for this. I'm out of here!" AJ shouts with quivering lips. The screen door slaps as he pushes through it, walking away from the crushing weight of tension in the kitchen.

I head for the door, but Austin's fingers close around my forearm. "Don't you run out on me again!" I try my best to wrench my arm from his tightly clasped fingers, but his grip holds strong. "I'm warnin' you, Casey Jane."

"Let me go!"

The morning grass is dewy under my bare feet as I run outside. "AJ!" He stops yet keeps his back to me as I get closer. Smoke plumes all around him as he dips his head and lights a cigarette. "What are you so mad at?" I pant, trying to catch my breath.

"You know what scares me, Casey? What would have happened if I hadn't shown up? How long would it have been before you ended up riding old Austin like Seabiscuit?" He turns and glowers at me, his gray eyes darkening to a terrifying shade of new moon midnight.

"That wouldn't have happened, AJ." My mouth says the words, but a grimace crosses my face knowing there may be a hint of truth in that statement.

"Oh, no? You sure jumped on my dick pretty quick!"

"That's not fair!"

"No! You know what's not fair? Not telling me that you're *living* with your ex-fiancé! All this time, I imagine you all alone out here, but you got John Wayne sleeping off the kitchen."

"Okay, fine! You're right! I messed up! It's not ideal, but it's how it is. Besides, it's not like you handed me a checklist of all your ex-lovers!"

"Well, I can assure you, none of my exes are going to jump out of the woodwork at you either," he growls through clenched teeth. "I shared everything with you. No matter how painful it was to open those doors, I did it anyway because you deserved to know what kind of man you were getting. It would have been nice to be given the same courtesy."

He brushes past me, but I stay hot on his heels forcing him to listen. "I was afraid if you knew what I did you wouldn't want me anymore." Desperation leaks from my voice like the fresh tears falling from my eyes. "The idea that I was innocent made you feel special. I liked making you feel that way, and I loved how it made you look at me. It made me feel worshiped and loved. I'm sorry if that was wrong, but it's the truth." AJ doesn't acknowledge what I'm saying; he just keeps walking away from the house. "I'm still the same person."

He whips around to face me, his eyes glittering in the morning sunlight. "I don't even know you."

Chapter 23

AJ

MY BRAIN FEELS like it's melting from information overload. What do I do now? I'm stuck in hillbilly hell with the woman who tore my heart out of my ass and a good ol' boy who looks like he wants to hand said ass back to me. What the fuck, man?

I need something to hit. If I had my drums, I could hide away and bang out my aggression until my head was clear. I knew how to handle this, but without them, everything jumbles together in my mind, making it impossible to think straight. J. Geils was right. Love does stink.

It feels like hours before I finally make the long walk back. Not because I want to, but because I have to. The only thing I have is a dwindling supply of cigarettes. I have no shoes. No shirt. All my shit's in the house. Including my heart. In addition to all that, it's hot as fuck out here already. I'm too depressed for this kind of weather. It should be raining, with demonic storm clouds overhead threatening to open up the heavens and pelt frogs down upon us. But the sky is clear and blue, as bright and bold as Casey's eyes. And hot. Actually, hot isn't the right word. It's the setting for London broil outside.

F-bombs flying from the edge of the barn catch my attention on the way. Grass and straw crunch under my bare feet, as I follow the clanging sound of metal smacking metal.

"I can help you with that if you're having trouble."

Austin glares at me from beyond the raised hood of an old Ford truck. A starter motor box lays at his boots. "What the hell do you know?"

"I know replacing the starter is probably overkill. Did you jump the solenoid?"

Austin gives me a dismissive look as I grab a screwdriver and step in front of the engine. "Start the truck."

"That ain't gonna do shit."

"For the sake of four hundred bucks and an hour's worth of your time, humor me, Hoss."

With the roll of his eyes, he reaches into the cab and twists the key forward. You don't spend as many years around cars as I do without learning a few tricks. I lay the shaft of the screwdriver between the starter post and the thick battery cable that leads to the solenoid. Sparks fly as the engine lurches, and the starter kicks over. "Bad solenoid, bro. Change that shit and you're good to go."

He grumbles under his breath and starts throwing tools into the box on the bed.

"You're welcome," I add for good measure. "Listen, man." I cross my arms over my naked chest and lean on the quarter panel of the dirty blue truck. "This morning was a shit show for both of us. But I'm letting you know right now, I don't want any trouble with you, bro."

I offer him my hand, but Austin just stands there, scowling at it. The last thing I need is adding fuel to this fire and beating Opie's ass. Yeah, he's taller than I am by a few inches, but I'm not intimidated by that. I've beat up dudes bigger and way tougher than he is. I'm a surprise. I can take a guy down faster than you can say "what the fuck?" They don't see me coming. I have East Coast rage and a street savvy attitude, not to mention a low center of gravity. The bigger they are, the harder they fall.

He cocks his head to the side, his eyes crinkling in the corners. "You think you're gonna come in here and steal what's mine, pretty boy? Think again. It ain't ever gonna happen on my watch."

Synapses fire in my brain, telling my impulses to bury this guy where he stands. He's provoking me. If he wants a fight, he's got one. I won't back down, but I'm not going to throw the first punch. "You had your chance, and you couldn't keep her. Casey's my girl now. This thing with you and her? It's done, bro. Just like this conversation."

I turn and head for the house, while the daggers of his gaze leave puncture wounds on my back. I don't lose. If he thinks I chased Casey all the way out here just to turn back now, he's mistaken.

★ ★ ★

A BLUE GINGHAM couch sits in the center of the huge family room next to a beige Barcalounger with a blue lace doily draped across the back. Fake ivy hangs across the enormous stone fireplace, and decorative oil lamps flank the mantle.

At first, I don't see the sunny blonde beauty curled up on the sofa fast asleep. A colorful knit blanket covers her almost entirely, but a halo of golden hair pokes out from the large woven holes.

I could leave right now. Pack my shit and go. Leave her a note; send her a text. Say goodbye and never return to this hellhole, but I can't. I'm stuck. Permanently attached to the girl who glued my cracked heart together with her own delicate fingers then sealed herself to me for life. Maybe she's not perfect, but she's perfect for me.

"Rise and shine, cowgirl," I mumble, peeling the blanket back. Warm pink circles dot both cheeks, and her light eyelashes still stick together in points. The idea that she cried herself to sleep on this couch while I sat outside and stewed like a baby makes me want to kick the shit out of myself.

Her eyelids flutter before opening. "AJ." My name comes out as merely a whisper. Two stupid letters given by my parents that somehow sound like a cello solo falling from her beautiful lips. Rays of light filter in through the flimsy lace curtains covering the windows and highlight her eyes in brilliant shades of cornflower and topaz.

Everything about her is bright. Like a rainy winter day, depressing shades of black and gray encompass me, but Casey is like the beach on the sunniest summer afternoon. She's the light to my dark, the sun to my moon. Just looking at her gives me hope. It makes me feel good in a way I didn't even know was possible until I met her.

The feel of her soft body against mine as I take her in my arms is all I need. Her floral fragrance wraps itself around me, making its home in my heart.

"I'm sorry."

"Forget it. It's over," I reply, stroking her hair. Apologies aren't necessary. I don't want to talk about it anymore. I just want to move on from here.

"I want you to know me, AJ." She leaves the room for a second and returns with a book. Stickers decorate the brightly colored cover, and the overstuffed pages cause it to take on the vague shape of a sideways V.

"What is this?"

"This," she starts, placing her hand on top of the book as if it were a bible, "is a glimpse into a life I can't keep runnin' from."

A hot pink paper sticks to the very first page, surrounded by more stickers and a blue ribbon in the corner. "Casey Jane, live at The Wander Inn," I read aloud.

I catch the corner with my fingernail and flip the page over. On the opposite side are photos of Casey in fancy dresses and princess crowns. The headline, *Pageant Queen,* cut out of construction paper curves along the top.

The entire album is like this. Bursting at the seams with fliers and photographs meticulously cut out and decorated page by page. Memorabilia from the past she's kept hidden until now.

I pull out a photo, and my eyes go wide. A much younger Casey is smiling on stage in front of a mic stand with a guitar strapped over her shoulder. The background is dark, but she stands out under the bright lights. On the adjoining page is a playlist of fifteen songs with her name and the date at the top. "Y-you're a musician."

"I *was* a musician. Now, I'm a bartender." Casey's lips press into a thin line.

"What happened?"

"Davis Cole happened."

The book slips from my fingers, but I catch it before it hits the floor. *Davis Cole?* Can't be the one I'm thinking of. There must be some coincidence.

As if she can read my thoughts, Casey adds, "Yeah, you heard me right. *The* Davis Cole."

"Who are you?"

The girl who doesn't date musicians not only turns out to be one herself but has some correlation to one of the biggest names in modern rock. I'm personally not a fan of Blood Sport, but you'd have to be living under a rock not to know who they are. Davis Cole, their volatile bass player, was always in the news. Guy was as deranged off the stage as he was on.

"This isn't who I am. It's who I was. I left everythin' behind to follow Davis. He took what he could and left the rest."

Blood Sport may be climbing the charts with their over pro-cessed brand of mainstream rock 'n' roll, but their biggest claim to fame was the celebrity death scandal that surrounded them. Just after the release of their debut album, news about the death of their bass player rocked the world. They found him in a dwelling unsuitable for human life, surrounded by enough dope to kill a horse.

"How do you even know him?"

Casey snorts out a humorless laugh. "Davis ain't shit. He's a bumpkin from small town Texas, just like I am. He coasted off my talent and used me as a steppin'-stone to pave his way through showbiz. Blood Sport's first album was written by me."

"Hold up." I lift both palms, urging her to slow down. "*You* wrote Fire and Brimstone? You don't even like rock music."

"I don't"—she sighs—"but I loved Davis. At least, I thought I did. And I'd have done anythin' to help him. Includin' set my career aside."

"What?"

"I started out as a pageant contestant. The fatherless daugh-ter of the town whore, no one even looked at me twice. Sure, I was pretty, but so were all the other girls. I was nothin' spe-cial." Casey slides the book from my hands and lets her finger-tips graze over the photo on the page. "But when I started to sing, people stopped judging and started listenin'. I wasn't just another Grainger disappointment. I was Casey Jane. All that fell to shit the second I saw him.

"Davis had a very enigmatic personality. He was handsome and slick and had a way of getting' inside you without you even realizing it. The no-name record label that picked me up paired us together. He played bass in the studio band, and we clicked right away. Two weeks later, we were in New York."

Casey's glassy eyes meet mine, but her face is impassive. "We lived in a roach-infested shit box that cost more money than I even care to mention. I was workin', savin', payin' our bills, and he was livin' the rock star dream. It wasn't uncommon for me to come home and find Davis in our bed with other women, naked and drugged out of his mind. If I got on to him about it, he'd only smack me around, so after a while, I just withdrew.

"Little by little, he'd taken it all. All our money, all my jewelry, and every shred of self-respect I had. All of it—just gone. Stuck in his arm or up his nose." She slides her hands through her hair, pushing it back and resting it on one shoulder, mangling the entire length with her fingers. "One day, I came home, and he was dead."

The air in the room is thick as she finishes her story. My heart smacks against my ribcage hard enough to cause bruises.

"That's why you stopped dating?"

She shrugs, looking away. "Ever seen a real dead body, AJ?"

The memory of my father crashes down onto to me hard. An icy chill rolls down my arms and freezes the depths of my belly. I feel my face contort into a look of disgust as I nod. Just once, and it was far too many times.

"Don't you see? It's my fault. I wished him dead. I blamed him for the mess I made of my life, and I wanted him gone, but I was too afraid to leave him myself." Casey lifts her gaze and stares at me through her long lashes. "I've spent so many years wishin' I'd stayed in Texas, but now, I realize everything happens for a reason. Funny thing about manure. It may stink to holy heaven, but the most beautiful things grow from it."

"What grew from yours?"

She lifts her hand and rests it on my cheek. "You. You're my beautiful thing, and I wouldn't change a minute of my shit life because it brought us together."

A cyclone of emotions spins inside me. Anger, confusion, anguish, love—they rotate so fast I want to reach out and grab one just to hold something for longer than a second. They all blur together, making my head feel numb and dizzy.

"If you want to leave, I understand."

My fingers catch under her chin, lifting it to meet my gaze. Her eyes are deep blue pools of fresh, unfallen tears. She's cried so much I can't bear to see them anymore. "None of this matters. The only thing I care about is you and me, our future."

"You mean it?"

I nod, and Casey falls into my arms, pressing her lips against mine. The salty taste of her damp skin trickles into my mouth as I press it all over her cheeks and eyelids, kissing away her tears. "You don't have any more giant confessions, though, right? You're not gonna tell me you used to be a guy, are ya?"

"No." When she giggles, the sound leaves me breathless.

Chapter 24

Casey

MAREN MORRIS'S SMOKY style hums from the speakers of the little radio Gran kept in the kitchen. She and I always fought because the moment she turned her back, I'd change it from the religious station to whatever I felt like listening to at the time. Right now, I'm yowling along to "My Church" at the top of my lungs, trying to pretend that I didn't inadvertently thrust us all into the strangest situation imaginable.

Austin spent the majority of the day making himself scarce. Either in the yard tinkering with the truck or minding the horses. He didn't even come in for lunch, which is a first since I've been back. Even when we weren't talking, he made an appearance in the house at least once. I hate that I hurt him, not once, but twice now. It's the last thing I intended to do, but I can't deny what's in my heart.

The pies are starting to pile up in the kitchen, and I'm almost out of flour when I hear the heavy sound of boots scraping the tattered linoleum behind me. Warm hands caress my back, sending a thrill slithering down my spine that snakes around my front just like the masculine set of arms do.

"Hey, baby."

A flour dust cloud flies into the air as I turn, expecting AJ, but run smack-dab into the chest of Austin Krehley. His hands hold firm to the butcher-block countertop behind me, caging me between his body and the cabinetry with nowhere to run. The scents of hay, cotton, and all things man waft off him, making the breath hitch in my throat.

Why do you still have this effect on me? Stop it. Stop invading my dreams, stop turning me on, just stop, stop, stop. I've chosen.

I've chosen . . .

"We gotta talk, Casey Jane." His voice is low and hushed. If there's a God above, he'll make sure AJ is far, far away from this kitchen and doesn't bear full witness to the way Austin sends an unmistakable flush growing along my skin.

"What about?"

His gaze follows the path of my tongue as I wet my dry lips, and he pulls his own between his teeth. The Austin I know is not this aggressive. He's not the type of man who takes what he wants. He doesn't chase. Doesn't fight. Yet here he is, pinning me against him and staring down at me with hungry, desperate eyes that are begging me to succumb to whatever this is brewing in the tight space between us.

"Why?"

"Why what?" My whispering voice comes out too sexy for its own good.

"Why him?"

"What do you mean?"

"I mean he's all wrong for you. He can't give you the life that I can give you. The love you deserve. You and I . . . we can run this ranch together—make it great again. *We* can be great again. He's gonna make a mistake, and it's gonna cost you everything. Jersey Johnny doesn't belong down here, and you know it."

"No. AJ wants to be with me, wherever I am." Uncertainty drips off my lips along with the words. With his thick black boots and heavy metal tees, AJ's an obvious fish out of water here. Could Austin be right? Am I making another mistake?

No. Austin is wrong. AJ wants to be here. We're good together. I'm sure of it . . .

When he leans in farther, another whiff of his masculine scent overtakes the sweet smell of fruit and sugar lingering in the air. His breath flutters against my ear. He's too close to me. I'm uncomfortable. "But do *you* really wanna be with *him*? Look at you. You're tremblin', baby girl. I've barely touched you, yet here you are meltin' like a pad of butter on a hot plate."

"You need to back up."

"Stop fightin' this. I know you still want me." When Austin shifts his hips, I feel his arousal beginning to take shape beneath the heavy denim.

"I said back up, Austin. I'm serious."

"And if I don't?"

"Then you're begging to have your ass kicked." AJ's voice cuts the tension, making both our heads whip toward the direction of the hallway. "She said back off. Or are your ears too full of horse shit to hear her?" he adds, stomping toward us. He grabs Austin by the bicep and manually forces him back. "Is this your game? Cornering frightened women when they're alone?"

Another duel in the kitchen is about to go down. A showdown at the OK Corral. Guns blazing, best man wins. This can't be happening.

I fly into action, pushing AJ back with one arm while pressing into Austin's chest with the other, holding back the bull about to charge. "Enough! Go to your corners!"

The tension in Austin's shoulders eases, but AJ's testosterone is still firing on both cylinders. He morphed from man to machine; ready to defend me from what appeared to be the start of an attack. If only he knew, the only attack I was suffering was of the hormonal variety. At any rate, we both need a little space from Austin and some time to clear our heads.

"Come on." The pulse in AJ's neck begins to slow when I thread my hands behind his back. "It's your first official day as an honorary Texan. We should celebrate!"

"Where you goin'?" Austin blusters.

"The Wander."

A slow roll of red rage creeps up Austin's face. "Course. Gotta show off your boy toy to all your fans," he grumbles, turning away.

"What was that?" AJ calls after him.

"Nothin'! Have a good time!"

"Ignore him," I say. "Let's go have some fun!

★ ★ ★

BEAT-UP TRUCKS SIT on the cracked asphalt in front of the only bar in town. During the day, The Wander Inn is a hole in the wall that serves greasy burgers and day old french fries, but at night, it comes alive. Right now, only a handful of people are milling about, but once the band comes on, the joint will be bursting at the seams. This was my stomping ground. My home away from home. I wasn't old enough to be in here, but when you're Brewster County's sweetheart, people tend to turn a few blind eyes. I owned this place. In the metaphorical way, of course.

The smell of cigarettes and stale beer greets us at the door as we step inside. It's been seven years, but the place hasn't changed a bit. A burned out Miller Light sign struggles to stay lit, blinking randomly over the old jukebox that I know for a fact is busting a gut with old Kenny Rogers's songs. A circular bar sits in the center, surrounded by a few scattered tables, a small dance floor, and a platform stage in the corner.

AJ pulls out my stool and waits while I sit. "Watch this." The bartender, a man with a handlebar mustache and gray side-burns, doesn't even look up. Just throws down two bar napkins and asks us what we want.

"We'll take a Bud and the biggest margarita you got," I say, a smile tugging at my lips.

Crystal blue eyes snap to meet mine. Ray's aged quite a bit since I've seen him last. His ear-to-ear grin is a little less white and his face a little more worn, but deep inside that warm, invit-ing gaze is the same old Ray who used to sneak me Cokes and chicken fingers under the table on those rare occasions when I was left in Loretta's care. "Casey Jane? Shit! Aren't you a sight for sore eyes? Get over here and give your Uncle Ray a hug!"

The smells of peppermint Skoal and Old Spice tingle in my nostrils as he reaches across the bar, grabbing me up in his thick arms. Yet another time machine scent sending me back. "Whatcha doin' down here in these parts?"

"Takin' a break from grass and hay." I smile up at AJ, who looks about as comfortable as a raccoon after sunrise. "My friend, AJ, here has never been to Texas. Thought I'd bring him down and show him off," I say with a wink.

AJ greets Ray with a, "Hey, man," and a hearty handshake, his voice just slightly deepened. He's still on edge from having to deal with Austin and playing Alpha Dog for the moment. As if he has anything to worry about. Ray's been kind of like a dad to me. At least, what I imagine a dad would be like. Not that I have any basis for comparison.

"We gonna get you on the stage tonight, pretty lady?"

Ray's watery eyes glimmer from the swatch of light beam-ing in from the kitchen side of the bar. His guitar was the first one I ever picked up. He taught me my first chords, my first notes, while Mama sat in the corner with her man du jour.

He told me, "Pretty voices are nothing if you can't pluck the strings."

"Nah. I hung up my voice. Kissed it goodbye for greener pastures." I press a kiss to my fingertips before adding, "Literally."

"That's a shame, Casey Jane. You have an amazing talent to be wasted on them horses." Ray makes quick work of preparing our drinks and sets them out on the bar for us. "On the house. Nice to meet you, AJ. You take care of my girl here."

As the night wears on, the crowd gets thicker, and the drinks go down smoother. I have a solid tequila buzz and a smile that makes my cheeks hurt. Old friends pour through the door. People I haven't seen or heard from in years, yet still manage to pick up where we left off, like no time at all has passed. They welcome me back with open arms, laughter, and tears. I'm happy. More so than I can remember being in a very long time, and it's not the booze, even though it helps. It's this place. My home.

"Holy shit! Casey Grainger!" The voice booms over the music playing on the jukebox. Before I even see where it comes from, I'm knocked off my feet in a bear hug. "When the hell did you get back?"

"Ah hell, Renee! Look at you!" Bar lights glint off the star-shaped badge displayed proudly on her ample chest.

Having grown up on the farm neighboring ours, Renee is my oldest friend. I've hardly a dirty-kneed childhood memory that doesn't include her.

"You're a sheriff's officer now? Didn't we get hauled in for trespassing on private property; drunk and disorderly . . . I don't know . . . a few dozen times at least?"

"Yeah," she says with a snort. "I'm off the clock now, though. My husband's with the band. I married Earl Hinderman. You believe that shit? Who you here with?"

I crane my neck and catch sight of the black Zildjian cap

bobbing near the stage setup. Naturally, AJ gravitated toward the band. Why am I not surprised? "Come on. I'll introduce you."

Grabbing Renee by her pudgy hand, I drag her through the ever-growing crowd of people. A guy I don't know balances a banjo on his knee. His drawl's so thick, he's incoherent, but AJ stands politely listening to him talk about Lord only knows.

"Havin' fun?"

AJ turns toward the sound of my voice and grasps my hips, pulling me closer. The man has this gift. A crazy habit of making the rest of the world disappear with the tiniest caress. Every touch sends sparks skittering along my skin and now is no different. A scorching burn courses up each side as his thumbs graze along the strip of exposed skin between my tank top and skirt.

"Rusty was giving me a quick rundown on the history of bluegrass."

That smile. I haven't seen it since our early days at The Wreck. The flirty, unsure of himself grin that sets my heart blazing now as much as it did then. Seeing it, feeling his sizzling touch, a pulsing pound begins to throb between my suddenly slick thighs.

I take a step forward, but the sound of someone clearing their throat brings my head back where it belongs instead of in the clouds where it flew the second AJ put his hands on me. We're not alone here.

The old Casey Jane is emerging from the cocoon of misery that's held me captive for the last handful of years. My wings are unfurling, and I finally feel like I could soar. I pull AJ's head to my ear and take in the clean scent of cotton and the smoky smell of tobacco. "Say hello to my friend then excuse yourself through that door on the right."

He pulls back with a raised brow but doesn't question my

motives. Instead, he extends his hand toward Renee with a respectful smile as I make introductions.

"Excuse me, ladies. I got to go hit the head." His smoldering gray gaze flickers past me as he turns away from us and saunters off.

"Damn, girl. You always had a thing for big, dumb animals. Cute, though. Does he know that's not the bathroom?" Renee asks.

"He's had a bit to drink. I'll be back."

I turn away from my friend, following AJ's path through the door clearly marked *Storage* on the front. A pull string swings back and forth from the naked bulb hanging above our heads. Extra tables and stacked chairs line each wall. In the corner, a broken down mechanical bull sits among its various pieces waiting for Rodeo Night to be set up for the ride.

AJ leans against its frame, his knuckles resting on the saddle, and his long legs crossed at the ankles. "Challengin' me to another ride?" I ask.

Without warning, my feet leave the ground, and my ass hits the bull sidesaddle. "My riding days are over, cowgirl. But yours have just begun."

Our lips crash together. The taste of beer and whiskey playing on his tongue teases me as it tangles and twists with mine. We're sloppy. Unbridled. The room spins around us in a drunken haze of booze and lust. Outside the door, the crowd of people gets thicker by the moment. Anyone could come in, but the danger of that risk fuels the naughty need already beginning to gnaw at me.

The band begins to play, and AJ starts inching up my skirt. The airy material flutters along my skin as he tugs at my underwear. I shift my hips from side to side, aiding in his hot pursuit to tear them down with clumsy hands, but the cheap elastic pops, snapping against my thigh like a firework.

Hooded eyes lock me in their hypnotic gaze. He drops to his knees on the brown tile floor. Stubble scrapes against my thighs, tickling the delicate skin as hot breath feathers along my damp flesh. My urgent need for him is agonizing. I teeter on the edge of the saddle, waiting for him to drive me into oblivion.

With rough hands, he grasps my thighs, forcing them wider. "This . . ." A calloused fingertip skims past my slick entrance, causing my hips to buck. "Is mine." A series of whimpers and whines falls from my mouth as he slips two fingers in down to the knuckle. "You want my mouth on this gorgeous pussy?"

I nod, writhing against his palm as he works me over with his hand. "Then say it. I need to hear the words escaping those pretty lips."

"It's yours, AJ. Kiss it. Fuck it. Take it. It's yours."

"I won't share you with that redneck fuck. Whatever you had with Austin is done. Understand?"

Another whimper, another nod. He's torturing me with pleasure, giving me a taste but holding back what I really want as punishment.

"That's my girl." Taking hold of my leg, he drops it over his shoulder. His tongue glides from bottom to top. One long, languid lick that sends a hushed moan tumbling out of my mouth.

"Moan louder. I want everyone in this bar to know who you belong to."

His stern voice vibrates deep inside me. "Don't stop," I mewl, dropping my head back as he flicks my already engorged clit with rapid-fire fervor.

The band is killing it on the stage. The erratic beat of banjo twangs loudly through the door, but as AJ delves deeper between my legs, everything becomes muffled. His hat lies forgotten on the floor at his knees. My fingers tangle in his unruly waves. I'm lost in the moment, drowning with desire. Holding his head and fucking his tongue until a muted shriek rips through my clenched teeth.

"Hold onto me, baby. I'm nowhere near done making you mine." Pleasure whirls through my body as his arms tighten around my backside and lift me in the air. He settles onto the bull with me on his lap. "Go on, cowgirl. Ride."

Still reeling with aftershocks, I fumble to position myself over him, sliding down his entire length until I'm straddling both him and the bull. The way he growls when I start to move is almost enough to make me come on the spot. No space resides between us. He fills me completely. Not just my body, but my head and my heart as well. Every part of me is his.

"Whose cock do you love?" he barks with a firm smack on the ass.

"Yours," I breathe, trembling with another impending release.

His palm comes down on my ass again. "Who owns that pretty pussy?"

"Oh . . . oh, AJ . . . you do." My nails dig into his shoulders as he jerks my hair and bites down on my neck hard enough to draw blood. Stars pop behind my eyes.

"Watching you fall apart is so fucking hot. Come for me again. Now."

The taste of me is sweet on his tongue as AJ attacks my lips, matching the beat of my body with his own slapping hip movements, as he slams upward into me hard. Fingers bite my ass. An unashamed cry tears from my lungs and thick spurts of heat overflow my insides.

"What did you do to me, woman?" Goose bumps prickle my oversensitive skin as AJ's hands roll up my back and slide under my hair. He's as affectionate as he is possessive. Owning me, yet loving me at once. Harsh and gentle; ruthless and tender. Everything I need tied up in one deliciously decadent bundle of muscle and man.

"What do you mean?" I giggle.

He pushes us up, and our bodies come apart with a pop. Gray eyes search my face. His gaze is earnest and strong, shrinking my smile and raising my heart rate. "Ever since I lost my family, I've wanted to start one of my own." He rests his palm on my cheek. "I still want that, and I want it with you. I love you, Casey."

Chapter 25

AJ

WHAT THE HELL is wrong with me? You can't fuck a girl in a dirty bar storage room then start talking about babies and shit. When did I become such an emo bastard? And . . . did I just tell her I wanted to marry her?

Her body just feels so warm next to mine, melting into me with its floral fragrance that drives me wild. Her hair is like a garden of lilacs, and her skin as soft as jersey knit cotton. Maybe it isn't the most romantic setting to be dropping the L word, but to me, the moment just seemed right. I love her, and I want her. When I close my eyes, I don't just see today; I see tomorrow and day after. Years in the future, with Casey by my side. My partner, my lover, my life.

Jesus Christ, I really am *an emo bastard! Fuck!*

Her mouth opens then shuts like a ventriloquist doll. She doesn't move, doesn't speak. My gaze snaps to hers, trying to read her mind before losing my cool. I've never seen a woman look quite this freaked out.

"Casey Jane? I know you're out there somewhere, girl. Get your cute little butt up on this stage!"

Until now.

"Shit!" she whispers, scrambling off me. The busted strip of panties falls further into her boot. She does a little hopping dance trying to grab it out to pull it off, then wads it in a ball to wipe what's left of my cum away.

"I can't do this, AJ. I ain't Casey Jane anymore. I can't sing in front of all these people."

An iota of relief washes over me, hoping that deer in headlights look on her face is a severe case of stage fright, rather than the rejection I worry is coming. "You are, and you can."

"How?"

"Just focus on me. Let all those other people fade away and stay right here." I point at my eyes with two fingers.

With a deep breath, she nods. "I'll go out first. Wait until you hear me talkin' and then follow. Got it?" She drops a kiss on the corner of my mouth then disappears out the door.

I look down at the soiled wad of cotton she pressed into my hand with a snort. *What am I supposed to do with these?* I stuff them in my pocket and adjust my fly. I'm still half-erect. Impressive, I know. The smell of sex hangs in the air; the combined fragrance of honey, flowers, and sweat all mingling together, making me want to go for another round.

Or two.

"Hey, everybody! How y'all doin' tonight?"

Her sweet voice melts under the crevice, beckoning me to come out. Opening the door, I slip through the crack undetected and force my way to the stage as the crowd erupts with applause. Show lights bathe her in a yellow and red glow. The stage is makeshift. A platform, really. A homemade mix of two-by-fours and plywood. But with Casey on it, it could be Madison Square Garden as far as I'm concerned.

She stands in front of the microphone with a shy smile, her dimples highlighted by the combination of lights and shadows dotting her face. Next to her, the burly dude with the ZZ Top beard slips the guitar off his neck and hands it to her. She hesitates. Her eyes dart over the crowd, no doubt looking for me, but I'm still fighting my way through, trying my best to get to her as promised.

"Looks like Casey Jane needs some reassurance," Burly Dude drawls into the microphone. A cacophony of hoots and hollers waves through the crowd, filling up the tiny space.

I saw the pictures, and I heard the stories, but seeing it first-hand is remarkable. All these years she's been gone, yet no one forgot. They all still love her. Want her. *Casey Jane* may not be the household name she'd hoped it would become, but here, in this tiny podunk Texas town, Casey is as big a celebrity as any.

Her hands shake when she reaches for the guitar and straightens the strap over her slim shoulders. Burly Dude claps and stands back, giving her the full spotlight.

"I hadn't really prepared anything . . ."

Seven years of silence is a mighty long time. Her lips tremble as she seeks me in the crowd, but calm when she finds me with her pool blue gaze. Her hands move over the strings, a haunting, purposely off-key tune plucked by her delicate fingers.

The words come out timid and weak. She pauses for a second but continues sliding her fingers along the frets. When she tries again, the song bursts out of her chest like a caged bird taking flight. I don't recognize the song, but it draws me in. The words are magic, washing over me. Nightmares, wreckage—a premonition falling from her angelic lips. I, too, have been sleepwalking. Living my life in burned-out ruin, unable to right the wrongs I've committed.

Chills break out on my skin. She looks different now. I always thought she was beautiful, always referred to her as an angel, but I never realized how astute that comparison was until right this minute. The voice that comes out of her is like nothing I've ever heard before. It reminds me of church at Christmastime. Beautiful, spiritual.

All around me, the crowd sways to the music. Some sing along, others just watch with half smiles plastered on their faces, while I look on with awe. They all want her, but I *have* her. She belongs to me, and I refuse to share.

Under the majestic yellow and red lights, her gaze locks on mine. The crowd disappears. It's just her and me and that sweet voice singing to my soul.

★ ★ ★

A HORSE STABLE isn't like the picture I had in my head. I imagined animals just hanging out, walking around, and sniffing each other's butts and shit. In reality, it's nothing like that. The large wooden structure looks like a house from the outside and fancy horse jail on the inside.

Long snouts poke out from each individual enclosure, lined up one after the other on the left-hand side. Each stall has its own door, both in the front and the back so the horses can enter the stable or run through the pasture. Along the right is a row of low shelves. Above them, saddles hang in a neat row one after the other on racks and, in between, hang various other items like ropes and blankets.

Just outside the stable, a concrete slab sits alone surrounded by wooden posts with a hose dangling off one of them. Today is grooming day, or so I'm told. Each horse gets a bath, followed by a treat for good behavior. Casey hands me a plastic bucket filled with brushes, shampoo, and conditioner and tells me to wait. A strange face in the stable can upset the horses.

The slow clop of hooves on dry earth turns the corner as Casey emerges with the first horse I've ever seen up close. His black coat gleams in the sunlight. She holds the rope loosely and lets the beast guide her, not the other way around. "This is

Barney." Casey's voice is tender as she strokes the horse's mane. "You ready for your bath, big guy?"

Barney huffs a breath out his nose in response but doesn't walk toward the slab. "Barney's a sweet old stallion, but he's a little skittish at times." She continues to comfort him, humming with the same gentle tone. "Talk to him."

This is crazy. The only thing that comes to mind are the old *Mister Ed* reruns I used to watch on late-night television, but I'm sure yelling "Wilbuuuuur" isn't going to win me any bonus points. "Uh. Hey there." I feel like an idiot. "You must be an earring. 'Cause you look like quite a stud."

"Seriously?" Casey asks with a laugh.

I shrug and smile. "I don't know how to talk to horses."

"Just say whatever comes to mind."

The only things ever on my mind are sex and music. Animals have no place in either. Then again . . .

The lyrics to the "Four Horsemen" tumble from my mouth like poetry. Cheesy, I know, but they popped into my head and found their way out before I had a chance to think it through.

Casey gives the rope a little tug, and the horse begins to move again. Who'd have guessed Barney was a Metallica fan? He walks toward me slowly and takes a step up onto the concrete platform. Casey ties the rope around a post before settling her hand on his back with a light scratch between his shoulder blades. "Good boy."

I remain off to the side, nervous I'll spook the animal if I get too close. "Barney's sweet spot is on his wither," she explains. "Never go straight for the face. Always reach for the base of the mane first. They like that."

"You know a lot about horses."

The dimples on Casey's face say it all as she reaches for the bucket and pulls out a comb. Her hands roam the horse's coat as she finishes combing then switches to a brush. She's a calming force. The horse knows she's in charge and allows her to work. *This* is her calling, not the stage. In the spotlight, she was unsettled, but on the ranch, she's in control.

She gracefully glides her hands down his leg, and Barney lifts his foot. I watch with wonderment as she picks the hoof with meticulous care then goes on to the next. "You're amazing, you know that?"

"Nah, I've just been doin' this a long time. Been around these animals all my life. Can you fill that bucket with water for me?"

Water sloshes into the bucket from the hanging hose and makes a *splish-splash* sound as I set it down next to her. She dips a cloth into it and strokes the horse's nose and face. As soon as she's done, she sprays his body down with cool water.

"I got a job for you."

The way she smiles and dangles the mitt out in front of her is so damned sexy. I never thought something like bathing a horse could have erotic undertones, but that would be a severe underestimation of Casey's power over me. Every move she makes drives me just a little bit crazy. This morning, I wanted to bend her over the sink after watching her brush her teeth.

I take the mitt and await further instructions. She squeezes a quarter-sized amount of shampoo onto it then covers my hand with hers, massaging Barney's coat with a small, circular motion. "Think you can manage that?"

"Yep. Just like washing a car." A big, breathing, furry car that could kick me ten yards away if it gets mad.

I work my way across his side, and Casey follows with the hose. Soapsuds foam and run off Barney's slick body into a puddle of water below him. The excess spray dapples my hot skin, soaking my shirt as we work side by side. With my free hand, I grab the back of my collar and tug it over my head in one swift move.

Casey's eyebrow slowly lifts as she watches my tee carry on the breeze and flutter to the grass. A lascivious smile passes her lips. She aims the hose and shoots water on my pants. "Ooops!"

"That's how you wanna play, huh?" My attempt to snatch the hose falls flat while she continues the task of rinsing the horse. Instead, I pick up the bucket. "You'd better run, cowgirl."

She does a double take before lifting her arms in surrender. "Okay, I give up," she says, dropping the hose and backing away from both Barney and me.

It's on.

Water flies from the bucket and spatters against her stomach with a splash. It soaks her shorts and trickles down her legs. "Aww, gross! That's dirty horse water! At least I hit you with the hose!"

"Well, then I guess I'm going to have to wash you next!" I take her by the waist and smash her against me. The cold water is already warm, heated through by both her body and the sweltering temperature outside. "Then again. I kind of like you dirty."

"Mmmhmm," she breathes against my mouth when my lips find hers. They instantly part, allowing my tongue to slip between them for just a moment. A tantalizing appetizer for what I hope is to come as soon as we're finished with work. "I plan to get very dirty. Just so you know."

My hands inch up the back of her shirt and glide down her silky skin. Casey sucks air between her teeth, shivering under my ticklish touch. "Then I'll have to bathe you extra thoroughly to make sure your coat is shiny."

A loud bang, followed by the echoing clop of hooves turns Casey's docile body rigid in an instant. I turn and follow her gaze. Clouds of dust kick into the dry air, followed by flying horsetail and a black dot getting smaller by the minute as it runs away from us.

"Oh, my God! Barney!"

I run, work boots thumping heavily on the mix of yellowing grass and dirt. My smoker's lungs burn, but I can't stop. This is my fault. I distracted Casey from her work, and the horse got loose.

Barney slows as he nears the fence, knowing he can't get past it, and my sprint becomes a jog. I don't want to spook him. With my hands braced on my knees, I hang my head to catch my breath before finding the strength to inch near the horse. I really have to quit smoking.

Singing the same song as before, I step forward. Barney's whinny is loud as he moves backward, butting up against the fence. My voice is quiet, but I don't stop warbling the words, standing still and waiting for the horse to calm. When I take a tentative step, he lets me. A few more steps and he meets me. My hand rests between his shoulder blades, just the way Casey showed me, as my free hand wraps around the rope still attached to him.

"I think we're gonna be friends, Barney." I sigh with relief, continuing to rub his back.

All it takes is a gentle tug, and the horse follows me back toward the stable. Casey stands at the edge, not far from the wash pad where I left her. A look of relief slides over her face when she sees me, but a snarl crosses mine when I see Austin. He's leaned against the wall of the stable, opposite Casey, so he goes undetected. His dangerous glare sends a shiver up my spine. Something about the way he looks at me. It's not just menacing. It's evil.

"It was you, wasn't it? You untied the rope!"

"What's going on here?" Casey's ponytail flaps behind her head as she jogs toward Barney and me.

"Your boy, here, is accusing me of endangerin' one of our horses!" Austin strolls over, all bowlegged and slow like he's

Doc friggin' Holliday. *"I told you he'd make a mistake!"*

"I'm not accusing you. I know you did it."

"AJ." Casey keeps her voice light and even as she takes the rope from my hand. *"Why would Austin do somethin' like that?"* She turns and leads the horse back to the slab.

Austin's mouth quirks. The bastard is grinning at me, and he's about to eat his own teeth for breakfast. *"You ain't gonna win. Best leave it alone."*

"You're begging for it," I warn, taking a defensive step forward.

"You gonna push me, little boy?"

"No." The slapping sound of skin ricochets through pasture as I crack Austin across the face open palmed. *"I'm gonna smack you like the little bitch you are!"*

Fuck being nice. He's been goading me since day one. I tried to make it work, but this is war.

His lips curl over his teeth in a vicious sneer. He throws a swing, but I duck and tackle him to the ground, sending his stupid cowboy hat flying. A dirt cloud plumes up as I smack Austin's head into the dry grass.

"AJ!" Casey is behind me in an instant. Her tiny hands close around my bicep and pull, trying her best to get me off Austin who's lying on the ground letting me beat him up. It makes no sense. He's been dying for a piece of me ever since I got here. Why now, when I've finally given him a reason to fight me, is he holding back?

I stand, brushing the dry, dead grass from my pants as Casey continues. *"So this is how it's gonna be now? Y'all are just gonna fight like a bunch of children?"* Her piercing blue eyes are full of blame as they narrow on me. *"This shit is gonna stop. I need to know right now from both a' y'all. Are we gonna have a problem here?"*

"No, ma'am," Austin mutters.

"Are we gonna coexist like adults, or do I need to get out Gran's spoon and give y'all an ass-whoopin'?"

"Yes, ma'am," he replies again.

"This is some hillbilly bullshit," I mumble under my breath.

"What was that?" When Casey steps closer, I notice the pulse vibrating in her neck. Her lips tremble, and her eyes shine with anger. She's yelling at us both, but she's furious at *me*.

"I know Austin untied that rope." I enunciate each word, clear and even. I'm not backing down on this. He's sabotaging what we have, turning us against each other, and he's winning.

"Go in the house, AJ. I'm too busy for this bull-spit."

"So you're taking his side?"

"I ain't takin' a side. I'm shuttin' this down. Austin and I have work."

I can't believe this! My mouth falls open as I listen to her stand up for him while chastising me as if I'm an insolent toddler. She didn't see the look on his face. I'm not wrong about this.

Casey and Austin both turn away, leaving me standing there wondering what the hell just happened. Today went from great to shit, and that fucker is behind it all the way. There's something underhanded about that man. Every time he walks into a room, it feels like a thousand spiders are crawling all over my skin. He smells like hidden motives, and I don't trust him. He may have her fooled but not me.

Chapter 26

Casey

MORNING SUN PEEKS through the blinds as the alarm starts to buzz through my room. The bed shifts behind me and the room goes silent, save for my sleepy groan. How is it morning already?

"You sleep, cowgirl. I'll feed the kids their breakfast." A soft yet bristly kiss falls against my cheek, forcing a smile on my tired face. AJ's taken to referring to the horses as "the kids," which I find adorable.

As AJ rushes around to get dressed for the day, Austin's words drift back to mind. He gave me doubts, but he was wrong. After a week on the ranch, AJ's entire demeanor has shifted. Back in New Jersey, he was troubled, reserved. Out here, he's happy. The sadness in his steel gray eyes has lifted, replaced with a cheerful twinkle and an easy smile. His presence here has added something this ranch was missing.

It gave it life.

I roll onto my back feeling lonely without him next to me and force myself to get out of bed. I've blown off so many chores to hang out with AJ, and things are starting to pile up around the house. It doesn't matter how long I let it sit, the laundry just isn't going to wash itself.

The dryer is full of Austin's clothes. I pull them out and fold them into neat piles then stack them into my basket to carry to his room. His bed hasn't been slept in. Ever since AJ tackled him in the pasture, he's taken to sleeping in the barn. He's always been so kind and gentle. Austin wouldn't even hurt a fly. AJ lost his mind that day. I know he's sorry, but things between him and Austin will never be the same. Not that they were very good to begin with.

It breaks my heart, but maybe it's better. Being around Austin only stirs up complicated feelings. He shouldn't still affect me this way. I don't know what to do about it. I can't let him go—his presence here is too valuable—but I can't keep walking on eggshells, afraid of how he'll react when he sees AJ and me together.

I set the basket on the small oak dresser in his room and shimmy open the top drawer to set his things away. Everything is right where it always was. Socks in the top drawer, tees in the middle, pants in the bottom, shirts in the closet. His room is simple, defined. Easy to navigate.

Hangers clang together as I begin to hang his shirts in a neat little row. My bare toe scrapes against something in the corner of the tiny closet, forcing me to the floor. A wooden box sits alone on the hardwood. Putting his clothes away is one thing, but going through his personal stuff is quite another. I kick the box back into the corner, but curiosity gets the best of me, so I slide it out and peel off the lid.

An instant lump forms in my throat. My gut is yelling at me to snap the lid back on and leave, but my heart won't allow it. The contents are a strange brew of items that no one else would bother to look twice at, but everything that grazes past my fingertip is something special: A small bottle of lilac lotion. Two movie tickets. A hair scrunchie. A small stuffed horse. A guitar pick. A heart-shaped rock.

An engagement ring.

A whole host of things from a life we almost built wrapped up tight in a little wooden box. A metaphor for the love we once shared, now dead, buried in a coffin deep inside a closet.

"What are you doin' in here?"

I gasp at the sound of Austin's voice and scramble to my feet. "I'm sorry. I was just puttin' your clothes away and . . ." The look on his face almost overshadows the sight of him wearing nothing but a towel.

Almost.

"Why did you keep all this?"

His hand grasps the knot around his waist as he walks toward the dresser and begins taking out his clothes. "It made me feel close to you."

Heat rises up my neck and into my face. I chastise myself for being nosy, but all thought comes to a grinding halt when the towel falls to the floor. A squeak hurtles from the back of my throat seeing his long body on full display. The muscles in his back ripple as he bends over to slip clean jeans up his thick thighs and over his lean, round ass. "You got somethin' to say?"

Dryness takes over my throat. My lips stick to my teeth as his gaze locks on mine in the mirror ahead. All I can muster in response is, "Mm-mm," with a head shake as I turn toward the door.

"Wait." He turns, gently taking my forearm. I force my eyes to stay focused on his face, and not on the trimmed patch of exposed hair showing beneath the tiny metal teeth of his open fly. "I've been tryin' to understand what's going on between us, but it's so hard."

"Austin . . ."

"Just listen for a second." He steps closer, his damp skin brushing dangerously close to my chest. The clean smell of his shaving cream blends with the scent of my shampoo on his hair, creating a masculine yet feminine fragrance that jumbles my mind and making it hard to know the difference between right and wrong. "It's been killin' me all these years, wonderin' why you left, but I think I finally figured it out. You were young, and I didn't want to make you feel forced to do anything, so I never tried. I waited for you to make all the first moves because I was too shy, too respectful. You needed a man. One who knew how to make you feel like a woman."

Dark eyes burn into mine as he continues to move forward until my back hits the wall with an "oomph." "I'm every bit that man, Casey Jane. You have no idea what kind of things I wanted to do to you. The things that went through my head, that still do." Hot breath blows against my mouth, as his head dips to mine. Once again, I find myself trapped in more ways than one.

Without waiting for permission, his lips claim mine. Every nerve in my body pops. He's rough and angry, devouring my mouth like he's punishing it. The hard lines of his body press against me. I feel him growing along my skin, going from flaccid to hard as he presses into the soft center of my stomach.

Aggression pours from his lips. I can taste it on my tongue, feel it simmering in my gut. It's unpleasant, and I don't like it.

"We both know you want this." His voice is gruff as his hand roams my backside and slides under my knee. "I want you in my bed. AJ never has to know."

"AJ already knows."

The hurt in AJ's voice is a punch to the gut. Austin's grip on me remains tight as AJ turns and storms away. "AJ wait!"

"Let him go. You don't need him."

"Austin, I love him."

I love him.

The realization hits me hard. I didn't know it until just this very second, until I was face to face with both men and backed into a literal corner. When forced to choose, my heart knew all along what my head couldn't decide. I'm in love with AJ.

All those feelings I have for Austin aren't real. I projected my guilt and held on to a life I thought I missed because I couldn't stand the one I had. I never saw a future with Austin because I didn't want one. When I look at AJ, I see it all. My entire life stretched before me, with a man who loves me. A man who I love more than I thought my heart would allow.

He forgave me once. I'll lose him now for sure.

I smack Austin's face and break free from his tight embrace, running up the stairs to my room. AJ sits at the edge of my bed with his head hanging in his hands. An empty pack of Marlboro Reds lies crushed in a ball near his feet.

"It's not what you think."

"Not what I think," he mumbles at the ground. When his head pops up, his gaze is dripping with acid. Knowing it's there because of me sends a few more cracks rippling through my already tender heart. I hurt him. "I don't have to think, Casey! I saw it!"

"I know it looked terrible, but please just listen."

"I'm done listening! You think I'm stupid? You don't think I see the looks? The way your shoulders tense every time he enters the room?" He stabs his hands through his hair, pushing it back off his forehead. It splits in the exact location of the scar, making it seem much larger than it usually does. "I tried, all right? I tried pretending it didn't matter, but it does. I told you flat out—I refuse share you, Casey! I need to know that I'm the only one."

The sound of drum beats rings through the room from the cell phone in AJ's pocket. He looks at the screen and sends the caller to voicemail.

"It was a mistake. You're the man I want, you always have

been. Austin works for me, that's all."

AJ runs a hard hand down his weary face. "No. It's not enough. He's not just on the ranch, he's still in here," he says, dropping his fingertips over my heart. "I need to be the only one inside your heart. Because you're the only one who's ever been in mine."

He turns, but my grip on his arm tightens. "Don't leave."

"Then tell him to!" The mini drum solo in his pocket starts up a second time. He sends the caller to voicemail again.

"AJ, please understand." The words stutter on my tongue as I try to hold back the tears I feel saturating my eyes. Staring into his sad face, the lust that consumed me just a few moments ago has vanished. Heartbreak, confusion, and regret have replaced it.

"I watched my mother die then my father. I stared death in the face a third time when he came for me, but I fought my way back and came out clean on the other side. All of that was nothing compared to this . . . this slow, agonizing torture that leaves me with nothing to fight for." His fingers trace the pink scar in his hairline, before moving his hair back in place to cover it. "After all of that, this is going to be what finally kills me. You chose him, and I can't stay here."

"I'm not choosing him. I love you."

Holding back the landslide of emotions building up inside, it comes out as a whisper. I'm not sure if he heard me over the loud ringing of his phone for the third time.

With a sigh, he looks down again and slides his thumb over the screen. "Not a good time, Jameson."

His incessant pacing stops as the pained expression falls off his face. He's a stone. A wall. A statue, standing stock-still and staring straight through me before falling onto the corner of the bed. "What does that mean? Is she going to be all right? Okay . . . Okay . . . I'm coming."

He drops his hand to his lap, still squeezing the phone in his fist. "Everything all right?"

The length of time it takes him to respond feels like an eternity. When his eyes refocus and snap to mine, all I see inside them is fear. "Have you ever heard of an ectopic pregnancy?"

My mind races back to my high school health class. "That's when the baby grows in the fallopian tube instead of the uterus, I think. Why?"

"Jillian's just ruptured."

Chapter 27

AJ

COMING HERE WAS a mistake.

I run around Casey's room throwing everything I own into my duffel bag. The sooner I get to the airport, the quicker I can get my ass home and replace this nightmare with a new one.

"What can I do?"

"You've done enough, believe me," I say, tugging the zipper on my bag closed.

"Don't shut me out, AJ. Let me help."

"Leave all this. Come back with me."

A lone tear breaks over the dam of her lash line and rolls down her conflicted face. "This is my home, AJ. I'm not goin' back."

And there's that swinging bat again, smashing me in the heart for the second time that morning. The wheel of emotions spins again. Past anger. Past confusion. Next stop: pain. Hearing her say it makes it too real. I ran all the way out here, but it was too little, too late. I'd already lost her.

"You're staying because of *him*."

"No." Blond hair brushes past her shoulder as she shakes

her head. My fingers tingle, wanting to slide through it, but I keep them at my sides. I can't touch her right now. *"I'm stayin' because this is where I belong. I may have lived back East, but I wasn't livin'. I was existing. Pourin' drinks in a dive, goin' about the motions like I didn't hate every second of every day that I was there."* Another tear falls, another twisted twitch of the hand that I refuse to move to wipe it away. *"Gran left me this place for a reason. I'm not gonna let her down."*

Heat radiates from her body, spreading through my chest and down my legs as she moves closer to me and rests her hand on my cheek. *"You of all people should appreciate that."*

I do. I know exactly where she's coming from, but it doesn't make it hurt any less.

I turn and head down the stairs, but she follows close behind. *"AJ."* Casey's soft voice stops me at the door. Rays of morning light cascade through her kitchen windows. It's too fuckin' bright. I can't stand it. The sky and the sun just remind me of Casey, and I never want to see either again.

It's funny how just a few months can feel like years. Casey and I have spent more time apart than together, but I still can't fathom the idea that things between us are over. I feel like the Tin Man, hollow and cavernous. If you bang on my chest, all you'd hear is an echo.

"All those things you said on the bull, marriage, children, I want that, too. Don't leave like this. Promise you'll come back." She steps forward and falls against my chest. Soft hair tickles my skin. Her lips move against my neck with a mixture of kisses and mumbling, *"Stay with me, stay with me, stay with me . . ."*

My head's not right when I'm standing this close. Her scent is all around me. Sweet notes of honey and flowers wrapped around my fingers and embedded into the fibers of my shirt. The girl gets under my skin. She's a predator posing as a house pet, determined to eat me alive the second I let my guard down.

I try to leave, but she stops me again. "Aren't you even gonna say goodbye?"

"How do I say goodbye to my heart?" I turn back toward the door and pull it open. The promise of a scorching day greets me, followed by the smell of hay and fresh cut grass. Without looking back, I step off the porch, feeling her gaze bore into my back.

Horses whinny in the distance. I look toward the direction of the stables one last time and see Austin saunter my way. "You win, dude. She's all yours."

"She was mine to begin with."

"Whatever," I grumble, turning away from him.

I shove in my ear buds to dull the serene sounds of Casey's home. Taylor Swift's ethereal voice comes through, followed by the gravelly twang of Tim McGraw. Instinctively, I start to sing along then stop myself. I know all the songs and all the names. Stupid country music has infected my heart the same way Casey has. That's what she is. An infection. Something I caught along the way but just can't shake, no matter how hard I try. No antibiotic can cure this horrible affliction. No. What I got, I have for life.

★ ★ ★

IT'S LATE BY the time I arrive at the house. One lonely light shines through the window, creating a creepy, horror house-type setting behind the shop. This grim, bleak atmosphere is more my speed. It's depressing and lonely, just like my life.

I let myself in and close the door with a quiet click. A thick swatch of red-orange hair dangles off the olive colored couch pillows where Marisa lays sprawled out on her back.

What the hell is she doing here?

"Marisa."

I gently shake her freckled shoulder. She rouses with a snort, her green eyes still consumed with sleep. *"You're back. What time is it?"*

"Around one. Why are you here?"

Marisa sits up, blinking herself back to the human race. Her orange brows pinch together and a tiny pout forms along her lips. I never noticed how many freckles cover her milky skin. Without her usual war paint, she looks ten years younger. *"Casey called me."*

I wait for her to elaborate, but she's still half asleep. *"And?"*

"She said your family had an emergency and needed me to babysit. Your sister and James are at Crestmere Hospital. Zakk's upstairs."

I'm too stunned to correct her when she botches my brother-in-law's name. Casey called in reinforcements to help my family. Why would she do that? Does she think this makes us even? Hopefully, for her, her little phone call helps her sleep soundly, but it doesn't change the fact that she tore through my heart like tissue paper then wiped her ass with it. *"I'm here now. You can go."*

Marisa's light eyes narrow into slits. *"You're a real asshole, you know that?"*

"Whatever."

"Case in point," she snaps, rising to her feet. *"And since you failed to ask, she's a wreck thanks to you."*

"Thanks to me? She was the one with her tongue down Austin's throat!"

"She's a human being. She made a mistake. And all that little kiss did was prove to her how much she loves you."

"Right. She loves me so much she used me to make her ex-fiancé jealous."

"If you really believe that, then you're a bigger asshole than I thought." Marisa shoves her feet into her shoes and grabs her

stuff before heading to the door. "And by the way. Your sister came out of surgery just fine. You're welcome."

★ ★ ★

JILLIAN LIES ON the couch propped up on pillows, watching cheesy music videos from the eighties on Vh1 Classic. Zakk stands at the edge beside her, grasping the cushions with both hands. He lets go when he sees me and falls on his diaper-covered butt before rolling over and doing it again.

A Johnson & Johnson commercial comes on the television, and Jillian's chocolate eyes well with tears. "Frig," she says, wiping them away. "These damned hormones. I can't stop crying." When she shifts and moans, Jameson runs to her aid like a hired hand.

He hasn't left her side for a second. If I ever doubted his devotion to my sister, I'd be a believer now. When he finally came home from the hospital, the red rings around his eyes were nothing compared to the Parkinson's-style shaking of his hands. He was a mess. Jillian was in surgery for hours. Apparently, she'd been suffering from abdominal pain and nausea for weeks but kept it a secret. She's always so busy taking care of everyone else that she never stops to worry about herself. This time was no different.

"The blood," he said. "I've never seen a person bleed so much and live to talk about it."

She's been home for three days now, and every time he looks at her, I can see the relief plain as the nose on his face. If he lost her, he'd have lost himself. They complete each other in a way that's rare and special. Apart, they were two halves, but coming together made them whole. I thought I had that with Casey, but I was wrong.

The lead singer from Zebra, a guy with the unfortunate name of Randy Jackson, screeches out of the television set, assaulting me with his words. Crying over the madness of giving everything and coming up with nothing.

Behold the bludgeoning of irony.

The weight of Jill's stare tears my attention off the television. "You have to call her."

I lift the brim of my cap and scratch underneath with a sigh. This conversation is pointless. Casey and I said what we needed to say. She's staying in Texas. If circumstances were different, maybe I'd consider starting over, but I can't. Austin's always going to be there; the third corner in a twisted love triangle that makes none of us happy. Removing me from the equation was the only way to resolve the problem.

She still loves him.

And I love her enough to let her be happy.

My silence doesn't stop Jill's incessant need to mother, however. "It was sweet of you to run home for me, but I'm fine. Your obligation to me is over."

Already, I feel the burning sting sweep across my eyes, and we've only tapped the surface of our chat. "Maybe I'm just meant to be alone. My purpose in life is to work and hang out. Not everyone gets a happy ending."

"You sound like a loser when you talk like that. You had the opportunity for happiness. You blew it."

"Let me ask you something." My hands start their twitchy need to bang on something, but I ball them on my lap instead. "What would you do if you walked in on Jameson kissing another girl? Seriously, Jill . . . what?"

She cringes at the thought. "Let me counter your question with this one: What would I have missed if I didn't at least try to work past it?"

Zakk chants "ma ma ma ma ma" as his pudgy little hands beat against the cushion, vying for his mother's attention. She strokes his hair and tickles under his chin. Giggly squeals erupt from his drool-covered lips, and he falls on the floor again. "What we have . . . it's worth fighting for. You and Casey had it. You sat in our kitchen deflecting our questions about your new mystery woman. I saw it then."

"All of this is moot. You forget the biggest problem here. She lives in Texas."

"So what?"

My top lip curls. Wow, she must be loopy as hell from the meds. "So . . . we live in New Jersey. I can't leave you. You guys need me too much."

She shimmies herself as close to sitting as her wounded abdomen will allow. "Listen to me. You're always going to be my big brother, and my best friend, but you need to stop. I found my soul mate. You need to go find yours. Even if it means moving to Texas."

"You're high. What the hell am I going to do in Texas?"

"Help Casey with the ranch. You hate fixing cars anyway."

"Why didn't I think of that? Oh, that's right! Because I don't know shit about horses or ranching."

"Yeah, but you know a ton about business. Morello and Tate is kicking ass because of you. You can do anything, AJ. You're smart, and you're driven. I can't stand seeing you like this anymore."

"Like what?"

"Empty. Brooding. When she was around, the old, fun AJ was starting to return. I miss that guy because, frankly, this new guy is shit."

I stew on the couch while Jillian's words sink into my thick skull. Can I really do this? If I don't try, I'll regret it for the rest of my life, but I'm having trouble turning my back on everything I know and taking the leap.

It's not just a new state. It's a whole new life.

"Look," she continues with a sigh. "I'm gonna be honest, AJ.

Straight up, no bullshit—you are one of my favorite people on the planet, but you are incredibly hard to love. Casey loves you. Don't take that for granted."

Jill's words are a sledgehammer to my ego, but I can't deny them. I'm a selfish bastard. Everything has to be my way. I'm moody and arrogant, pigheaded and dismissive. Casey changes me. I'm a better man just having been with her. She moves me. She gets me dancing, makes me sing. With her, I feel invincible, lively, and playful. I want to be that AJ. Not the judgmental asshole I've been.

Making a big life change is scary but not nearly as much as regret. I'm done with those. I'm in love with the girl. I need her. Her effect on me is greater than all the songs, all the drum beats, and every loud, growling heavy metal vocal. She's the rock to my roll and the soother of my soul. All this time, I expected her to fit into my life, but that was wrong. Maybe I'm supposed to fit into hers.

The opening chords to "Love Song" by Tesla float from the screen and stab me in the chest. Eyes as blue as the sky cross over my subconscious. The chorus belts out, loud and proud for all to hear. It's a sign. Even Jillian telling me to go wasn't enough. I needed fate to intervene, and here it is. It's screaming at me with pure rock ballad fervor, reminding me that love will find a way.

Chapter 28

Casey

"Y OU EVER GONNA talk to me again, baby girl?" Austin leans against the doorframe with each thick forearm.

"I ain't your baby," I say without missing a beat.

"It's been a week. How long you gonna keep this up?"

I grab the bag of Safe Choice off the shelf and start measuring it out, spilling half the contents in the process. "I haven't decided yet. Maybe forever."

"You can't stay mad at me forever. We have to live together."

"Do we, Austin?" I ask, scooping up the fallen feed. "Because I've been seriously contemplatin' that."

"Why? You going somewhere?"

I roll my eyes. He's going to keep holding this over my head for the rest of my life. Nothing I do will ever make up for it. It's always going to be that third person in the room hanging out between us. My monumental fuck up and the ruination of Austin Krehley. I've spent far too long punishing myself over it. I refuse to live like this.

"No. You are."

Austin's body fills the space behind me. "You are not kickin' me off this ranch, Casey." His already deep voice turns into a scary baritone that I've never heard come out of his mouth before.

"I'm not?" I challenge. "I kept you on for Gran's sake, but I've about had all I can stand from you."

"The sign out front may say Grainger, but you and I both know this here's my land. I've been a slave to these pastures for the past fifteen years. You left. I stayed."

I look up from the floor. His brown eyes darken to a menacing shade. Once warm and inviting, they now look cold and bleak. I stand. "This isn't about me at all, is it? You don't want me. You want the ranch."

I suddenly see Austin in a whole new light. Sweet, kind Austin. The man who bent over backward for my family. The one who never stopped pursuing me, who wanted to marry me the second I turned eighteen. It all makes sense. He knew Gran would never leave this place to Mama, and he sure as shit knew she wouldn't leave it to him. In order to take over, he'd have to marry in.

"You diabolical son of a bitch."

"Hey, hey, that ain't right." His hand closes around my forearm, biting my skin with its rough grasp. "You and I? We're destined. You'll see soon enough that marryin' me is the best choice for both of us." His handsome face twists into a scowl.

"Austin, you're scarin' me."

"Ain't no reason to be scared, baby." His voice is placating, but his grasp on my arm doesn't falter. Skin bubbles between his fingers, and I'm sure I'll have a hand-shaped bruise when he finally lets go. "Just so long as you know that I will kill you before I see you with another man. Got it?"

He jerks my arm, pulling me closer. "That hurts!"

Suddenly terrified of the man I once found far too gentle, I don't know whether to cry or scream. Austin's finally snapped.

I can see it in his eyes. His piercing gaze bounces around my face, bopping with senseless fury. Did I drive him to this? Or was I so wrapped up in young love that I never noticed the evil dancing along the edges all along? I'm starting to wonder if everything I knew about Austin was a ruse. A ploy for my attention, but all the while hidden beneath that quiet exterior was a psychopath waiting to emerge at any given moment.

"You made me look like a fool. Now, you owe me, and I'm takin' what's mine."

"What do you want?" I squeak out, timid as a church mouse.

"I want it all!"

His mouth crushes mine just before he throws me to the floor. Straw scratches my back; the smells of fertilizer and feed surround me. Hoofbeats clop near my head as the horses snort and whinny in their stalls with nervous energy.

Austin turns for a split second. I use that as an opportunity to scramble away, but I'm paralyzed with fear when I see him turn back with a rope. "I'm sorry, Austin. Please don't hurt me."

"You don't know what pain is, you fuckin' bitch! Pain is seven years lost! It's workin' your whole life toward something only to have it ripped out from under you! It's watchin' the woman you love get fucked by another man in the home you've kept for her! You took everything from me, and now, I'm takin' it back!"

The rope cuts into my skin as he wraps it tight around my wrists before moving to my feet. "Don't fuss, now," he cajoles as he twists it around my ankles. The combination of tears and terror blur my vision. He pulls on the rope, and my wrists and ankles join. Leave it to Austin to know how to fasten a perfect Boy Scout knot even when he's hog tying a person.

"You cryin'? Shit, you know I can't stand it when a woman cries." The last thing I see is his arm reaching out to snatch one of the horse blankets off the hook before daylight disappears.

The blanket muffles my screams as he starts tugging at my shorts. *"Remember that night you snuck into my room to seduce me? You were so sweet. You just laid there and let me break you."*

AJ's face pops into my mind. Staying was a bad idea. A string in the long line of awful decisions I've made throughout my life. I don't know what Austin plans to do with me, whether he intends to kill me or what, but my biggest regret to date isn't choosing to stay. It's that AJ will never know how much I love him.

Sobs echo in the stiff fabric as the salt water leaking from my eyes collects in my ears. I feel the denim shimmy past my hips, but I can't move to stop it. Austin continues his insane ranting in a tone more akin to reminiscing over tea than attacking a person in cold blood. *"I told you then that I was gonna marry you, and I still intend to. Soon as we're done makin' up for lost time."*

I feel his hardness poke the back of my thigh, and I know he's taken his pants down. The blood rushing my ears soon becomes a shrill ringing. I'm sucking in a breath, but I can't get enough air in my lungs. Even under the blanket, I can see my vision begin to pixelate, starting around the edges and moving slowly inward. It's fuzzy, like static on an old television set. It's then that I realize I'm about to pass out.

Voices tunnel in from a far off distance, echoing in my mind like a dream sequence. The scuffling of boots, the clopping of hooves, then crashing, yelling, cracking, grunting. Intense heat flares up all around me. Then . . . nothing.

Chapter 29

AJ

TWO THOUSAND MILES doesn't sound long when you say it. *Two thousand miles.* However, while sitting behind the wheel of my truck, hauling the tiniest trailer with all my belongings inside, it feels endless. It never occurred to me how little I cared about anything until I had to decide whether to pack it. In the end, all I took was my drum set, some clothes, my tools, and a photo album Jillian put together for me. The tears on her face as she watched me pull away broke my heart, but she's right. It's time to move on. Jill and Jameson will always be my best friends, but Casey is my life. Her embrace is my home. Her bed is my church. I just hope it's not too late.

Thirty hours on the highway alone leaves a guy with a lot of time to think. First, I apologized to Marisa for being a douche-bag. It was awesome of her to run to my sister's house the way she did. She's a good friend, and I've never treated her the way she deserved. Together, we worked up a speech of all the things I need to get off my chest. I want to tell Casey I'm sorry for not trusting her. That I don't care about her past with Austin because I want to be her future. And, most of all, I want to kiss her until her lips are red and raw and until her body aches for only me.

Adrenaline courses through my veins at a rapid-fire pace as I pass the sign for Grainger Ranch, but the sound of bloodcurdling screams flying from the open door of the stables turns my fiery blood to ice. *Casey.*

Wind whips past my face as I take off across the pasture, running at top speed. What I see when I get there is a nightmare come to life. Casey's bound like a pig on a spit. Austin is on his knees behind her, toying with her, talking to her, touching her in places that send a molten river of rage flooding into my veins. *"Get off her!"*

"What the . . . ?"

I lunge at Austin. He falls into a garbage can full of feed, knocking it to the ground and sending tiny pellets rolling all over the floor. The crook of my elbow closes around his throat in an instant, dragging him across the stable. He's big and heavy, but the adrenaline still drives through my body, adding to my already brute force.

His elbow lands in my gut, knocking the wind from my lungs as I fly backward. *"You don't fuckin' learn, do ya?"* Austin runs toward me, but the butt of my palm catches him in the nose. Blood splatters from his face like a broken water balloon. Temporarily blinded, he doesn't see me running toward him again.

I ram my shoulder into his gut, and his feet leave the ground. We fly through the air, crashing into another garbage can, this one full of oats. Punches send daggers of pain shooting up my side, but it doesn't slow my attack. The kiss was nothing. Seeing him manhandle her, hearing her pleas for help—that was my breaking point.

A punch to the kidney forces me to my side. Then he's on me. His hands wrap around my throat, squeezing my windpipe. Unable to get enough air, my vision grows fuzzy. I'm fucked. He's going to strangle me to death right here in the stable, and Casey's going to have to live with the ghost of another dead body emblazoned into her memory forever. That thought alone gives me one last surge of strength.

My sloppy, flailing arms find his face. I jam a thumb into an eye socket. A brutal bellow rings through the stable as Austin falls to the side.

I scramble onto all fours, sucking wind and grasping my throat while Austin groans behind me. His moans soon become maniacal, super villain laughter as he pushes to his feet. Sunlight slices in through all the windows in the stable, creating a blinding shine glinting off the Zippo in his hand.

My Zippo.

A brilliant shard streaks across his blood-smeared cheek as Austin faces me with a smile. His boot lifts me off the floor with the force of his kick. "Y'all can burn in hell, you sum'bitches!"

The Zippo sparks. With an evil sneer, Austin drops it to the ground. The tiny flame catches the dry straw covering every inch of the floor. It ignites fast, spreading through the stable like a brush fire. The horses scream in their stalls, bucking and clamoring to find their way out.

Smoke fills my lungs. My eyes tear and burn. Austin comes toward me, walking through the inferno like the Devil himself. The second he's close enough, I take one last chance. I lunge again and catch him in the knees. He falls hard, smacking his head on the corner of the shelf with a nauseating crack. The blaze burns all around him, melting the saddles, devouring the dry wood, and licking up the walls of the stable, but he doesn't move. I don't know if he's alive or dead, and I don't care. I only care about Casey.

I cover my nose and mouth with my shirt and drag her outside. Knowing she's a safe distance from the fire, I run around the stable and unlock all the doors. My lungs are on fire, and my whole body aches. The horses dart out one by one, running to the safety of the pasture as I run back to where my girl lies still bound in the grass.

"Casey!" I tug at the rope, loosening the knot, and her arms and legs fall dead at her sides. "Wake up, Case. Come on," I urge.

With clumsy fingers, I search her neck for a pulse as I call 911. She's alive, but I'm afraid to touch her. Her breathing is too shallow. I don't know if she hit her head, suffocated, if he choked her . . . Giving her a quick onceover, she appears okay, but I can't tell for sure.

I fix her clothes and gently slide her onto my lap. "God," I start, looking up at the sky, "I know we've been on shit terms, but if you're there, please, please make her all right."

Ash blows across my face in the wind, lifting my messy hair off my forehead. I lost my hat in the fight, but it doesn't matter. She is the only thing that can't be replaced.

Heat rolls up my cheeks. It stings my swollen eyes and blurs my vision. I can't breathe past the lump in my throat. Even my nostrils burn. At first, I think it's from the raging inferno that's encompassing the stable, but when I wipe my face, I find it wet.

Fuck.

My cheeks, my chin, even the neckline of my shirt, all of it covered in the salty water leaking from my eyes. Now that it's started, I can't get it to stop.

"Don't do this. Don't take her from me. I can't handle losing her, too," I sob.

I jam my eyes shut in an effort to hold back Niagara Falls from pouring down my face, but all I see behind my closed eyelids are my mom, my dad, Jillian, Casey—everyone I love, vanishing before my very eyes. I can't live through it again.

Tears break through my lashes and fall down my face as I

finally grieve for the first time in fourteen years.

Quiet sirens fill the distant air, getting louder the closer they get. Cops, firefighters, paramedics—they all run toward us doing their jobs, but I'm glued to the ground, crying like a bitch. The stable is gone, and so is Austin.

Everything's going to be fine. I chant it repeatedly as they strap Casey to a gurney and load her into the ambulance.

It's going to be fine.

It has to be.

Because if she doesn't recover, neither will I.

Epilogue

MOANS ROCKET OUT of my wife's mouth. My face is buried so deep between her thighs that I'm going to have to come up for air soon. I know she's close, and I don't want to break the rhythm that has her sucking wind and tearing the hair from my scalp. It's early, and she's so tired, but it's been so long, and I want her to come. Not having been able to touch her for weeks has made me a little overeager.

A cry tears from the monitor near our bed, and my head pops up on instinct. Casey lets out a drawn-out sigh and flops both arms over her face. "Dammit!"

"Don't worry, cowgirl. I got it." I rise to my feet, stretching my body—and my overworked jaw—before heading out of our bedroom.

"How's my girl this morning?"

Gabriella's scrunched up face matches her pink pajamas as she cries and kicks her cotton covered feet. Gabby was a surprise, one neither of us expected. After three boys, a little girl finally graced our home, making our family complete. She's just as pretty as her mama is, and she stole my heart just as fast. Cradled against my bare shoulder, she begins to root. Babies this young are like animals. It's all about food to them.

Shoving the pacifier into her tiny mouth seems to appease her for the moment. After the first three kids, I'm a pro at this.

I can change a diaper in the dark and have her back in her pjs before she even realizes the tiny hunk of silicone isn't going to start spouting milk anytime soon.

"Here you go, baby. Breakfast is served," I murmur, placing my newborn daughter into Casey's arms.

Ten years ago, I never, in my wildest dreams, could have imagined my life would turn out the way it did. A gorgeous wife, four amazing kids, and acres of farmland as far as the eye could see. It's light years away from where I came from, but it's perfect. I wouldn't change a single thing.

Except for Austin.

Getting past it was hard for both of us. It took months of therapy and good old-fashioned time to move on. Casey and I never talk about it anymore, but it's there. Lodged in my brain, unable to forget no matter how hard I try.

Casey has let it go. Exonerated him for his sins and absolved him of his crimes. She says the only people her anger was hurting was us. Austin isn't around anymore to feel her pain. He's gone, and we need to thank God for the second chance he'd bestowed upon us.

I'm not that forgiving.

For a long time, I blamed myself. Thoughts about what would have happened had I not returned when I did still haunt me. Visions of my girl bound and tied, almost raped and burned by a violent lunatic replaced my dreams of wreckage. Paramedics said the blanket saved her. Without it, she would have inhaled enough smoke to suffocate for sure. It worked as a filter, keeping her airway clear. For that, I'll always be thankful.

"Luke! Jackson! Up and at 'em, kids. Animals ain't gonna feed themselves!"

Bleary eyed, my two oldest boys ooze out of their beds. Ranch work never ends, and I need to have Mr. Pritchett's truck fixed by noon, which means I need a little help from my homemade crew.

I make sure the boys are on their way to getting dressed then go wake up the little one. "Come on, buckaroo, daylight's wasting!"

"But, Daddy, I'm tired!" His little voice is raspier than usual, as he jams his tiny fist in his eye and shifts under the covers.

"I know, buddy. But we got work to do before Aunt Jill and Uncle Jameson get here this afternoon."

He shoots up in his bed. "They're comin' today?"

"Yep. It's April second."

My own smile reflects back at me on the smooth face of my four-year-old. Between the three boys, Beau is the most like me. Same dark hair, same eyes, same olive skin. Ironic, since he's the one who carries my name.

Anthony Morello III but we call him Beau after Casey's grandfather. He emulates me, from his ball cap to his work boots. He's my shadow. Wherever I am, Beau is sure to be right behind me.

"Are you and Mama playin' a jig tonight?" His little hands touch the sky as I help him pull off his pajama shirt.

Once a month, Casey and I headline a show at The Wander. Covers mostly—heavy metal/country combos recreated by a strong Southern chick and a hard rockin' guy whose combined love of music couldn't be suppressed. It's not the neon dreams Casey once fantasized about, but up on that silly plywood stage in a local bar in nowhere Texas, she shines like a star.

"I think you mean gig, buddy." The look he gives me is so innocent that I can't help but smile. He has trouble with words. I try to correct him but hearing him substitute F for the TR sound in truck always makes me snicker. I may be almost forty, but I'm still a big kid myself. "And yes, we are."

"Does that mean Miss Sally's comin' over to watch us?"

Dark waves spring up out of the neck hole on his tee as I

pull it over his head. "Sure does. I don't want to hear that y'all have given her trouble like last time, ya hear?" Beau pulls up his socks with an overstated nod. "All right, then. Let's go get some grub."

After a quick breakfast, the boys and I get to work. We have two ranch hands helping with our day-to-day tasks. Good men who've been with us for years. They work the land then go home to their families at night, but we trust them enough to leave the ranch in their care on the rare occasions we head back East. Today's a special day, though, and Brock and Jorge have the day off.

In addition to horses, we also have chickens, a dairy cow, and a small vegetable garden. Casey gives riding lessons, but she's on maternity leave at the moment. We each do our jobs, and the morning goes without a hitch.

Casey's shrill whistle echoes from the back door. That's her way of calling us all in. The boys grapple over one another on their way up to the house, and I meander in behind them, already exhausted from my half-day's work. When it's just us on the porch, I press my lips to hers. Moments alone are so infrequent these days, but I never miss an opportunity to kiss my girl whenever I want.

"You still owe me one later, city boy. Don't forget." She giggles.

The hair on my arms stands on end. Ten years together, and that little laugh of hers still makes me tingle all over. "Don't you worry, cowgirl. I'm gonna plow you like fertile land," I joke, patting her on the ass before I head into the kitchen door to greet the family waiting there for me.

It's been a year since we've all been together, and I'm happy they're here. We try to talk as often as we can, but life gets in the way. They're busy, we're busy; it is what it is. The visits are never as long as I hope. Morello and Tate is left in good hands, but business awaits and they can't stay. However, we all agreed this day is the one day of the year that we will all be together, no matter what.

"Hey there, bumpkin."

My sister's embrace is so tight it strangles me, but I don't pull away until she does. I feel the wetness in my eyes, and it doesn't embarrass me. Dad was right. Family is everything.

"I hear your dad's got you helping out at the shop. Don't let the old man boss you around," I say to Zakk, whose lazy smile reminds me so much of his father I want to smack it. He still resembles me a little, but this kid is a Tate in every way. Sarcastic as fuck and super chill.

An original Morello and Tate tee hangs on his slender frame as he casually leans against the counter. At ten, he's almost as big as his mother is already. He's even gotten in trouble at school for kissing girls, too. I always said Jill was going to have her hands full, and I was right.

"Can I hold the baby?" My niece, Nikki, bursts into the room. She's six, the same age as Jackson, but she's not shy like he is. She's just like her mother: little but with a personality that can suffocate a room with its size.

"Me first," Jill coos, cuddling Gabby in the crook of her neck. "Jameson, look how sweet she is. I want another baby."

"Oh, jeez. I'm going to have to get a vasectomy after this trip, aren't I?"

"Y'all are crazy. C'mon, I set up lunch outside." Casey grabs a platter of salad and ushers everyone out the back door, while I head to the sink to wash up.

Through the window, I see them all laughing and playing. Talking like no time has passed at all. The bitter sting of emotion hits me as my gaze falls on the pasture. It is a perfect day. The sky is like a painting. It's one of those stop-and-take-it-in kind of moments. Everything I ever wanted is here, except for the one person I miss most.

"What'd I miss?" I ask, joining them in the yard.

"Jameson was tellin' us about the time y'all were sellin' Christmas trees by the shop."

Laughter cracks the sky as I throw my head back; encased in a memory I'd long forgotten yet remember like it was yesterday. Business took a hit that year, so to supplement our income my dad got the brilliant idea to sell Christmas trees off our lot after the shop closed for the day. He hired Jameson and me, only fifteen at the time, as his lackeys. "We froze our asses off! What a nightmare that was!"

"Seriously, dude. Your dad was a sheisty bastard!" he cries, rolling with laughter so heavy it's pooling in his eyes. "To this day, the sound of Christmas carols still gives me the chills, and not in a good way."

"Man, the things he used to make us do. Remember when he took us down the shore and insisted we all wear matching sweatbands? Mom refused because she was worried about her hair."

Jill smacks the table, sucking in wind while cackling like a hyena. "Oh, yeah! Mine was pink. I was so pissed!"

I grab a plate of uncooked burgers and carry it to the grill, still laughing. He would have loved this. I feel his presence all around me and see it in the smiles of my children, but it's not the same. He should be here. Laughing about old times and sharing a cold Bud with us. The life I live isn't the one he'd planned for me, but I know he would have been proud of the man I've become anyway. He would have been sixty today, and not a day goes by that I don't think about him.

The cold meat sizzles on the grill, and I turn to back toward the table. "To Dad." I raise a beer, and everyone follows suit. "Thanks for the laughs, old man. Until we see each other again."

Playlist

Twisted Sister—"I Wanna Rock"

Judas Priest—"Touch of Evil"

Johnny Cash—"Ring of Fire"

Pantera—"Cemetery Gates"

Jason Aldean—"She's Country"

Tim McGraw—"Meanwhile Back at Mama's"

Luke Bryan—"Move"

Lee Brice—"I Don't Dance"

Queensryche—"Spreading the Disease"

Luke Bryan—"Pray About Everything"

Carrie Underwood—"Heartbeat"

Metallica—"Fade to Black"

Randy Houser—"We Went"

Florida Georgia Line—"H.O.L.Y"

Jason Aldean—"Burnin' it Down"

Kansas—"Dust in the Wind"

Tesla—"Love Song"

Rush—"La Villa Strangiato (An Exercise in Self-Indulgence)"

Carrie Underwood—"Starts with Goodbye"

Iron Maiden—"No More Lies"

Guns N Roses—"Estranged"

Lee Brice—"You Don't Sound Like You"

Eric Church—"Springsteen"

Jennifer Nettles—"Unlove You"

Scorpions—"No One Like You"

Dierks Bentley—"Say You Do"

J. Geils Band—"Love Stinks"

Maren Morris—"My Church"

Cam—"Burning House"

Metallica—"The Four Horsemen"

Tim McGraw—"The Highway"

Zebra—"Tell Me What You Want"

Chris Young—"Who I Am With You"

Garth Brooks—"You Move Me"

Cole Swindell—"You Should Be Here"

About the Author

J ANE ANTHONY IS a romance author, fist pumping Jersey girl, and hard rock enthusiast. She resides in the 'burbs of New Jersey with her husband and children. A lover of Halloween, vintage cars, & coffee, she's also a cornucopia of useless 80's knowledge and trivia. When not writing, she's an avid reader, concert goer, and party planner extraordinaire.

Jane loves hearing from her readers! Connect with her on these social media sites, and don't be too shy to say hello!

janeanthonyauthor.wixsite.com/romance
twitter.com/JAnthonyAuthor
facebook.com/JaneAnthonyAuthor
facebook.com/groups/JanesRomanceAddiction
instagram.com/janeanthonyauthor
pinterest.com/janeanthonyauth
tinyletter.com/janeanthonyauthor
goodreads.com/JaneAnthonyAuthor
amazon.com/author/janeanthony

Other novels by Jane Anthony

Secrets and Promises
"He was everything I desired except for one thing
I needed most: My brother's approval"

KADE: A Second Chance Rockstar Romance
One night. No rules. No strings
. . . until he fell for her.
Now, Kade Black is returning to claim what's his.

Acknowledgements

"THE END." THOSE two words leave such bittersweet finger-prints on my heart, and this time is no different. The Morello family has always had a special place in my heart since the first word I wrote in my first book over a year ago. Jillian and James-on had such a sweet love story, I couldn't help but fall for them, but AJ's story had gone untold. The amount of people who asked me—actually BEGGED me—to give him a story all his own was astounding. I hadn't considered the possibility before, but the more people asked, the more his story came to life in my head. He started banging around in my brain and wouldn't stop until he finally had the happy ending he deserved, and boy, did he make me work for it. At times, his brooding, selfish be-havior was enough to make me curse his name. He was stub-born and we fought a lot. In addition to that, Austin literally came out of nowhere! I hadn't intended to write a love triangle, but his story flew from my fingertips and once it was there, that was it.

That being said, I didn't do it alone. I have so many people to thank for making this story a reality that I don't even know where to start! So, I guess I'll start at the top. . . .

My master-betas—Robin W., Jenny G., Devon C., Jamie O., Betty Shreffler—you guys are absolutely amazing.

Robin—you are my "master-beta" in every sense of the word. Girl, you put up with so much! All my questions, all my comments, all my "what do you think of this?", "What do you think of that?" so on and so on. Even from Oxford, you never kept me waiting and were willing and happy to catch the brunt of my insanity. I don't think I could release a book without you at this point!

Jenny—you've been my cheerleader since day one. You read this manuscript not once but TWICE in one weekend because I lost my mind and rewrote it after sending it to you! You have no idea how much your effort and support means to me.

Devon—I love how much you hate AJ! HAHA You brought such an amazing aspect to the table—the hard-handed feminist point of view. You humbled AJ; knocked him down a few pegs. He doled out so much shit, and you called him out on it EVERY SINGLE TIME. As usual, your brutal honesty is what helps make my work what it is.

Betty—when I desperately needed another person's POV you jumped in with both feet and offered to read it. Your notes were wonderful, your help was invaluable, and your support through all of it gave you a permanent place in my heart. We haven't known each other very long, but thank you so much for being such a good friend to me.

Jamie—this was the first book you beta'd for me and I was not disappointed! You went beyond my expectations. I can already tell that you're going to be a fantastic addition to the team!

I need to give a special little fist bump to Cordelia Michelsen, Sandy Ebel, and Hope Pennie as well. All of you read snippets, gave me your opinions, and talked me off the ledge more than once. Sometimes, just having a sounding board there to listen when I'm "thinking out loud" is all I need to get it together. Thank you for always being there, and double thanks for the delicious man candy!

Stephanie H.—what is there to say that hasn't already been said? You're the wind between my cheeks, sister. Love love love to you always.

Candice Royer—you made the leap from Beta Reader to Editor and did an amazing job! I'm such a pain in the ass, I know. I keep making changes, relentlessly pick at things, and never stop rewriting! You not only helped polish this manuscript, but you shouldered all my crazy with a smile. At least, I imagined you smiling . . . ;) I've said it a zillion times, but I truly can't stress how much your opinion means to me. If it doesn't pass 'the Candy test,' it's not worthy of putting out to the public. Period.

Marisa Shor at Cover Me Darling—OMFG this cover! Seriously, the cover is art! When I have zero idea what I want (which is, pretty much, always) you wave your wand and create a masterpiece that is so perfect that I can't even believe it. You're amazing.

Speaking of pretty—Holy effing sh*tballs, Dani Rene'. The teasers you made are too gorgeous for words! You are seriously unbelievable! Thank you so much!

Christine at Type A Formatting, this is the third book we've done together and working with you is always delightful. Even though I technically write this before it's formatted, I don't have to worry because I know that it's going to be beautiful!

Same goes for Jenny at Editing4Indies! I know even before you get it back to me that it's going to be perfect! My grammar is crap on it's best day, but I know you'll always be there to fix it. That's if I don't take it back from you to add/change more stuff!

To all the bloggers—there aren't words in the English language to thank you enough for all your hard work! You guys are an indie author's BFF. Our life's blood. We'd be nothing without you! Special love to Socially Awkward Book Nerd for always taking the time to pimp me out.

As usual, I saved the best for last—my readers! I love all of you—especially my Addicts! Getting to know you has been a privilege for me. Your messages, posts, comments, and shares have warmed my heart more than you will ever know. This was the first story I wrote not only for me, but also for you. You wanted AJ to get his ending, and I hope it was everything you hoped for.

Thank you!

66365534R00133

Made in the USA
Charleston, SC
17 January 2017